OUT ON THE DRINK

D1738486

BILL BUNN

RECEIVED

OCT 2 3 2018

Published by Bitingduck Press
ISBN 978-1-938463-51-8 (trade paper)
ISBN 978-1-938463-52-5 (electronic)
© 2017 Bill Bunn
All rights reserved
For information contact
Bitingduck Press, LLC
Altadena, CA
notifications@bitingduckpress.com
http://www.bitingduckpress.com
Cover art by Jeff Delierre
https://jeffdelierre.carbonmade.com/

Publisher's Cataloging-in-Publication data

Bunn, William   [1963-   ]

Out On the Drink/by William Bunn—1st edition
p. cm.

ISBN: 978-1-938463-51-8

[1. Young adult—Fiction 2. Alcohol abuse (teenage)—
Fiction 3. Pirates—Somalia—Fiction] I. Title

LCCN 2017938458

To Ken, Diana, Randy, Brad, Chris and lovely Linda.
How could I improve without you?

This is a work of fiction. The events and characters depicted are entirely fictional, and any resemblance to real persons, living or dead, is entirely coincidental.

The cruise ship depicted, the Lyubov Orlova, is real. It sat off the coast of Newfoundland between 2010–2013, then became a floating derelict, the "Russian Ghost Ship." Its fate remains unknown.

The chapter heading art is an adaption of the photograph "Lyubov Orlova derelict dockside in St. John's, 2012," by Dan Conlin, Creative Commons License CC BY 3.0.

PROLOGUE

To whoever finds my body:

My name was Sean Bulger. OK. I'm skippered. I've never written a goodbye note to the world before. How are they supposed to sound?

It might be important to say that I wasn't murdered. And it wasn't suicide. It was stupid. This situation is the hangover that won't go away. Well, it will, when I kick off. I just hope the next life is much better than this one was. I was a drunk and a jerk, and that's kinda what got me here.

Please tell my mom I said goodbye. I should say sorry, but she'd better, too. Her name is Tanya Bulger, and her phone number is 709-465-6782.

Goodbye? Sincerely? Much Love? 10-4 good buddy?

Sean Bulger

P.S.

This will either be a short note to explain how I died, or, if I live long enough, it might turn into a story. Right now, I think I'm going to die. Feels like it. Dehydration, I'd guess. I'm surrounded by water, but I can't find any to drink on this floating tin can. I can't find food.

If I do get rescued, and there's a chance I might, I'll just hurl this overboard, and the words will drown instead of me.

P.P.S.

This is turning into a long goodbye note. Mr. Nutman, how many words does a goodbye note have to be?

Okay. It seems like I'm going to live another day. But

I'm pretty thirsty. Twice thirsty. I need a drink of water. My mouth feels like an ashtray in the July sun. I found a half-finished water bottle rolling around the deck in the hallway. Cigarette butt floating inside. Drank it. Yes, it's disgusting. But it was either that or die, right?

And my head is pounding like a marching band locked in a closet. I need a drink. By that, I mean alcohol. Without a drink, I'm going straight. And going straight hurts. I hate straight. Can't take life that way.

Going to look for water and/or gin. I need both to live. Back in a couple minutes.

Small search. It's creepy here. I'm too afraid to go too far. No gin. No water. But I did find a lot more paper and pens. School paper. Lord thundering, take a gawk at that. I'm haunted by homework. Next, I'll probably find an essay assignment, or a stray English teacher looking for his forever home. Now that I think about it, the presence of an English teacher would suggest I've already died and gone straight to hell.

Homework always survives. It's kind of like 9/11. I remember watching the towers come down. In the midst of the death and destruction, the chaos, what escaped? Paper. In all that fire and brimstone, everyone's homework survived. I remember watching clouds of paper slice through the smoke as the cameras focused on the scene. Homework doesn't leave anyone alone.

Speaking of English teachers, Mr. Nutman would be proud. The old coot would call it poetic justice. I'm probably going to die of thirst. Can't find a thing I need to live, but I did find paper and pens. The pen may be mightier than the sword, but it's not quite as good as bottled water, or a 40 of rum.

Rum, my dear friend, where are you? Help me, please. What happens if you pray to rum? First time for everything.

This is turning out to be a stupid goodbye note. I

should throw it out and leave one that would get me an 'A' in death. In case there's a mark. Mr. Nutman probably has a rubric for death notes. Thesis would probably be the fourth sentence, and sort of a combination of the topic sentences of the three body paragraphs I should write. But just like real assignments, I'm too lazy. So, I'm likely to get a low grade for failing to die correctly and for writing a terrible note.

Note to Mr. Nutman: You probably gave me the rubric for death notes at some point. I have either lost it or I skipped the class where you gave it out. I'm winging it here. Give me some marks for passion, you son of sailor's arse (I'm only calling you that because I know I'll be dead, and I wanted you to know how I truly felt about you).

I also don't have the internet. My phone just died as I was about to send a text. So I can't download someone else's death note and give it to you, either. Whose life would I plagiarize if I could?

If I die before I wake, please look after Sailor, my cat. I let him down, big. I'm his only friend. He needs more food and water NOW! My mom will not be paying attention to him. If he's home, he'll be under my bed, hiding. He hates her. Don't let him out, either. He's not fixed. If he gets out, I'll never see him again. Please make sure he finds a good home.

Oodles of time but no distractions. I'm so bored, I might actually end up writing, unless of course I die.

PPPS

My head is hammering like a demolition crew is taking it out. Booze is your best friend until it leaves.

Like my mom's last boyfriend, Greg. Decent enough guy until he drinks, she drinks. Then all hell breaks loose. He kicked the crap out of the apartment. Smashed stuff, punched holes. Some with his fist. A couple with my mom's head. A couple with mine.

We end up moving in the middle of the night because we can't pay for all the damage he did. He's skipped town, too. Too bad my head wasn't a crappy apartment. I'd leave.

My cell phone's officially dead now, too. No TV. No computer. Nothing. God bless my cotton socks, I must have been born on a raft. Lots of time. Lots and lots of time. This feels like Chemistry class with Mr. Godfrey. I can see him droning on and on, like watching the government on TV, with his right hand tucked into the front of his pants. The school clocks were ones that clicked back briefly before the moved forward, each minute. So as Roger Ferguson and I sat there, just behind May-Britt Brugger, we counted each minute as it clicked by. That's what this feels like, except the clock. Lots of time, nothing to drink. Nothing to do. I might as well start jogging.

P.P.P.P.S.

It looks like I'm going to make it a few days here. I'm going to stop thinking I'm going to die every day. The melodrama ends now. I'm so hungry I could eat the arse off a low-flying duck.

I'm about to write how I ended up on this ship, and what's happened so far. Anything happening earlier than now is generally true. I didn't make it up, that is. I just have trouble remembering. That's what drink does to me. So it's generally true, but not specifically, if you know what I mean. The best I can remember.

Mr. Nutman, I won't rewrite this first part, but tomorrow, I'll start the story. That should be worth a few marks, shouldn't it? For Sailor's sake think of my self-esteem, you frustrated old man.

Sincerely,

Sean Bulger

PPPPPS.

Warning: I also happened to find a dictionary. The homework gods have seen to outfit me properly. I've actually started looking up words because I'm bored. I'm in some sorry state, obviously. Be warned.

1

As best I can remember, I lay in a drunken slump in class, head resting on my crossed arms. Nausea clawing up my throat. Grade 11 English class.

"A group or herd of rats is called a mischief." Mr. Nutman—a thin, hawk-nosed, ginger-headed, tug-sized English teacher—frowned. His brown polyester pants ride high. A big ball of gut makes the top part of his pants balloon outward. He's wearing a shirt that was supposed to be white, but seemed to be turning yellow. "A mischief." His lecture was interrupted by the sputter of the public address system. "A flock of crows is known as a murder of crows." Aware of the class's distraction, he stopped and looked up. The PA loud speaker, painted white and mounted in a chocolate brown box just above the classroom's door, crowed feedback. Mr. Nutman winced.

"A group of students is called a class." From the class clown, Navdeep. Someone guffawed.

A group of drinks is called a drunk, I thought. My brain pulsed like a beating heart. The last stop before puke-ville. The sea-sick feeling just before a full-blown hurl.

I need a drink. By drink, I meant half a 26er of hard liquor, at least. Rum, preferably.

"The school administration has canceled afternoon classes because of the coming blizzard. Please travel home safely." The shrill, nasal voice lisped through the school's PA system. An old-fashioned January ruff. For me, timing couldn't be better. A weak cheer rippled through the building, along with the rustle and clunk of students closing their books and minds for the day.

11.45 and school let out. I stood in front of the school and swayed in the cold. The cool air tamed my nausea a little. I think I can take the bus without getting sick. And with that, I staggered aboard the yellow machine. The bus driver sat in his seat, a baseball cap hiding his bald noggin.

A younger boy fanned his nose as I walked by. "You smell."

"Shut up, you little tweak, or I'll puke on you," I growled. His grade 5 eyes widened like moons, like he was going to cry. But he held back.

I took a seat and rested my head on the seat in front of me. The bus swayed and slid on the snow like a carnival ride. The rocking and heat slowly brought my nausea back to a boil. After a few minutes, I was nearly as close to hurling as Donald Trump is to idiot. I raised my groggy head. Which kid did I promise to puke on?

The bus stopped for a moment. There was a pause. There was some muffled chatter at the front of the bus, which slowly became clear. "Sean? Sean? Are you all right?" The entire bus load, including the bus driver, was staring. Took me a while, but I met his eyes. The Esso patch on the driver's blue ball cap looked like a third, unblinking eye. The bus driver gestured to the open bus door. "Your stop, buddy."

I stood and blundered forward. I aimed my hangover at the middle of the open bus door and plunged through the exit. I made the sidewalk before I fell to my knees and let 'er fly. The technicolor yawn. The bus didn't move. I could picture the entire bus watching, wide-eyed and horrified, as I heaved myself empty. And then some. I heard the driver sigh, and the roar of the bus driving off, abandoning me under a black blanket of diesel smoke.

From all fours, I slowly rebuilt my stance. I stood still

for a moment, reeling. Funny. When you're drunk, the whole world feels like a ship in a storm. The hardest rock moves like a ping-pong ball on sea water. The world was spinning, counter-clockwise at the moment. I drink, and the world spins. When I drink, shouldn't I spin and the world stay still?

I took a few careful steps, trying to steady the planet under my feet. My ribcage felt like someone whacked me with a baseball bat. My throat scalded with stomach acid. The cool air and odd orphan snowflake helped me find enough sobriety to make it home.

I found myself in front of our apartment door. Getting the key to go in the lock was a bit of a trick. My hands shook like a flag in a hurricane. I stabbed at the lock hoping to get lucky and run the key home. The point of the key chipped a divot into the door wood. Little chips and dents surrounded the door knob like a constellation. Evidence that my hands weren't often steady. To be fair, neither were my mom's.

After several tries, a lucky strike. I landed the key in the lock and threw the door open.

I slung my backpack near the door and stumbled to the kitchen in search of nourishment, as Raphael, my mom's boyfriend—two back—called it. As I scanned the open table and countertops, Sailor—that's my cat—stared me down, as if I had done something wrong.

"Shut up, Sailor," I blurted. He blinked and buried his head in a dirty pot.

Filthy dishes wedged into a heap in the sink. Rotting fruit, still in its plastic bags from the store, lay on the counter. Empty chip bags. Insects buzzed in clouds over the decay. The putrid tang of a loaded litter box wafted through the kitchen. The war of smell made me want to ralph again. I needed a drink.

I swayed around the filth on the floor. Mom wouldn't be home from the bar or bingo, or wherever she was, for a while. It'd be easy to find a stash or two. Kitchen cupboards were the first stop. Chocolate brown cupboards with copper knobs shaped like satellite dishes. I scanned through the cupboard contents, looking for the bottles. The top cupboards, then the ones under the counter. No luck. Nausea began to build again. I felt jittery and leaned on the counter to still myself.

"Where? Where? Where?" I pounded a fist on the counter. The dirty dishes clicked with each pound. Sailor meowed his complaint. Think like an alcoholic mom. "Cleaning supplies." I shuffled to the kitchen sink, slumped into a lopsided squat, and inched open the cupboards underneath. "Ha!" Success. In the box of cleaning supplies, at the back, a 26 of cheap vodka. Third full.

With renewed vigor in my grasp, I spun the cap off the bottle and guzzled it straight. The empty dropped to the checker-tile floor. Then I bent over the table on straightened arms to wait while the alcohol soaked in.

It's a feeling like no other. Yes, it makes you sick and dizzy—all the time. Which is not pleasant. How do you describe the good side? Problems, when they get big enough, turn into bullies, bullies that live in your own head. When you're having a bad day, all your problems push you around, say nasty things, make you feel like crap. But say you watch a good movie or TV show. All those bullying problems, they're still there, but they back off. They shut up. You feel a little better. That's the good side of alcohol. It's like liquid movies. You drink and your problems back off, but only while you're drunk.

FYI. Alcoholics, in case you didn't know, are optimists. A bottle is never two-thirds empty. It's always one-third full. I held out a shaky hand. I watched as the tremor faded to calm.

"Mmmmmm." A close call. The nausea slowly melted away. My thoughts settled. "Steady as she goes, boys."

Once the buzz began to build again, I retrieved the

plastic bottle from the floor. "I'm back." Poured a little water down the bottle's throat until it looked as full as it had been when I found it. I snugged the cap in place and replaced the bottle in the crowd of cleaning supplies. If she'd had enough to drink, Mom wouldn't be able to figure out who finished it, even with just the two of us in the apartment. Well, three. But Sailor didn't drink alcohol.

Most of the stuff in her bedroom will be gone. She always drinks in her bedroom. The living room was my next guess. She spent a lot of time passed out on the couch or in the recliner. There had to be a bottle or two around somewhere. The buzz deepened a little and eclipsed more of the nausea. I need a little more, just a little more, for later. I drifted to the living room.

Sailor snaked around my feet as I searched. "Don't worry, buddy. I won't forget. I just need my medicine first." I flipped the couch cushions up. Sailor sprung onto the couch bed, trying to follow my gaze, it seemed. He bonked his head into my leg and bowed his head slightly. That means he wants me to scratch under his collar. So I did. He seemed to enjoy it and then attacked my arm, biting firmly down on the webbed skin between my thumb and forefinger.

"Ouch, you little sculpin." He looked at me hungrily. I shook my hand away from his paws. Like me, he's not much to look at. He looks as though he was once all black, but then sprinted through a deep puddle of cheap white paint. He's one of a bad batch. Sloppy manufacturing.

A gleaming green bottle with a peeled label. As I picked it up, I could tell it was empty. "Dead soldier." I replaced the bottle, swept the cat out of the way, and punched the cushions into place.

I dropped to my knees and lifted the couch apron. The DVD remote control lay on the floor, its battery cover a few inches away and a couple of yellow and black generic batteries scattered beyond that.

Jackpot!

A brand new 26er of white rum cleverly wrapped in a section of newspaper. I flopped into the filthy recliner and closed my eyes to savor the moment. I found another bottle, empty, in the recliner's outside pocket, along with a package of cigarettes and a lighter. Sailor launched himself into my lap.

"Life is good, Kitten, ain't it?"

I'm not a smoker, but I pocketed the pack and lighter. They make for good trade.

It was tempting to relax in the recliner, but I couldn't rest on my laurels. I struggled out of the chair and resumed the search. The small bookshelf under the living room picture window held a flask with mouthful of rum, which I downed.

Now Sailor. Sailor is my best buddy, after rum. Though I'm not sure he would agree. Not the way he attacks my arm when I scratch his flee-bitten neck. He's only calm and loveable sometimes. And it's impossible to say when that might be. It just happens.

I poured him a generous bowl of kibble. Topped up his water dish. I shoveled the chunks out of his litter box, bagged 'em, and topped it off with the fresh stuff. All the while Sailor purred and rubbed and turned eights between my ankles.

The front door flew open. My mom burst through the door like an angry, psychopathic gameshow host off her meds. "Who left this door unlocked?" I abandoned my search and ran down the hallway toward my bedroom. Sailor sprinted ahead of me, disappearing into my room. I stowed the liquor in my bedroom and walked to the front door, to make it look like I was just leaving my room. She met me in the hallway, swaying like a hula dancer glued to the dash of a rush-hour taxi cab. Or maybe I was the one swaying.

"You little sleeveen. You been drinkin' again? You

been into my hooch?" She raised a fist. I flinched. She lowered it. "Quit bein' a baby. You ain't captain of this ship. I am." She poked her chest with a thumb." I relaxed, too soon. An explosion of anger and she knuckled the side of my face. "If I find a drop of it gone, you'll be in for some." I massaged the side of my head. "That's for skippin' school, ya streel."

"I didn't skip. We were let out early for the snow," I whined. She carried a brown bag with something inside.

She wagged a skinny finger with bulbous knuckles at me. "Shut up, ya boiled boot. It's time for The Young and the Restless. You keep it down, or there won't be enough a' you to pray over."

I returned to my room, massaging my cheek, and lay down on my bed. I plugged in my phone. The little charging logo appeared on the screen. Like me and alcohol. The bottle is my battery. Plug a bottle or two into my mouth, I'll kinda wake up.

Now that my brain was properly pickled, I could focus. The phone buzzed. It'd taken on enough power to wake up. A few things buzzed and binged. I checked them all. Phone. Facebook. I stalked a few profiles. Ah. A friend of a friend of a friend.

A party announcement. Carly's house. Her parents were in Toronto for a couple of days. There'd be alcohol. 7 p.m., 138 Queens Road. "My friends will be there," I muttered. By my friends, I meant bottles of hard liquor—alcohol, not actual people.

Sailor worked up enough courage to join me on the bed. I scratched under his collar and behind his ears. "I'm goin' out tonight, buddy. But I think you're set up until I get back." His purr hummed rough as a gravel road.

The low groan of my mother wafted through the door. She's getting weepy.

When she got home, she'd often take a good belt from one of her stash bottles. It'd take the blade off her anger and she'd go into deep, unending apology and blubbering regret. I'd had my supper from a bottle. I gotta get while the gettin's good.

I leapt to my feet, and grabbed my coat.

The groan widened into a moan. I jogged down the hallway to the apartment door. The moan broke into a soupy sob. Mom blubbering in front of the TV, again. "Sean, Sean. I'm sorry, son. Come here, my baby boy." Before she could ask again, I hoofed it out the apartment door. "Sean!" Her voice was hoarse and haggard. I threw the door closed. "Sean!" The door's slam muffled the sound of her begging.

A rose-colored sky began to let loose. Flakes hit the open skin of my face and stung like needle pricks. With nowhere to go, I wandered up and down streets, wherever my druthers took me. In the general direction of Carly's party. Which was still two hours away. I fondled the new rum bottle in my pocket. Something to tide me over. Technically, I didn't need any more hooch from the party. The one bottle should get me through until tomorrow. But, one can never have enough, can one? Maybe I could keep some of this bottle for tomorrow.

To conserve my supply, I waited until the buzz wore down a little.

Staying drunk is a bit of a balancing act. Once I get to my happy place, I got to drink just enough to keep my bullies at bay. Too much, and I get a whole new set of problems—hospitals, stomach pumps, addictions counsellors, and all that stuff. Too little, my bullies come back.

I found a glassed-in bus shelter on Queens Road and uncapped the rum bottle. I sipped a little until the buzz strengthened. So did the storm. January's fist about to fall. The odd flake became a steady snowfall. The snowfall thickened until it brewed into porridge.

As the light faded, the snow slowly turned from white to a darkening blue. Night had begun to fall. Good and drunk, I checked the time on my phone. 6.45. Seventeen missed calls from my mom. No kidding. I could see her in her chair, dozing and waking, and every time she woke, speed-dialing me. She was between boyfriends then, which made it worse.

I nipped small sips to hold my buzz steady. I ended up hanging out on a bench in a gazebo in the middle of a park, part way up Becks Cove Road. Then back to the glassed-in bus stop, on Queens. Back down to the gazebo.

From my pocket I pulled my phone, again, and blinked a few times to clear my sight. The party was about to start. 6.58 p.m.

I surprised myself. The bottle had about a half-inch of rum left. I would need more alcohol, after all. I drained the bottle in a final swig and hurled the bottle onto the street where it smashed. From there, I lurched toward Carly's party.

The sidewalk led me up Queens Road, alongside the park.

Carly's house. 138 Queens Road. An orange neon guitar hung in the window. Bass notes burped through the walls and into the night. A few doors down from Carly's house, between two lines of homes, a convenience store. I took shelter in the parking lot against a westerly wall, and waited.

I wouldn't be welcome on my own. The last time I got into a party, it ended with me in the hospital. So I'd have to crash the party with a group. A couple of singles approached the door and entered. The sound of music and voices spilled into the street for a few seconds each time the door opened and shut.

A clump of teens moved up the street. They looked 16ish. About my age. "Ah ha." I nudged the wall away. There were a couple of guys and three girls. "Perfect," I purred.

"We're here," one of the girls chirped.

"Time to get wasted," one of the guys screeched. The group exploded with a choir of whooping and laughter. I let them pass and fell in behind. I trailed them to the front door, slowly closing the gap between the group and myself. Like a joke, timing is everything.

The door opened. A blare of music slopped through the door. The group pushed through the front door into the house, and I pushed in behind them, head down. My drunken buzz meant that I stumbled over the sea of shoes arced around the front door. But I was lucky. No one noticed me. I kicked my shoes into the corner and headed into the kitchen, coat on. My coat has lots of pockets.

"Lookin' for the good stuff," I hummed to myself. A bottle or two ought to do.

The group who had just arrived slammed the fridge door shut after adding their stock. The appliance jangled like a Christmas Santa. Sounds like bottles, I thought. Though the good stuff won't be in the fridge. I scouted around and found a forest of hard liquor bottles on the kitchen table nested between snacks. A string of Christmas lights wound through it all. As Kelpy, one of my mom's old boyfriends used to say, I was gone right out of her. My buzz cut strong and deep, making it hard to think. Just the way I liked it.

Time to take things to the next level.

I drew up to the table. There stood my best friend.

2

RUM. YOU LITTLE DEVIL. GOOD to see you!

A couple of fingers of it left at the bottom. One good belt. I found a plastic cup, and drained the bottle. Swigged it straight. The cup went into the kitchen sink. It had been silly even to look for a cup. The kind of drinking I do doesn't require any stinkin' cup.

Back to the forest of bottles. Most were open, uncapped, and full. I lingered in the kitchen until a large group congregated, chatting and devouring the food. I could see another open bottle nearly full of brown rum. I reached for it and pulled it away. The cap next to it rolled on its side right into my other hand.

I turned to face the counter as if I were going to pour myself a drink. Crowned the bottle with the cap and spun it closed. Slipped the entire bottle into the mickey pocket of my coat. I picked an empty wine bottle from the counter and returned it to the crowd of bottles on the kitchen table. No one noticed a thing. Smooth, right?

One more, maybe two.

I turned back to the table and scanned the necks carefully.

Not the wine. Not the beer.

A 26er of gin, possibly. But unopened! At the back of the kitchen table, against the wall.

I waited until the crowd around the table thickened. Then pushed in and got my hand around the neck of the bottle.

A thick hand grabbed my wrist.

"Sean, you son of a gun," the voice attached to the hand said.

3

EAN?" SOMEONE IN THE CROWD complained.

"Sean's here," Charles said. He held my wrist steady.

"How'd he get in?"

A quiet groan broke through the group as the news spread. Carly strode into the kitchen. "Ah, man. You aren't welcome here," she spat.

Charles, the owner of the thick hand, was a Frenchman from Montreal. We called him Charles. Not Chuck. Not Charlie. Not Chaz. Charles. "You gonna take my drink, Sean?" he asked. "You weren't even invited, were you?"

Carly leaned into Charles. I could hear her loud whisper. "How do we get rid of him? I want him out. Please."

"I was just gettin' a drink, man. Chill," I slurred, smooth as a used car salesman. "I got a Facebook invite." Carly shook her head.

"Sure, I did. Kinda."

Charles released my wrist, and sniffed the air. Maybe my breath. "Holy man, you're pretty wasted already," he noted. "You trying to get your stomach pumped again?" A menacing group of guys formed and stood behind Charles.

I backed up to the counter and looked for an out. Last down and ten yards to go. The exits were blocked. I'm not exactly a linebacker either. No way I'd break through that line.

"Awww, man. I just came for a drink, fellas. Just one teeny tiny drink." I held my thumb and forefinger up to my eye to show how small. I don't know why I bothered. When you're drunk, you don't think straight. That's what's good about it. That's what's bad about it.

Charles wasn't a bad guy. Tough and fair. But the boys congregating behind him, another sort altogether. More like sharks. The kind that smell blood and circle until they get an easy piece.

Another beating on the way. Did I mention the beatings before? I'd had a few. For some reason, people don't like it when you steal their alcohol.

4

CHARLES EYED THE GROWING CROWD and turned to Sean. "I got an idea, Sean," he said. "I'm going to save your ass. Here's the deal. I will give you my 26er of gin if you do me a small favor." Charles paused.

"Sure," I squeaked. "Does this mean no Christmas gift this year?"

He laughed. I reached for the bottle of gin. Charles grabbed my hand again and pulled it away.

"You know that ship that's abandoned in the harbor?" he asked.

"Yeah," I replied. Everybody knew. The Lyubov Orlova was a small Russian cruise ship. Two years ago, the crew had docked, and the company went bankrupt. The ship had been seized because the cruise company owed money. Now, a new owner was going to tow the boat to the Dominican Republic for scrap.

"I want you to get me something from that ship, and bring it back here for me. Then, I'll give you the 26er."

"You'd let me back into the party?" Too easy. Way too easy. "Where's the catch?"

"We'd let you back in," Charles said with a nod. "And you can drink all you like."

"Sure, no problem." A mission was better than a beating, wasn't it?

"I'll give you a couple of beers for the road, too."

I grinned. Big mistake, Charles. I'll be right back and I can drink better than anyone here, I thought.

Plus, they hadn't found the bottle of rum I'd already taken.

"I have to be able to tell that the thing came from the boat, right?" Charles watched me to make sure I understood.

"OK. So like something with its name on it, like a life saver ring, or something. How about something with some Russian writing on it? A brochure with the ship name?"

Charles nodded. He went to the fridge and retrieved a couple of bottles of beer.

"One more?" I begged.

Charles eyed me for a moment, and pulled another off a loaded shelf and passed it to me.

"See you in a stitch," I announced and staggered from the room and fetched a pair of shoes from the shoe sea. I may have found my own shoes, but honestly, I have no idea. Then, I drunk a deep breath and dove through the front door into the storm. I heard a faint cheer behind me.

At the time, I was pretty excited. I hadn't been beaten. I had a few pockets of alcohol. And I got a free ticket back into the party, and all the hooch I wanted. That's pretty much a perfect scenario for me. That's as good as my life got, at the time.

Just a simple souvenir from the Lyubov Orlova and I'd be back. How hard could it be?

The ship docked three blocks away. A short trip down Becks Cove. The blizzard stewed flakes into a blinding white screecher. The last cup of rum began to thicken my stupor. I had a little too much in my system at the moment. It would wear off. It always did.

My steps were uneven. I made it a block away, to the park, before I realized I hadn't zipped my coat. I stopped under a street lamp. The zipper ends swam before me, rubbing my fingers raw with the saw-tooth draw of the zipper before it caught and closed against the storm.

Then an inventory. The rum bottle, check. Three beers, check. My phone, check. My vision blackened for a moment, and then returned. I dropped to my knees and then to my butt, waiting for the nausea to pass.

Focus. Weather eye out. No more drinking 'til I've got into the boat.

My pants were now soaked. But what does a drunk person notice? Not much. Which is the point, after all. After a short sit on sidewalk snow, I continued my stagger down Becks Cove Road to the ship. Becks Cove opened into Harbor Drive and the docks. The stern of the Lyubov Orlova hulked dimly through the storm. I needed to find a way on board. Should be easy. The ship was a floating garage sale, not a fancy cruise ship. No security.

I bumbled towards the bow. About two thirds of the way forward, I noticed a gangway leading to the ship entrance. The gangway stood on a steep incline covered in a layer of sticky, slick new snow. At the top, a plywood door. At least, that's what I thought I saw.

Between the deck of the gangway and the aluminum railings stretched nylon netting to catch anything or anyone who might accidentally fall from the gangway. With any luck, it would keep even a drunk dude from falling into the water. I climbed the gangway, clinging to the aluminum railing on one side. I couldn't keep my footing and stumbled onto my knees several times. I could feel my pants grow heavy and thick as they sponged up the storm snow. My hold on the railing was a little sloppy. Didn't get far before I slipped skidded on my knees all the way back to the dock level. Bottles clanked and jingled as I slid. Slush and snow now jammed up the inside of my pant legs.

This might be harder than I thought.

I stood and wormed up the gangway again. This time I clawed at the nylon, and after a bitter climb I reached the ship's door. The door was dark and well worn. Did I mention padlocked? Took me quite a while to figure that out.

"I'll be jiggered!" I yelled.

I grabbed the lock and shook it. Below the padlock, a metal handle had been bolted to the plywood door. I blinked slowly and grabbed the metal handle and shook it. Heavy sigh.

I lowered myself to the gangway decking and dropped the last few inches onto my butt, clinging to the nylon net.

It's all about letting go.

So I let go. And skidded down the gangway to the dock. Another mush of wet snow shot up my pant legs. And the gangway ribbing gave me a profound wedgie. Almost sent me into another dimension. The cold shock cut into my buzz. The back side of my legs enjoyed the brace of a fresh chill.

Staggering to my feet, I tottered to the ship's bow.

The rust-scabbed hull of the boat rose easily fifteen to twenty feet above me. I paused by a heavy metal T-shaped post, called a bollard, attached to the dock. I followed a series of two ropes from the bollard through the opening in the boat decking to a loop around the timberhead.

The world tilted the wrong way and I stumbled forward to the dock's edge. The black water clicked and churned below. The odd stipple of water blinked orange as it jumped into the dim dock light. Not a nylon netting in sight.

Fall in there and I won't be coming back.

5

RAN MY HAND ALONG A rope as thick as my forearm and followed it with my eye as it stretched to the bow.

Too steep.

I wobbled a circle and headed toward the stern. The hull didn't get any lower. But, near the stern, the hull's wall opened to an aft deck. The deck's surface was only a couple of feet above the level of the dock.

I stood next to a bollard, exploring the three sets of hefty stern lines tied to the metal post. The forward set wouldn't work—they led straight to the hull wall. The set to the aft weren't right either. One line was frayed and stringy. Plus they were too far apart.

The middle set might work.

The middle lines were three four-inch ropes side by side. The three ropes together formed a kind of bridge. The ropes hung about the length of a car over the black boil of seawater below. I knelt over the ropes. I touched each of the three lines to be sure my good friend rum wasn't playing tricks. Yep. Three. They'd hold me easily.

I couldn't see the water between the dock and the ship, but I could hear the waves spit and sputter. Without much more thought, I straddled the three lines, and sat on them. Dangerous. Stupid. These are words that come to mind as I think about it now. At the time, I wasn't thinking at all. I inched my way towards the ship. It was slow work, but before long I'd managed to cross halfway.

"I can do this," I sang to myself, visions of liquor bottles dancing in my head. The second half of the crossing was a little more difficult. I'd reached the bottom of the ropes' arc and now had to pull myself up an incline. But I persisted, and soon I was close enough to the ship to touch the aft deck's railing. I grabbed the railing with both hands and shifted my right foot to the deck's surface and pulled myself forward. As I did, my left foot grazed the rope and my running shoe tumbled into the black water.

One shoe in Davy Jones' Locker.

I bent over the deck railing and pivoted on my stomach until my feet cleared the railing and touched down on the aft deck. I was on the ship.

6

STAGGERED BACK AND FELL ON my butt. Vision dimmed again for a moment. I waited to see if I might pass out. After a minute or two, my vision strengthened again. Half done. Time for a little party.

I pulled out a bottle of beer and struggled for some time with the twist-off cap.

"A little nourishment," I announced. "Cold and refreshing." That's what beer drinkers say, isn't it?

An ooze of wet snow began a cold invasion of my left sock. I swilled the beer in seconds and dropped the bottle into the water. "There's a drizzle at the bottom for you, Davy," I announced. "A little something to wash down the shoe."

Now to find something to prove I was here.

I turned to look for a door of some kind. There were a couple, but both were locked. On the lower quarterdeck, a hallway ran toward the bow on the dock of the deck. The hallway looked creepy. A strangled orange light from the sodium vapor streetlights broke up the shadow a little. I rounded the far side. No staircase. Just another hallway running into darkness toward the bow. I returned to the wall to examine the doors.

A ladder! Actually, a steep set of stairs. Almost a ladder.

Bolted to the wall, the steps led to the deck above through a small, square hatch, which was open. I patted the ladder with each hand, one at a time, to make sure I actually had its rails in my hand, and I climbed to the next deck.

The deck below was spooky, and the second deck no less so. I let the beer push aside any thoughts that the ship was haunted. I had to press forward to get the prize. From this deck, an actual stairway led to another deck above. I trudged up the stairs to a deck that seemed to hold some promise. There were large windows facing the back of the ship. There was a set of doors in the middle of the space. I went for the doors. Locked.

A thought of the 26er of gin flashed in my mind, so I looked around for inspiration. I found it in the form of a piece of wood, baseball-bat-long and thick. I stabbed it through the door's plate glass window. I reached inside, and twisted the bolt's thumb turn to unlock the door.

I moved slowly into the dark of the carpeted room. It was a big, empty space, like a dining room maybe? Something scurried away as I walked. In my drunken state, it took a full few moments before I recognized the mold smell assaulting my nose.

"Eeeew." I squinched my face.

But it was much warmer inside than out. No brainer. So I continued in. I'd only taken a few steps inside the room when I doubled over and vomited. Guess I over did it, again. The contents of my stomach flew in a black torrent to the floor. I fell to my knees in the pool of muck, and threw up again, and again. My body spasmed to rid itself of every ounce of alcohol. I nearly passed out and slumped into the puddle of puke.

But I didn't. Pale orange ribbons of saliva stretched from my mouth to the floor. I crawled backward to steer away from the small ocean of puke. Exhausted by my journey and the excruciating exercise of vomiting, I wanted a little nap. I crawled a little further through the dark room until I came to a room with long padded benches, or couches, maybe. I picked a bench and slithered up onto the cushions.

The awful taste of bile filled my mouth. So I unzipped my coat a little and fished out the rum, and unscrewed the cap. In my stewed state, it took a moment to find a way to place the bottle neck in my mouth. A few mouthfuls spilled over my chin and down the front of my coat and shirt. In order to get rid of the awful taste, I took a mouthful, ran it around the inside of my mouth and swallowed. I took a deep guzzle to make up for the rum I'd just lost in my vomit. Time I was done, there wasn't much left in the bottle.

Might as well finish it off, I thought. Bottoms up!

I hoisted the bottle over my head and downed the contents. The ship was in a spin, so it was a trick to get the liquid down the throat. Fortunately, I'd had some practice. The bottle was a little less than half full. But, in my current state, it was far too much for my body to handle. Like I said before, the good thing about being drunk is that kills thought. The bad thing is that it kills thought.

I laid back on the cushioned seat for a few minutes, waiting for the nausea to pass. But as the rum rushed to my head, the room lost its substance and turned to black. I threw up again, I think, off the edge of the seat. And passed out.

7

WHEN I AWOKE, I WAS in complete darkness. My head felt as though it had been split open by an axe, and a zombie was gnawing on my brain. And it was hot.

Feels like a sauna in here. Where am I?

Not in the hospital. Bummer. The hospital was a good place for me. I groaned. My lips had dried and knit together. My tongue felt thick, and it was glued to the roof of my mouth. The taste in my mouth: a sour gym sock. A smell of vomit and mold. Weird sounds. And motion, maybe. Still drunk, so it's hard to say.

An edge of fear shaved thoughts close. As I lay on

the seat, I didn't dare move. I couldn't remember exactly where I was. Memory came back to me like a cloud of houseflies. Little flying bits of recollection landed in thought. They shifted around a little, taking off again, until the I had a general idea of my current location. I'm at Carly's house, probably.

I patted my coat pockets.

One beer. Two beer.

Then a half thought. Maybe this isn't Carly's house.

I fished a bottle out of my pocket. It was warm. Weird. Twist off.

I could feel the tremble as I grasped the cap. My muscle felt loose and weak. I couldn't seem to summon enough strength. I had to work hard to get the bottle open. I tore my lips apart. And poured the beer in my mouth.

Gave my tongue a beer bath. After it had soaked for a moment or two, it loosened from the roof of my mouth. My stomach snarled and popped. It wanted food. Great.

Whatever room I was in, it began to slowly rise as though it were climbing a steep hill. It seemed to hold for a moment, and shudder before plunging in the opposite direction. The space filled with groans and creaks. Maybe there were a lot of people in my condition waking up at the same time? The room again tried to climb slowly, then dropped away again. I am so drunk, I thought. The room is still spinning. This must have been a humdinger of a party.

It was so dark. I couldn't see anything. I couldn't see my hand. No light anywhere. I honestly couldn't tell whether I'd gone blind or not. Something wrong with that, too.

Phone.

I fished through my pockets until I found my phone. I tapped the screen until it woke up. The screen read 2:17 a.m. A thin sliver of red colored the bottom of the battery logo. It was almost finished. In little words underneath, it read Thursday, January 24. A small thought wormed into my brain.

Wasn't the party Tuesday night?

Maybe I read the day wrong. Though my mind felt thick, I made it work its way back to the beginning of the week.

I thought the party was Tuesday. Wasn't it? Which should make it Wednesday morning 2:17 a.m.

I studied the screen again. The readout insisted it was Thursday, as the room plummeted again. Another idea: Someone's probably messing with me. Someone changed the time on my phone.

I grinned. Of course. Hilarious, man. I'd been sleeping for a few hours. Pretty easy to get my phone and change the settings. But why so dark?

I used the light from my phone's screen to look around. I was lying on a couch of some kind. It was beige with brown stripes. The couch was part of a sitting area: two couches faced each other. Behind me, as I rolled onto my back, an outside wall, with a row of windows. All of the furniture seemed rough. Carly's basement, maybe? The upholstery was worn. Stuffing blossomed through tears in the fabric. Wait, it couldn't be Carly's basement. Old furniture in a musty basement. Basements don't move, do they? Or was it me?

I am so drunk, I thought.

Better shut my phone off, I thought. I might need the power later.

I sat up. As I did my stomach began to do loops. There were several similar seating areas in this room. My stomach instantly soured and an overwhelming nausea took control. So I lay down. My stomach tamed a little. I attempted to sit up again a few minutes later, but my stomach wouldn't let it happen. One option, really. More sleep.

8

A FEW HOURS LATER, I AWOKE to daylight. A standard St. John's winter gray sky. My mouth parched, again, still tasting like I'd eaten the sock of a construction worker with a foot fungus problem.

I took a few minutes to get my bearings again. I was lying on an upholstered bench in the middle of what seemed to be a library. Above and between the seating there were bookshelves. Many of the books had been pilfered, like a mouth missing most of its teeth. The room still hiked and dove, but not like it had felt the night before. Not Carly's basement. Basements don't have windows—at least, Carly's wouldn't—and they don't move. Unless I'm still drunk, which is the most likely scenario.

I inched myself upright. My stomach didn't appreciate it, and complained. The smell of stale vomit didn't help, either. I took to my feet. My left foot was numb with cold. A memory started to knock on the wall of my brain, like a starving insurance salesman who knows you're hiding in the house, refusing to answer the door.

A ship! The thought bobbled around like a caffeinated five-year old on a trampoline. I'm on a ship.

My whole body shook. My hands wouldn't sit still. They leapt around, like two ADHD children with oppositional defiance disorder, high on sugar. My insides felt delicate and raw. My left foot was a block of ice. I checked it. No shoe. What? I checked my right foot. A shoe. I'm missing a shoe. Panic began to brew and bubble in my chest. I tried to remember, but chunks of my brain seemed dark and empty.

Stupid shoe, I thought. I got to find something to walk home with.

I carefully turned to look out the windows. The

window hosted a waterfront view of a vast body of water. The North Atlantic? I blinked a couple of times. The brew of panic began to boil over, igniting the rest of the neural network inside my brain.

"I'm on a boat," I yelled. I had no idea how I'd arrived there, or what it was all about. I vaguely remembered arriving at St. John's harbor. For what? But the North Atlantic wasn't something you'd see from the safety of the St. John's harbor. Maybe, though, I'm just on the wrong side of the boat. Maybe the other side.

This is the side of the boat opposite the dock, I reasoned. I won't see much.

The thought calmed me for a moment. Until my thinker started to work a little better. And the flame of panic returned.

I should see the opposite side of the harbor, though.

I took a couple of careful steps to remind my legs how to walk, then surveyed the area. I looked for the closest door. There was an open set of double doors to my right. In the daylight, I could see well enough to make out a bar of some kind. My panic went on an instant vacation, my heart instantly hot with drink lust.

"I can use a drink," I said to the bar, like it was an old buddy.

I trotted to the bar. Not a drop to be found. The entire area had been ransacked. There were empty bottles on the shelves behind the bar. The boat rocked back, and the bottles on the floor behind the bar clinked quietly as they met, like ghosts taunting me with a toast.

The boat pitched forward. I nearly lost my footing. A runaway bottle hurtled toward the back of the ship, bumping and bumbling toward the bow. Through the bar was another set of doors. At those doors I found myself in a hallway. The hallway was dimly lit, except at the far end. I moved toward the light. The hallway opened into a large dining room. At the far end of the dining room, a set of double glass doors led onto the stern's observation deck.

I moved quickly, now fueled by adrenalin instead of alcohol. Without a drink my fear ballooned and eclipsed my need for a stiff one. I was drawn to windows on the far side of the dining room. The view put me out of my mind.

I should leave this part out, since I'm the author of the story. I should just say that I looked out and laughed in scorn at my situation.

The window should have framed a view of the St. John's hillside—the quaint houses, businesses, and narrow streets that flowed down from the hillside to the harbor front. Instead, all I could see was the gray white-capped stipple of the sea.

Arcs of emotion sparked and sizzled through my chest. I smashed furniture, and chucked stuff around. Meltdown: full on. Tears and blubbering and everything. Cursing, swearing. Tantrums. Praying. Surprised my tears didn't sink the old tub right there. The tide of emotion slowly ebbed away, and left me exhausted but calm.

Tears and blubbering and everything. Cursing, swearing. Tantrums. Praying. Turns out, nothing helped.

How far away from town am I? I wondered.

I twisted from the windows to the back of the dining room, where doors would let me out to the deck. I'd be able to grab a wider view. Not that it should be necessary to go outside to see the harbor. I mean, St. John's should be somehow visible from the windows I'd been looking through. Maybe the ship had broken loose from its moorings and had floated free, right? But I couldn't be that far away, could I? Someone would come out with a tug to haul it back to the dock.

I strode toward the double doors. Too late I saw the smashed glass on the dark carpet, and not until I felt a sharp prick in my left foot. I shifted all my weight to my right foot and hopped to a dining chair lying on its side.

I righted the chair, and sat down to examine my foot. A small piece of glass stuck out of my foot like a pin in a corkboard. I wanted my right hand to pull the glass sliver out. But my right hand danced away from what I'd wanted it to do.

I concentrated for several moments just to convince my fingers to grasp the glass shard. I pulled the glass out and threw it to the floor. This time, I checked the floor beneath me for glass and got to my feet. Then hopped on my right foot to the double doors and out onto the aft observation deck.

No land in sight, from the stern. I limped to the starboard side, and looked towards the bow. No land that direction either. My heart began to pound as a storm of panic broke loose in my chest. My breath came rapidly, in shallow mouthfuls. I buried my head in my hands.

"Oh, oh, oh, oh, oh. Oh, God, please. Please no."

I slapped my face a few times in case my pickled brain was lying to me. Scrubbed my eyes with my thumbs. Blinked a few times until I could feel the tears lubricate my vision. Looked again.

Tears began to tumble down my face again. My body began to spasm as the rhythm of tears fought with my panicked breathing. Once again, my vision began to fade.

My phone, I thought. My phone. Maybe there's cell coverage.

I groped my pocket for the phone and pulled it out, nearly dropping it on the deck. I powered it up. My hands still didn't want to cooperate, so it was a struggle to push the power button. There wasn't much battery life. But I had a bar of signal!

Contacts. Home. Dial. The phone began to complain of low battery. The phone rang at home. One ring. Two rings. Three rings.

"Come on," I prayed. "Pick up."

Four rings.

"Hello?" My mom answered.

"Mom?" I yelled excitedly.

"Sean, you low life," she began. She was drunker than a skunk. As any zoologist can tell you, skunks like to drink.

"Mom," I pleaded. "Just listen."

"No, you just listen, mister. You missed three days of school, an' everyone's wonderin' where you are. You selfish jerk. Get back here, now. Now, hear me?"

"Mom, I'm stuck on a ship and it's drifting out to sea. Please help me." I began to weep again. I had called the wrong person. But I only know one person.

"Crying ain't goin' to help you this time. You gonna get it, and not just from me," she slurred. "They gonna take you away from me...." The line went dead. Then a thought of Sailor. He'll be starving.

I punched the text button, and thumbed a message:

Mom,

I'm trapped on a boat that's drifting at sea. It's called the *Lyubov Orlova*. Call the Coast Guard. Please feed and water Sailor. Please send help.

Sean

I hit the *send* key. The phone said "sending," then it beeped one last time and died.

"Mom, no! No. NO. NO. I'm all alone," I screamed. I fell to the deck in a ball, rocking back and forth. Began to whimper. "I'm all alone," I whispered. I rocked back and forth on the green metal decking, drowning in fear. I wallowed until I realized I was ice cold. My left foot had become a frozen lump.

The sun glowed orange and balanced on the edge of the horizon. Long shadows lay across the deck.

The storm of fear calmed a little and thought returned. Without much of an idea of what I would do next, I decided to return to where I had slept. I felt awful, jittered and jumpy, like I needed to sleep, or at least lie down.

Inside it was protected. Warmer than outside. I wanted more water and a bathroom. I hopscotched on my right foot through the shards of glass.

Interspersed between the glass fragments were black things, like raisins, scattered over much of the floor. I picked up a raisin to inspect it. And just before I popped it into my mouth, I realized it was crap. Something had crapped all over the floor. I hurled it to the floor. A mouse or a rat or something. It was hard to tell with the pattern of the carpet. But the floor was dotted with the stuff. A novel's worth of punctuation with the words missing.

My bladder reminded me that it was good and full, too. Another reason to keep looking around. Before I lost light entirely, I would need to find a bathroom.

Through the bar, to the forward end of the dining room. Bathrooms need to be near where people eat, right? On either side, at the head of the dining room, there were cabins. I picked one that read "506." I tried the door, but it wouldn't open even though the latch assembly had been removed. I tried the cabin opposite. The number was missing but the cabin door swung open and closed with the ship's motion. The door swung closed on me, but I shoved it open and walked in. As I did, I interrupted a rat. The fat creature had parked in the middle of the cabin floor, between two single twin beds. It studied me before scurrying into the mattress of one of the two single beds. There was a tiny bathroom to the left of the sleeping quarters. The toilet was dry. Clearly the plumbing was out of order. I used it anyway.

On my way out of the bathroom, I investigated the sleeping quarters to see if I could find anything useful. One bed, the one where the rat had disappeared somewhere in the mattress, had rat-crap raisins covering the bedclothes. Other than those two things, the bed looked inviting. The bed opposite had an avocado-colored blanket and a bed sheet balled up in a corner.

"I'll take those." I carefully pulled the bedclothes out of the corner, making sure to shake them onto the cabin floor before I called them mine. Just a couple of rat-raisins. No rats. A good thing. "Time to set up camp."

A small dresser was fixed to the floor between to the two beds. I quickly rifled through the drawers. The Gideon Bible in the top drawer would be no help. Otherwise, the drawers were bare. The evening light drew dim.

I hauled my finds back to the library. When I walked in, a few rats were lapping up the lake of puke I'd spewed the night before. They scurried away when I arrived.

To warm up, I wrapped myself first in the sheet, then in the blanket, and hunkered down on the couch I'd slept on the night before.

How's this even possible? How can a ship tied alongside end up loose and alone on the Atlantic? I should have been able to walk off the ship onto the cold, hard rock. This is some weird, boy. The drink has made me daft. I just have to wait until my head's ship shape again. I'll probably find I'm in English class again.

If it's real, I'm missing the words to describe my surprise. I would have a hard time figuring the cut between being tied up at a dock, and ending up in a twist on the wide ocean with nobody around. That's plain crooked. Mighty squish, as my mom would say.

A maze of confusion set over me and chased me in loops. Liquor smashed memories came back in pieces, though no clear idea of where I was or how I'd gotten there emerged. I lashed any good thought to the deck. I spent a long time reviewing my brief conversation with my mom. Would she have learned enough to figure out where I was? Did the text send? Was help on the way? My emotions flip-flopped from terror to giddiness and back again. I tried to wrestle them into a good space. But the dark shadows of my predicament wouldn't quit chasing me. Um. Maybe I haven't mentioned it, but this is typically when I'd want to drink. A lot.

After a long while, I decided that if this is the way my noggin was going to play it, I'd better play along. It's some crooked and it doesn't like it when I argue with it.

"What have I got with me?" I said aloud.

Carefully, I scooped out the content of my pockets and placed it on a battered table between the couches. One remaining beer, a lighter, and cigarettes. A forged parental note for school, and a dead phone. One dime. Boogered balls of pocket lint. I'd lost my wallet, somehow. I moaned as fear overwhelmed me, again, for a few minutes.

The discovery of the beer caused my heart to leap with joy. After a little struggle, I raised the uncapped bottle to my lips and sipped the glorious amber liquid. Though it was warm, I drank slowly. As I did, I realized that I wouldn't be drinking alcohol until I got rescued. Which wouldn't be too long, would it?

Hopefully mom got the message. I'll be rescued tomorrow, probably, I thought.

But Sailor. "Sorry, buddy," I said aloud. "I screwed up. They'll find you and take care of you. I hope." The one life that needed me. The image of Sailor darted behind my thoughts as I tried to grab hold of my new situation.

I raised my right hand to my eyes and tried to steady the last beer. My hand trembled like a tap dancer after guzzling a case of Red Bull. I contemplated the brown bottle. Once it was gone, things would become difficult.

Though I wouldn't have called myself an alcoholic, that is, in fact, what I was. I hated life sober. I can't handle life straight. The future's so dark, I need a stiff one.

What am I going to drink after this?

9

TILL WRAPPED IN MY BLANKET, I was motivated by the taste of the beer to visit the bar again. In the dying light I checked the entire area again for liquor containers of any sort. There were lots of bottles, to be sure. If there were a bottle depot close, I'd be good. I sorted between bottles that were dry, and those that seemed to have a drop or drizzle in them. I let the sheet and blanket drape over my shoulders like a cape so I could haul that the hopeful bottles to my sleeping area. After a few trips back and forth, I had collected twenty-two bottles with a drizzle of alcohol at the bottom.

The bar fridges were old, moldy, and empty. I found a bottle opener and a corkscrew. There were plenty of wine glasses, shot glasses, and utensils of various sorts. I took the best of what I found, just in case.

A bottle at a time, I poured each drizzle and drab into a tumbler. My shaky hands meant the lip of each bottle clanged the tumbler's rim like a bell. Twenty two bottles later, and I'd pulled a mouthful of liquor together. I quickly downed the remainder of my beer, and turned to face what may be my last drink for a while.

In reverence, I stilled my hands as well as I could, took tender hold of the tumbler, and in a swift movement downed the shot of alcohol in a greedy gulp. It tasted like rat puke, but didn't care. I needed that drink.

The last of the beer and the drops-and-drizzles drink didn't even begin to touch my tremors. My hands still shook. I wanted to search for more, but it seemed like my two little drinks served only to remind my body of what it was missing. I felt a wave of nausea break over me. All I could do was hold onto my body and try steady myself. If I'd been honest with myself, I would have known there was no way I could keep exploring for more booze. Even so, I tried to stand up.

It felt like a valiant act, but it was pointless. Between the nausea and the twilight, I couldn't see a foot in front of my face. If I'd had a flashlight, I'd have kept going. The ship is pretty big. But without a flashlight, the dark was too deep. The kind that makes you feel as though you've given your eyeballs away. So I'd have to wait for the morning, and try in the new light.

10

THOUGH I LAY DOWN, SLEEP would not visit me. If my body was spasmodic before, it went into total freakout. I felt like a fresh flopping cod under a disco curse. Lord thunderin'. When you live drunk, your body gets used to it. Then, when it doesn't have it, it's going to let you know. Mine was acting like a four year-old on a long road trip. I needed at least half a forty of hard liquor, stat.

My gut also wanted some food. It jumped and bubbled, trying to get my attention.

To add to everything, twilight succumbed to darkness. Quickly. Like someone switched off the lights. Complete blackout. A cloudy night, no moonlight or starlight. No light from anything I could see. Another night of deep darkness. I strained to see anything—opened my eyes wide, and nothing visible.

My eyes were hungry to see something. Anything. I'd even take a Justin Bieber poster. I could hear the scurries and scrabbling of creatures, probably rats, as they moved around me, but my eyes were starved for light. I opened my eyes as wide as I could, but the night was utterly dark. The dark almost drove me mad. Serious body pain. Not a stitch of light.

As I strained to see something, anything, a rat came into view. Which was weird. I think I just told you how dark it was. I shouldn't be able to see anything.

A rat with an unusually large head approached me. It seemed unafraid. The rat sported a hole in the middle of its forehead. Did I mention it had a top hat? Dorothy, this ain't Kansas anymore.

11

HAD A FUNNY FEELIN' I knew what was on the way. I'd been there before. At home, I drank hard so I wouldn't go there again. But drink-starved, I had nothing to keep myself from alcohol's revenge. This time, it was personal. And it showed up in style. A rat with an extra hole in its forehead, topped with a top hat.

The rat swaggered toward me, a perverted Mickey Mouse. Close to the couch it leapt up onto my chest, like I was a stair on a stage. Sounds funny when I write it now, but I was so terrified at the moment, I believe I pissed my own pants. I tried to scream, but I was far beyond sound by then.

The rat reached towards my face, plucked out my right eyeball, and tossed it into his jaws, swallowing it whole like a pill. I watched as my eyeball rose like the sun in the hole in the rat's forehead. The eye popped up backwards, a red map of veins at first, then slowly spun until the pupil rose like a moon and focused on me. The rat now had three eyes. One of them was mine. The two on the bottom glowed an evil red. The one on top was one of my cute old blues. Once the new eye took its seat, all three eyes began looking in different directions. The rat seemed to grin, and from behind its back produced a gentleman's cane. He leaned forward over my face, on the cane, and whistled for his buddies.

Suddenly, a sea of rats poured out of the darkness and flowed over me where I lay. The sea of fur broke over my head, so I couldn't see out of my remaining eye.

The sea parted to reveal the rat in the hat. The rat raised its cane, and that somehow set me free to scream and thrash. Which I did. Full-on freakout.

"Get away. Go, go, go," I begged. I screamed. "Get off me!" The rats crawled all over my body, and under my coat, and shirt. Down my pants. I sat up and tore the coat from my body.

"Get off me!" I screamed. I ripped the shirt off and hurled it away. Then I began to claw at my own skin. "Get away. Get off me."

So you're thinking this is weird, and you'd be right. But it's also normal when you're coming off a big drunk. I bet I'd stayed mostly drunk for most of a month. At least. Trouble comes to visit when you run outta booze.

My stream of cussing and screams dissolved into something more primal. Noises of abject terror. "Ahhhhhhhhh. Woahhhhh." Some of the sounds I made defy the alphabet. I have no idea how to write them down.

A steady river of rats flowed slowly out of the dark and over me. Fangs and fur, nipping and biting as they went. Like a rat buffet, where I was the all-you-can-eat main course.

Long smooth rat tails snaked over my skin. Sandpaper fur brushed deep into my flesh. The whites of bared fangs, digging in. Squeals and whimpering sounds escaped from my lips. As I twisted in place, I fell off the bench to the floor. A few yards away, the rat with three eyes supervised the attack from a table top. He seemed pleased with how things were progressing. A creepy grin as he watched.

I slapped, and pinched, and flailed to keep the rats at bay, but they coursed endlessly over me. I caught the odd one in my hand and tossed it like a squealing hand-grenade across the room. Another I caught by the tail and slung into the wall on the opposite side. I gagged on fear as I tried to fight them away.

Though I hurt any rat my hands could find, there were far too many. I couldn't win. I couldn't even slow the rat torrent. I glanced at my midsection. The rats had eaten through my flesh. I could see my own ribs, and the dull glow of my innards caged underneath. One rat noticed me noticing, and dug through my ribs to pull out a string of my intestines. He held them up as though they were party streamers, ready to be hung. Another rat grabbed the loose end and it turned into a tug-o-war, over my dead body. The rest seemed to catch on and began to use my organs as sort of edible athletic equipment. One of them cut out a kidney and tossed it to his companions like a football. Between plays, several of them would take a bite.

I fought and fought. How long this continued, I can't say. It seemed like forever. The next time I looked down, I was empty. Organs gone. They'd taken me down to bone. Rats lounged in my pelvis like it was a couch. I'd shoo them away with my skeletal arms. But another pair of rats would only take their place. Nothing of me left by the end of it.

For some reason, I kept fighting, defending myself, even though there was nothing of myself left. The war raged on through the night, until I was beyond exhausted. Somehow, in the middle of the combat, I fell asleep.

12

AWOKE IN AGONY. SUNLIGHT SLAMMED my head like brick. Teeth chattering with cold, naked. But pleasantly shocked.

I still had skin. I had scratched myself viciously, but it was there. Yay, skin. Love skin. Good to have skin. The organ party I'd witnessed before was only a living nightmare. Legs. Arms. Two eyes. And a headache that suggested my head had been the game ball in a World Cup soccer game.

Yes, I had taken all my clothes off during the horrendous rat battle. And I'm mighty white. I was stiff and freezing, like a vanilla Popsicle. My mouth, dry as an English essay on Shakespeare. Tasted like I'd snacked on rat raisins all night, after stewing them in my own vomit.

Lying on the lounge floor. Every muscle screamed in pain. My heart pounded in my chest. My body bruised and battered, gouged end to end, head to toe; most of the scratches had drawn blood. My gut was tied in sailor's knots. And thirsty beyond anything I'd known. Rum, sure. Water first, though, please.

I remembered the rat in the top hat. Who could forget him? I remembered some of the war. Clearly it wasn't real, right? Maybe some of it was. Maybe a real rat had come and sat on my chest, and I'd made the rest up. Who could say? It's a tad embarrassing to admit that my hallucinations had encouraged me to beat the crap out of myself.

Hello. Police. I'd like to report an assault. A bully beat the crap out of me. Name of the bully? Me.

I pawed my T-shirt and held it out for inspection. Shredded. My coat I had torn off my body. The coat body was fine, but the zipper had been ripped out by the seam. My underwear dangled like a flag of surrender from a library bookshelf. My pants were in decent shape. I found one sock. Just one. What is it with socks anyway? Only one shoe. I shook my head in disgust.

I dressed myself in these rags. The sheet and blanket, upon examination, were fine. I hoisted them over my shoulders and wrapped myself up, trying to rekindle some warmth. Nausea exploded, beginning in my head and oozing quickly through the rest of my body. I lay down on the couch. It helped slightly.

I curled up and lay there for a while. As I began to doze, the image of the rat stealing my eye returned, and with it the start of a panic I'd felt the night before. I opened my eyes to a feast of daylight. I poked a hand through the sheet and blanket and touched both eyes to see if they were still in place. They were.

The rat didn't happen, I told myself. Just a pickle problem. I wasn't pickled, which was a problem. My brain, the big baby that it was, resented the lack of alcohol. So it put on a bit of a show. Big drama. Brains can do that, apparently.

I tried to let it know that it wasn't my fault. But brains just like to complain when they're unhappy. They make trouble. That's why I like to keep mine drunk. A sleepy, drunk brain leaves me alone. A perky one, awake and itchin' for things to do, gonna find a lick of trouble to get into.

I dozed for a while, until I was overwhelmed by the urge to go to the bathroom. I left my blankets behind and limped toward the cabin with the open door. The rat I'd seen the other day in the middle of the floor wasn't there when arrived.

On my way out, I paused at the door threshold.

I might as well look around the ship a little. So I did. A little.

13

XPLORATION NUMBER ONE: ON MY right, the remains of an exercise room with the odd bit of old exercise equipment inside. There were a couple of dumbbells on a bent rack near the back of the room. An old-school stationary bike. The remains of a treadmill. On the left, a cabin. The door still in place, 506. The door was missing its latch. I jimmied the door until it opened and walked in. A small stack of cardboard boxes piled in the center of the room. Rat droppings scattered around the room. Two single beds, and a bathroom, just like the other cabin. Garbage strewn about the room. I opened each box, one at a time. Files and paper. Letterhead, with the name of the ship on top. For a moment I wondered whether Charles would accept that as payment for the 26er. But it was now a moot point. I found a box of matching envelopes and cheap pens with the ship's name embossed on them. The drawers in the dresser—Nothing of note.

I turned to go up the hallway, but the darkness demanded too much courage of me. Who knows what lurked in this tub? Could even be another person or two on board, couldn't there? With my luck, I'd find an axe-murdering hillbilly.

I stood still, facing the dark hallway. It wasn't dark like night. The dark had a feeling to it. Sort of a personality. Like the darkness had eyes. Like something or someone was watching.

Instead, I chose to follow the light.

My hands began to shake slightly and the shake began to grow. This time the shake had less to do with alcohol as a lack of food and water. Maybe. Who knows, I'm not a doctor. I felt feeble. Weak. So I shuffled back to where I had been sleeping to lie down for a while. The sheet and blanket were working. Thank god for low-tech stuff.

I took a good gander out the windows again. I couldn't see anything in any direction. I don't know how it happened, but I seemed to be drifting on the open sea.

This seems utterly impossible. Everything I see defies everything I know. I was beginning to think I might have to actually put up with this situation. It could be real.

One thought kept trying to sink me. When I tried to throw it away, it returned with a vengeance. Like a yo-yo. Here's the thought: I could die out here.

14

HEALTH CLASS 101: A PERSON can live three days without water. I got no water. I also believed I couldn't live a day without rum. I was alive. Probably not for long. I'm not exactly a Boy Scout or anything.

I picked up the pen and paper and wrote a super dramatic note, in case I didn't survive. I hope my mom and English teacher cry when they read it.

I dozed for a while, imagining I'd wake in a new day, when in fact I woke maybe an hour later. Hard to say. My tongue nailed to the roof of my mouth again. My lips sandpaper. I tried talking: I was going to say something quite witty and deep. But was having difficulty because of the dryness. I believe I said "Maaaaaaa." It sounded like a sea cow with diarrhea.

Getting   close   to   a   moment   I'd   call "water or die."

15

WATER" I ATTEMPTED TO SAY. It probably sounded more like "Waaaaa."

"I'll take water for 100, Alex." That's what I wanted to say. See I'm brave that way. I make jokes when I'm pretty near dead. Very manly, I thought.

I slammed through a set of double wooden doors that led outside. Outside, I found myself on the deck, in a covered hallway. The ship's starboard was right there, but instead of an open railing, the ship showed me a covered hallway, with windows. I couldn't see the sun, though it was bright enough that I had to blink until my eyes adjusted. Up the hallway I walked, toward the bow.

I passed a couple of cabins. Apparently, some had doors to the outside of the ship. 502 and 501. 502 had a door and a latch. I tried the latch, and the door opened into a cabin twice the size of the ones inside one. Luxury, I thought. This is where the fancy people sleep.

I lurched into a sitting area with a couch and a table. An old TV sat on an open shelf. The sleeping quarters held two twin beds, in a separate room to the right. Note to self: No rat raisins. I couldn't see one anywhere.

There were a few bits of garbage lying around. In the middle of the garbage, I found a half-finished water bottle, with a cigarette butt and specks of ash floating on the water's surface. Gross, right?

Wrong! Lifeline. I pounced on the find. I tried to fish out the cigarette butt, but ended up losing a few tablespoons of water on my blanket. Screw that. I hoisted the bottle to my lips and keeping my teeth closed to strain out the chunks, drained the water in an instant. The cigarette butt fell against my teeth like hair in a shower drain.

Smoked water. I suppose it's a delicacy somewhere, like smoked salmon, maybe.

I'm sort of the opposite of a boat. A boat tries to keep the water out. A human needs to keep water in.

After a detailed inspection, I took a seat on the bed to let the water sink in. The pun intended. Sorry about the joke. Even bad ones seem to help.

I found a bunch of dirty, discarded laundry, including socks and a pair of small running shoes. Sadly, the shoes were far too small for me. Two matching socks. Weird, right? I nearly threw one overboard just to set the universe to rights.

The room had a porthole on either side of the cabin door, facing the covered deckway. The portholes were large and let in a lot of light. This cabin still had bedding on the bed and pillows. Someone had been sleeping here regularly.

I realized the cabin was closed off from the inside of the ship, which is where the rats liked to live. The working door would keep any rats out who happened by. Hence, this was a good cabin to set up camp.

The light, my discoveries, and the half a bottle of water brought on a small improvement to my mood, and infused me with the chutzpah to explore a little longer. From Cabin 502, I wandered into the one next door: Cabin 501. A good door and latch. It was a larger cabin, too. The layout was a little different than 502, and it had a forward-facing window in the sleeping area, which I liked. You could keep an eye out in two directions. No signs of rat life in this cabin either. I searched the furniture, the wardrobe closet, the cupboards, looking for anything. I found a right rubber boot, size thirteen, the size of a small ship. My own feet are nines. I eased it on to my left foot. As I looked in the mirror, I felt five years old again, trying on my stepdad's boot. Some stupid kid idolizing an abusive, king-sized moron. I paced around the cabin a little. It felt like I was wearing a canoe, but it would do.

Lame as it sounds, exploring those two cabins wore me out But they were prime real estate.

"I'll take both of them," I say to my imaginary real estate agent. The views will do, I suppose." Then I wave him away. "I'll pay what they're asking. No quibbles."

I made it back to the library, to my old sleeping spot. Though I liked the two cabins, I didn't take possession until the next day. That right there is another joke. Underline if you must.

Ah, when will I stop? Will I have to send myself to the principal's office for my unstoppable humor, on top of a restraining order I've taken out on myself? These are all questions I will tackle tomorrow, dear reader, assuming I continue to live.

16

READ MY GOODBYE NOTE OVER again. With a shaky hand, I added a couple of things to it. My additions were a little less panicked than my original note, but if you're reading this, you know that already. Night was coming quickly. On the water, night doesn't descend gently. It falls with the weight of an unabridged dictionary. The sun was there, and then it wasn't. So I needed to make the world disappear through the magic of sleep. All the writing and relentless joking tired me out, so I tucked in and fell asleep.

I remember falling asleep after the most embarrassing parent-teacher interview. Grade six. My mom was totally smashed. She met my teacher, Mr. Gorman. Mr. Gorman and I got along well. We had a groove and it made school fun. But when she met him, she thought he was pretty cute. She was shopping for a boyfriend at the time. So instead of being normal, she sat in his lap and put her arms around him like he was Santa Claus, and tried to whisper her Christmas wishes into his ear. Mr. Gorman was horrified. He was newly married with a young baby. Needless to say, he would hardly look at me for the rest of the year. I remember it being so awkward, so weird. The only relief I could find was sleep, at the time.

Sleep has always been a good hiding spot for me. Before I learned to drink. When you don't like life that much, sleep is a good getaway. Makes sense that depressed people want to sleep all the time. Sleep is a wonderful friend for those of us whose lives suck.

17

AWOKE IN A GRAY AND growing light of morning, somewhat refreshed, though my mouth felt like I'd eaten a bowl of Sailor's used kitty litter, dry. My stomach snarled as if to say "not funny." I held my hand up and studied it as it quavered. I worked my mouth a little to get my joker up and running for the day.

"Nurse? Cancel my surgeries," I say to the ship. "I won't be operating today." I nearly smiled at my own joke.

My stomach had a lot to say. The groans became more articulate, almost like words. "Shut up," I told it. "I know what you're trying to say." Here's what my stomach was trying to shout: Today's agenda involves two things, in order of importance, water and food. You'll notice that rum has dropped off the list entirely, and not because I don't think about it all the time. This is how Sailor must have felt when I forgot to feed him or top up his water bowl.

I moved up the outdoor hallway toward the bow until I found another set of double wooden doors leading inside. Let's try it, shall we? The doors opened, and I stepped inside. Both doors had large windows. A fringe of morning light shot through the black fust. The room's guts were an ocean of shadow. Who knows what I'd find? But my choice was the same as yesterday. Survive, or die.

18

SCREWED MY COURAGE AND STEPPED inside. It looked like a lounge-style seating area with a dance floor and small stage...for the undead. I could hear a rustle as fleets of rats parted everywhere I walked in the room.

The wrong-footed rubber boot did help a little. I think it was steel-toed, too. I could walk with a little more confidence. Even in the few steps I'd taken, I could feel a blister the size of a hamburger forming.

There were several large windows covered by some thick orange-red inserts designed to block the light. The inserts were in rough shape, so they leaked a little light around the edges. The windows were twice as tall as me. Light is becoming my friend, so the inserts had to go.

Judging from my location, I guessed they'd look out over the ship's bow. I approached a window. The inserts were snapped in place. I popped the snaps out. The top line of snaps was too far above me, so I undid the bottom and two sides and pulled. The last snaps refused to let go, preferring to tear off instead. The insert fell on top of me, but released a huge belch of sunlight into the room. The light caused a huge rat panic. I could hear the room explode in activity.

There goes my damage deposit.

I pushed the insert off of me. The window glass was huge. I was right. It offered a view of the bow deck. There was a huge crane mounted on the deck out front. Kinda cool. I pulled the other four inserts out of their windows. An awesome thing. The heat of the sun through the glass warmed the room nearly instantly. I actually took my coat off for the first time since the rat dream.

Now, with maximum light on my side, I turned to explore the rest of the room.

The carpet was a bright orange, and the seats blue. A tarnished wooden dance floor sprawled in the middle. No wonder the ship went out of business. Décor, people.

The carpet didn't have a pattern, so it was easy to see the rats liked to party here.

The lounge stretched from port to starboard, too. On either side, thick royal blue curtains kept out much of the view. I took aim at the curtains, pulling them out of the way. Most of them had catch cords so they could be held back easily. A couple didn't, so I tore them down. Between the garbage on the floor and my efforts, the place looked like my own room at home. Sure, ugly and filthy, but home sweet home.

Then, pure gold. A half-open flat of water bottles. No kidding. There were more than a dozen bottles! If I'd found a stack of hundred-dollar bills, I'd have left them alone, and taken the water instead. If I'd had more energy and a football in my hands, I'd a done an end-zone dance, and slammed the ball into the dance floor.

I tore one out the packaging, and spun off the cap. I guzzled the water instantly, and hurled the bottle. Goodbye kitty-litter mouth. And grabbed another. Then another. After the third bottle, I got sick. I might have drank too much too fast. I hurled again on the hideous carpet.

I'd have to say, the golden color of my vomit actually improved the décor.

"Slow down, big boy," I said. If you're on your own, once in a while your inner Scout leader will talk to you. I took another bottle out of the flat. This time, I dropped into one of those blue seats and took my time. Instead of guzzling, I sipped.

"I can't afford to vomit this stuff," I lectured. "This is life."

I sipped the bottle dry, and fumbled with the flat's plastic wrapping to extract another bottle. All the excitement reminded my hands to shake spastically. I fought with my own hands to get a hold of the plastic cap.

"Stupid hands!" I cursed. "Do what I tell you to do!"

My hands blundered until I got hold of the cap and with considerable effort, twisted it open. After a few more sips, and a few more minutes, my mouth could salivate again.

Stupid old-person saying: You don't know what you've got 'til it's gone. Surprised to find that it's pretty true.

True, if you're talking about saliva. I'm pleased to report that I'm good at salivating again.

Okay. Time to get serious and focus. Finish searching this room. The water helped me feel pretty good. My gut was hungry and thirsty, and so far I'd been able to supply half of what it demanded. While I searched, my gut sloshed like water in a bucket. So it stopped talking to me for a while.

I found a ship map. This room is apparently called the Forward Lounge. I can say, now that my search is done, that the forward lounge had nothing much to offer: Another couple of old TVs and a collection of DVDs. A couple of file folders of notes for talks, including a few books on the Arctic, Antarctic. A bulletin board with the banner "People's fates are like the fates of ships." Underneath the banner there were black and white photos of a woman—the lady the ship was named for, Lyubov Orlova.

A faded dot-matrix printout summed up her life in a few sentences. A Russian film star. Stalin's favorite actress. Born in 1902. Died in 1975. And this ship had been christened in her honor in 1976. In most of the images she sported a black and white Hollywood grin. The eyes seemed somehow sad. As though she was sad, maybe even disgusted that her namesake ship had come to this sorry end. Or perhaps she was distressed by the orange carpet and blue seating.

Back to the flat of water bottles. I sat down and sipped another. I had eight bottles left. I hauled the flat back to the port-side library, my current sleeping quarters. With a little more courage, after a major success, I took on the ship's shadows again.

Just the way the ship was laid out, it felt like the far end of the library might connect back to the room with the lounge entrance. So instead of going out on to the deck and around and into the lounge from the outside deck, I pushed forward into the dark end of the library. At the far end, a door. I pushed the door open. The ship's inner darkness greeted me. I took a deep breath and stepped over the threshold.

A dark hallway. But somewhere ahead, some light. I plunged into the deeper shadows. The hallway zagged right. I passed a few doorways, and opened them one by one. It was hard to tell what was in each room, because none had windows, but they appeared to be offices. Office-y stuff. File cabinets and pens. Desks and paper clips. And complimentary rats.

The narrow hallway fattened up into a long narrow room. On my right, a kiosk of some kind. A long counter in front with a little gap at one end. There was enough light to spare to give the general shape of objects and things. A single shaft of reflected light from further up the hallway shot against the wall, like the beam of a flashlight. I stepped into the shadows behind the desk. I picked up shadowy objects and held them into the shaft of light. Paper. Pens. Keys. Sewing kits. Individually packaged tabs of Tylenol, small shampoos, soaps, and hotel types of things. This was important. I pocketed a few things, but left most of the stuff there.

I popped a couple of expired Tylenol, and downed the two tabs with a gulp of my precious water. After a little more searching I found a board with room keys. Many of them were missing, but some still hung on their hooks.

Bingo. This boat isn't huge, but it is a cruise ship. Basically a floating hotel. This was the front desk.

I stepped out from behind the counter and journeyed a little further up the space, toward the bow. I could see what looked like a cabin door waiting just to my right. A room just ahead was filled with light.

On the other side, another kiosk-like notch in the wall. This one had several glass displays, which suggested a small store. There were racks for postcards, candy, and chips. Display cases and refrigerators for cold drinks and other things.

I admit I got my hopes up. A can of Coke and a bag of chips would have been pretty awesome. Just the suggestion of food reminded my stomach that I hadn't brought it everything it had asked me for.

"Orb." That's what my stomach just said. Mouthy, eh.

Ahead were a couple of long squares of light beaming on the floor and just in front of that, the entrance to the Forward Lounge. My old sleeping spot.

I would have done another touch-down dance. It meant I had basically explored and conquered a whole floor of the ship. Level. Deck. Yes, deck. Ships don't have floors you idiot, they have decks. This is probably the aloha deck. Captain's deck? Holodeck? No, wait. That's Star Trek.

My thirst required another water bottle. So I retraced my steps with confidence. I ended up staring at a dark door, one without a window, outlined with weak lines of sunlight. I patted the door until I found the handle and pulled it open. The glow of the library in the afternoon light greeted me.

"My name is Sean. I'll be your tour guide," I told the ship.

Observation: When you're not drunk, it's way easier to figure things out.

I donned my bedsheet and pea-green blanket like a superhero cape. I settled behind a table and sipped another two bottles of water, one after the other, until my thirst had been slaked. When I was done, there were six bottles of water left.

As I tossed my last bottle onto the floor, like garbage, I had a brainwave. I should keep those bottles. I may need to store water in them at some point.

I'd have to strike out on a search soon. Hunger was coming at me like a killer Pitbull. I gotta find something to eat.

"Why haven't I tried the water taps?" I asked myself. I moved to the bar, stepped behind to the sink, and tried the hot water tap. The water line simply belched. I tried the cold tap. The faucet gasped.

"What kind of cheap-ass cruise is this?" I yelled. "I want to talk to the manager. Now!" My yelling seemed to cause a furious scrabbling sound behind the cabin wall.

Back to the library. I sat with a pen and paper to try and plan things out.

After some deliberation, I wrapped myself in my sheet and blanket, scooped up all the stuff I'd collected so far, and took everything with me to cabin 501. Cabin 502 had a better layout, I realized, but 501 had the porthole that looked forward. I took the time to put my belongings into the dresser drawers and closets. This was officially my home base until I either get rescued or I die.

I hadn't felt much hunger since I'd ended up on this rusty tub. When you're drunk, hunger was kind of like one of my mom's boyfriends: not around much. Thirst had been the big thing. But now that thirst was taken care of for the moment, hunger began to throw a temper tantrum. I'm gutfoundered. No way to fire up a scoff. It didn't help much that I began to imagine all my favorite meals. Hamburgers and French fries. Poutine. Pizza. Man, I'd kill for a milkshake. And a good stiff drink.

The sun dropped out of sight, as if disgusted by what it saw, and night began. A deep gut hunger jumped around my stomach like a kangaroo on a pogo stick. I honestly had no idea what to do. It's not like I'm going to go exploring the ship any further. Not in the dark.

Instead I sipped water, keeping a close eye on my water bottle collection. I bet rats would like the water, but their paws are too small to open the bottle lids. Can't do it. Lucky for me.

I selected another bottle of water. I say "selected" because I had the choice of four. The other three I decided to save for tomorrow. With this bottle, my stomach was not impressed. It could now see the difference between water and food. So it decided to throw a full-on fit, which made it hard for me to fall asleep.

In the daylight, I'd have to forage for food, mainly. I'd also need to work on my water supply. Three bottles ain't much of a backup plan.

I wondered how Sailor was doing. Probably thirsty and starving under my bed. We're probably in the same boat, I think. Metaphorically speaking.

I am kinda expecting to be rescued at any moment. I don't think people are allowed to put a big ship like this into the world's bathtub and let it float away. Someone's got to pick this hunk-a-junk up, don't they? Talk about littering. My rescue theory did not impress my stomach.

"Ooooorrrbb," it replied.

19

DESPITE MY FANCY NEW ROOM, and the free shampoo and mini-soap bars, I didn't sleep too well. I had some wicked dreams. Probably that's the drink makin' trouble as the last of it leaves. I slept for a few minutes. I woke up. I slept for a few more. The three-eyed rat with a top hat stopped by to say hi. Finally, dawn began to dilute night. Until morning broke. Probably. I hesitate to call this morning without the witness of a proper clock.

The North Atlantic. A light gray cloud blanketed the sky. The sea a deep gray with white-fringed waves breaking over the horizon as far as I could see. The ship heaved gently on the swells. No ship, no land visible from the cabin windows or the portholes that looked onto the Orlova's starboard side. Fight to keep the lingo, boys. She'll be easy to lose out there.

Today is a day for major exploration, I declared. Gotta find me find some food and water.

I did the aloha deck yesterday. There was a deck above me, which wouldn't be too hard to search. Lots of windows. Lower decks—not so many. There were at least two lower ones. Plus, there was probably a service deck under that, places for engines and hot water tanks. The ship map didn't show one, but it was a map meant for the tourists. And I don't think I qualify as a tourist. I'm having to work too hard here.

The light wasn't strong yet, so I decided to start at the top and work my way down. The strongest daylight I'd use to explore the dark bowels of this beast.

What do I need? Water. Check. I took one of my last three bottles out of the nightstand drawer beside the bed. I uncapped it and sipped a little.

My stomach instantly stormed in protest. Like dropping cold water on a hot stove burner. I thought a sip of water would be like a peace offering. Not bloody likely. My stomach started to churn and chatter, making the boil of stomach juice say things I'd never heard it say before. If I didn't know any better, I would have thought my stomach was swearing at me in German.

Search time. I made sure I closed my cabin door, just in case a rat thought of stopping in for a visit. Toward the bow, I walked.

I followed the covered deck, past the set of wooden doors I'd entered yesterday. The deck led forward, and the covered portion of it ended, opening to the bow. This was not a place to hang out in the dark. In the middle of the deck, a giant square hole in the deck led down into the depths of the bow. It was wide open. The white crane I'd seen earlier is just on the other side of this giant square hole. It was probably designed for workers to take stuff off the dock and drop it down the hole so it could be stored. Like pallets of food, maybe. If a guy was just walking around, and didn't watch where he was going, it'd be easy to fall in here. It looked like it went from the top of the deck straight down to the hull bottom.

At the bottom of the hole, a swill of water fussed. A couple of smashed deck chairs spiked out of the soup. Bunch of garbage. Nothing much. The crane's arm leaned over the hole, the base strapped to the deck by a chain. The crane's arm turned back and stowed securely to the bridge behind. There were several coils of rope, as thick as my arm. At the tip of the bow, a tiny set of stairs leading up to a small platform. I stepped up. I made sure the railing was secure. Hate to die drowning.

I got a free view of the bow of the boat. You know that scene in the movie Titanic where that guy and girl are leaning over the front of the boat? Like that, minus the girl and the music. Same sinking feeling, though.

I looked over the front of the bow, down to the sea. The sea is a hungry monster. Its name is Dave, apparently. I know it wants to eat the ship and me. It would if it gets the chance. I got the shivers, like when someone walks over your grave.

Enough of that. Down the stairs and around the port side of the bow. Port is the left-hand side of the ship, when you're facing the front, the bow. So says the ship map. (You may have been wondering how I knew the names for the parts of the ship. Now you know. The ship map taught me. Did a better job than Mr. Nutman, if you know what I mean.)

I passed a crooked set of stairs heading up. Left them alone and walked down the port side of the ship. The port side had a covered and windowed deck, just like the other side. A matching set of wooden doors, like the ones on the other side. Past a bank of windows looking into the library. Then the bar, and finally the dining room.

The covered deck ended and opened into a small covered area at the back of the boat—the stern. A set of exterior stairs led up, and one led down.

Up I go.

20

CLOMPED UP THE STAIRS TO the next deck, which had a small sign that read, "Observation Deck." Duly noted. I shall observe.

On the green decking, in the middle, a giant yellow "H" with a circle around it. A helicopter landing pad. Might be important at some point. Behind it, tucked into the back portion of the deck, was a battered-looking oval swimming pool. Blue. Small, though. More like a big, deep hot tub. The matching blue tarp that had once covered it, now weather-shredded, sagged into the skiff of green murk that coated the top of the gallons of fluid sloshing at the bottom.

It smelled like a rotting corpse, or what a rotting corpse might smell like. There were these things that looked like balloons made of fur bobbing in the green goo. Cereal bits floating in leftover milk. I stood at the top of the dented chrome pool ladder and studied those fur balloons.

The ship heaved a little in a wave, and one of the balloons rolled. It had a huge, twisted grin on its face. Oh, wait. Not fur balloons! A few rotting rat carcasses. Not cereal. Stew. So, yes. It smelled exactly like a rotting corpse, or rotting corpses to be specific. Yeah, if I get hungry enough, I got me a chunky-style stew, with real meaty hunks. I'll be tempted to eat it with a fork, or a big-ass spoon.

This deck I decided to explore clockwise, so I started on the port side. The first thing I saw: lifeboat hulls. The boats themselves were tucked up tight against the ship on the deck above this one. This deck hosted huge arms that arched over the deck leading to the outside hull. The arms were there to help a launching lifeboat clear the side of the ship.

Note to self: Check out the lifeboats. Don't they have to have supplies in them? I think they're supposed to be motorized and fueled, too. I walked underneath the arms, looking up at the lifeboats' bottoms. The deck ended abruptly. I had two choices. A door to the inside, and a set of stairs up to the next deck. I opened the door and peered in. Inside, a lobby with a set of stairs going up and down. The door on the bow end of the lobby carried a sign that read "Officers Mess."

I know what you're thinking. It's the mess that belongs to the officers. Mr. Nutman, you'd accuse me of missing an apostrophe. For the record, I didn't. Not me. Not sober, anyhow. I pushed open the door. It was a small dining hall. I think "Mess" is supposed to mean "place to eat."

In this case, it was classic understatement. Litotes, right, Mr. Nutman? A better name: "Officers' Disaster." Apostrophe supplied at no extra charge.

The place was trashed. More garbage than anything. No furniture. A few boxes strewn around. A few cabins up front. At the far end of the mess, a few offices and cabins. Nothing useful. Letter openers, a good stapler, and box of staples. A working pencil sharpener. Another couple of dirty pairs of socks, which I did keep. A couple of pairs of tighty-whiteys. I kept those too. Gross, perhaps. But think about it. These could be important at some point. A set of mechanics' overalls. Kinda dirty, but otherwise OK.

Back to the lobby area and out the door. Time to try the stairs, which I did. A narrow green corridor, view totally obstructed by three lifeboats tucked tight against the deck. The gunwales—that's the top edge of the lifeboat's sides—swung about head level. But there was a three-rung metal handrail. A perfect ladder. So I stepped up the rungs and flopped inside the first boat.

I stood and my heart sank. None of the three boats were tarped. If everything's right, and all the supplies are there, the tops are supposed to be covered to keep the weather out. Like plastic wrap on supper leftovers. That way, when all hell breaks loose, they're ready to launch. No tarps would probably mean someone had been inside and taken the good stuff out.

The ship, as it is, is kinda like a floating island. Even if I see land, or something, I can't get there. I might need a way to get off this tub at some point. I mean, I might see something, like a deserted island with coconuts and bananas or something. Worst case scenario: This tub sinks. Then I go from being stranded on an island to living on this dinghy. No, thank you very much.

This lifeboat had a huge hole in the bottom where the motor and stuff had been removed, and no oars. It wasn't launchable.

There was a little trunk of supplies at the bow of the boat. It should have all sorts of handy things: food, water, flares. But honestly, my hopes weren't high.

As I sat and studied the boat, I remembered. I'd heard on the news that when the ship had sat in the harbor, the crew had run out of food and supplies. They had probably begged, borrowed, sold, or stole nearly anything good. Sure enough, the trunk was empty except for a crushed pop can. That's worth a nickel at the corner store.

The other three lifeboats were essentially in the same condition, except that whoever took the engine and prop out of one of them had left the bottom intact. One had a couple of wrenches and a hammer. And a picnic-style ice chest. I took all of it and set it at the top of the stairs at the rear of the deck to pick up later.

This deck ran like a horseshoe around the back end of the ship. At the front end, the deck ended and with a door to enter the bridge—the place where they'd stand to steer the ship. Bridge sounds way cooler than "steering place."

The bridge looked like it had been parked too long in a bad neighborhood. Utterly ransacked. The bridge hosts the ship's main controls: It's like a huge car dashboard. The dashboard had lots of empty slots and holes where equipment had once lived. Bouquets of wire sprouted from the holes. Nothing food or water related, anyhow.

I did find three empty plastic water bottles. I've decided to save them now. I put the three water bottles in the ice chest I'd stowed near the stairs on that deck. That made me think of all the empty liquor bottles in the bar. If I find a water source, I could fill them all. And when I get to shore, I'll get a good fifty bucks from the bottle depot.

Up another deck, on a set of metal stairs tucked just behind the bridge. The top deck. Not much up here. The entire deck was open bow to stern, sandy steel painted green. At the front, a white tower, probably for equipment: the communication and navigation arrays. About three times as thick as a streetlight post, it sported a ladder that went up probably twenty feet with tiny foot decks at the half-way point and near the top. The valuable parts had been plundered, leaving open holes and gaps in the tower.

In the middle of this open deck was the boat's funnel— the thing that looks like a giant smokestack. On the side of the funnel's back starboard side, a ladder led up. What the heck. I took it. Obeyed my curiosity.

The funnel's top was flat, broken only by the ends of a few protruding pipes. There was a tiny deck on the top. No railings. I stood in the middle, the entire ship below my feet. The boat heaved and rolled a little. The waves seemed to be gathering strength. I stood as though I was surfing and rode the motion.

Up here there was no wind protection. The icy breeze sliced through my clothing. I was instantly freezing. But the view extended three-hundred sixty degrees. Ocean in every direction. Nothing breaking up the long gray-green surf. Beautiful and haunting at the same time.

"When are you gonna get here?" I yelled aloud. "Don't forget to send someone, Mom. Don't let me down." I paused. "And Sailor needs food and water." The universe is listening, my mom told me once. I'm not sure.

After my major announcement, I stepped back down to the decking below and listened. The breeze whistled gently through the ship's rigging. The breaking waves hissed. The odd wave clapped and slapped against the ship's hull. Quiet creaks and groans issued from the ship itself. Not a mechanical sound. No airplane. No sirens. No traffic hum. No people as far as I could see in any direction.

I have never been so alone in my life.

21

TURNED FROM THE RAIL AND retreated to the back of the deck. I stepped down the stairs to the bridge deck, where I had left that ice chest, then toward the narrow deck toward the bow, to the bridge. A few windows looked in on offices.

Back into the bridge. As I stepped through the door, a couple of rats scrambled for cover.

No steering wheel, I noticed. No one trusts me to drive. "I'm sober now," I told the ship. "I am the designated driver." A small bank of buttons, all labeled in Russian, did nothing but confuse me.

Who knows, I thought, maybe one's an emergency beacon or something. I pushed them all, especially the ones that had a "do-not-touch" look. Nothing happened.

I ran my hand along a metal handrail at the base of the banks of controls and exited to the deck on the opposite side. Besides the one to the bridge, there didn't seem to be other doors.

Down a set of stairs to the captain's deck. The deck was wide and open. Against the wall of the ship, several wooden benches faced the sea. As I moved forward, I could see a brown wooden door leading inwards. I summoned some courage and opened the door and stepped inside. A scurrying sound began as I stepped through. Surprise! Rats.

Note to self: Rat encounters seem to be increasing today.

Just through the doors on the left, was a corridor leading aft. A sign on the wall read "Clinic" with an arrow.

"Yes," I trumpeted. "The doctor is in."

In the dim hallway light, I could make out a couple more doors. The first door on the left was some kind of office. The second on the left I opened, to a loud squeal from inside, as several rats chirped to protest my interruption. The rest cleared into corners. Three rats hustled out the door, scooting right over my booted foot.

Nausea instantly crowded my throat.

A storage room, I think. Maybe some food here, if the rats indicate anything at all. I didn't want to go into this space unarmed. I need a weapon of some type. I backed into the hallway.

The clinic itself reminded me of a doctor's examination room, which is probably what it was. The room looked as though it had been searched. Drawers pulled out and their contents spilled on the floor. Garbage so thick the red carpet was almost obliterated. Most of the supplies had been pilfered. There were a few bandages, slings, and crutches. I located a few sample packs of medication. I jammed everything I wanted into a discarded box. Wait. Idea.

The crutches.

I ditched the supply box outside the clinic door and

grabbed a crutch.

"Time to kick some rat butt," I yelled.

I returned to the storage room with the rats, and threw open the door to chorus of squeals. In my right hand, I clutched the crutch like a spear.

"You flea-bitten varmints," I yelled, a clever blend of Yosemite Sam and Arnold. "Payback time. And this time it's personal."

The more sophisticated rats seemed to appreciate this joke and squealed as I stepped further into the room. I left the door open, in case any wanted to flee.

"Stay where you are," I yelled. Hopefully, these were English-speaking rats.

There were no obvious rodents as I glanced around the room. You got to give them credit. They know how to hide.

The room had stored boxes of prepackaged snacks of various kinds. Wrappers lay everywhere. Several boxes had fallen off the shelves and lay on their sides on the floor. I nudged one open with my crutch. Inside, a mottled ball of gray with two grim eyes stared back.

I calmly stepped backwards. Ha, ha. Not really. I threw a full on squall. I screamed like a sunburned baby dropped into a bath of hot water. I ended up tripping over a drawer behind my feet and falling back against the storage room wall. I sat down on a pile of file folders and balls of paper. Under my butt was a large lump. The lump began to move—a disco tumor. It could only mean one thing.

I'd chosen to sit on a rat.

22

ROLLED ON ONE BUTT CHEEK like I was doing a one-cheek sneak. The terrified critter shrieked and streaked away like a fart in a hurricane.

When he screeched, it was as though the alarm had gone off and the entire room was on fire. The room exploded into a squirming sea of fur. I jumped to my feet like toast in a restaurant of truckers. The rat I'd found in a box decided to make like superman and leap out of the box. And the rats bounced and careened around and out of the room like pool balls after an opening break. I wanted to run, but my stomach was pretty excited to think there might actually be some food in the imminent future, so it made me stay.

"If there's anything to eat in this room, I'm gonna find it," I promised my stomach. I thumped the crutch on the floor. "Let's do this."

Box by box, I searched the room. The crutch served me well. Though there was a lot of potential—shiny chip packages, chocolate bars, and snacks—the rats had managed to pick every one of them clean. If I'd found a single rat-nibbled cookie, I'd have scarfed it. Seriously. You have no idea what I would have done for a single chocolate chip at that moment.

This was a snack-food cemetery. My stomach was excruciatingly disappointed and bellowed as I crutched through the wrappers. Shiny wrappers did their job. They got me all excited about eating some pre-fab food. My stomach was thrilled by the thought. It had a few big ideas as to what it might get. But it was like having a birthday that everybody ignored. Better not to have one at all, right?

Actually, it reminded me of my thirteenth birthday.

I'd been wanting a bicycle badly. And my mom and her then-boyfriend, Doug maybe, had announced that they'd bought me a bike for a present. So, naturally, I was over the moon. Jumping. Yelling. Thrilled.

They tell me where the bike is. So I go running out of the building to the storage locker. Nothing there. I run back and say it's not there. Oops, they say. With a big laugh. Try the trunk of Doug's car. So I run out again, with the keys. Nothing there. They keep me running around for a good forty-five minutes. That's how stupid I am. Ha, ha. Funny, right? That's how my stomach now felt.

"Sorry," I said to my stomach. If nothing else, I could apologize.

I retrieved my clinic loot, met up with my ice chest, and dropped everything off at my cabin. The room-to-room searching was scoring me a few things. There had to be a kitchen on this bathtub, didn't there? I suppose it wouldn't be up in the nicer parts of the ship. It'd be down in the bowels.

I adjusted my crutch grip. The crutch became my new weapon. I went back up to the bridge deck and finished searching the last few rooms: a couple of offices and sleeping quarters for crew. A board room, for meetings. A chartroom for navigation course calculation. There were a few maps, or charts as they call maps when they're on a ship.

I even found one a couple that marked the waters up the East coast of Newfoundland and Labrador. There were a bunch for the Antarctic, too. Torn and stained. Pretty. Good poster material if I decide to decorate my room.

Interesting general philosophical point: Maps are only useful if you steer yourself somewhere. If you can't control your direction, maps are as good as toilet paper. I'm being super deep here.

Related point: Maps are only useful if you know where you are in the first place, or you can find out somehow. If you don't know where you are, a map is as good as another Justin Bieber album.

Out of the entire search, I found two boxes of gift pens, with the words "M/V Lyubov Orlova" embossed in gold on the side. Free pen, for the next two hundred visitors. Act now to get yours! The first one is for Charles, in case he doesn't accept the letterhead.

There were also two unopened packages of foolscap, whiteboard pens, and a few sets of batteries. A smashed plastic flashlight and a smaller, disposable flashlight. And a binder titled International Maritime Dangerous Goods Code.

Now that I'm back in my cabin, looking at my swag, I'd have to say the captain's deck seemed like a lot of work for nothing. Maybe half the day is gone now. My stomach is beginning to yell like a first-class passenger waiting for service.

I DEMAND FOOD.

23

THE UPPER DECK SWEEP WAS a little more productive. I surprised the crap out of another group of rats in a small kitchen just off the dining room. When I threw open the door, there were several rats on the counter. The rats were feasting on the rot left behind by humans. One, sitting on the stainless steel counter top just inside the door, caught my wrath. I launched the crutch, smashing its hind leg with the crutch's rubber foot. The rat leapt from the counter to the floor and limped after the rest of the rats who had scattered into the dining area.

The kitchen had been ransacked. First by humans

abandoning ship, then by rats, now by me. Rats had cleaned up anything rotting, but in the process had left rat scat over everything. But in a corner, under a stainless steel counter, I found several large plastic tubs that were sealed well enough that the rat hordes could not invade them. I found a tub of sugar, I guess about a pound or so. A tub of flour. Maybe three pounds. A six- or seven-pound tub of rice, and a four-pound plastic jar of popcorn, unpopped. Four packages of Quaker Instant oats.

Hallelujah! I've been saved. It's not forever, but it is for today. I guess I'm going vegan. I have an unlimited supply of gluten-free pizza: the ship's carpet. Call me a health nut.

Time for a feast. I tore open the four oat packages and basically drank them. They were a little dry, so I helped them down with a little water. Now dessert. I sat down and dipped a battered three-quarter cup tin measuring cup into the sugar and downed it. Diabetes, here I come.

Though the tubs weren't heavy, their bulk required that I horse each tub to my cabin one at a time.

There were a few utensils, too—kitchen knives, some ladles, and large spoons. An old 2008 "Puppies and Kittens" calendar hung on the wall. Oh, so desperately cute. Two salt shakers, with a fair amount of salt in each. A couple of pots and pans. I took whatever I thought I might use and stowed it in my cabin hideaway.

The rest of the upper deck seemed to be mostly crap. Most of the day was gone, it seemed. I had time to do one more deck. But before I did, I headed back to the cabin to get that crappy disposable flashlight. The beam was weak, but the two floors could only be accessed by hallways and stairwells in the interior of the ship, which could mean little light. Sure the flashlight wasn't much. I know that. But it would prop up my crappy courage.

I began by heading into the main lobby, near the hotel desk I was telling you about. There were two sets of stairs, one at either end. At the bow end, a straight set going down. At the stern end of the lobby, a spiral set. I was close to the spiral set, so I used them. In my left hand I held the flashlight. In my right, the crutch, ready to do business. I thumbed the flashlight on. It emitted a nearly useless anemic glow.

The spiral stairs ended in a small lobby, or maybe a T intersection, with a narrow hallway on either side, one for the starboard cabins, and one for the port. Port is scarier. Why? As my mom used to say, left is not right.

As I stepped into the hallway, gray and brown fur streaked every which way. I could see fairly clearly because even though I was on the shadowed side of the ship, daylight still glowed through those open doors. A stupid rat at the end of the hall seemed bewildered by it all, but when our eyes met, he caught on and cleared out. Most of the doors swung in unison with the rocking of the ship. The door latches and locks had been removed.

These cabins were small. Me, I lived upstairs, on the good side of town. These cabins were small, claustrophobic. Some of the cabins even had bunk beds. Wow. Juvenile, or what. A small porthole lit the interior of each one. There wasn't much in any of them. I found a couple of pairs of women's high-heeled shoes. A few discarded suitcases. A few moldy lifejackets with the name of the ship stenciled on them.

The search was quick. Down the port side. Up the starboard.

I took the best two suitcases, opened the larger of the two and set the smaller one inside to make them easy to carry. Toward the back of the ship, I found a few doors for the crew. One lead to a large laundry area. The laundry was heaped with sheets, bedding, and towels. Rats and rat crap. Near the door, I stabbed a pile of towels with my crutch and hoisted them one at a time into the hallway to make sure they were rat-free. Six towels and I was done. The room seemed to melt and move. But it was just the rats in the flashlight beam.

I found another larger kitchen, right underneath the dining room. It too swam with rats. There were some porthole lights into the space, but I hadn't the courage to take on so many vermin with just one crutch. I returned to the spiral staircase and left the suitcases on the stairs.

The search had taken less time than I expected. The daylight still seemed strong enough. Maybe I could finish the last batch of cabins today. Get it out of the way. That would free up some of my schedule tomorrow. Ha ha.

The final deck awaited. I slowly stepped down the stairs with my combo flashlight and stabbing crutch. The darkness, at least in the stairwell, was thick and putrid.

The boat seemed to get sicker the deeper I went. It was damper with less light and air flow.

I visited the lower deck cabins. Rat hotel. Rat infested, and nothing much in them at all. At the back were some more "crew only" doors. One of them led to an engine room, which, though it was lit by a few portholes, seemed far too creepy to enter. I found another room, built like the inside of a small warehouse. On the floor lay a white, grease-stained XXL T-shirt, which I picked up to add to my stash. The selection was terrible, so you take what you get.

The shelves were bare, except for garbage and rats. Another few rooms of ship equipment, and a shop for fixing things. On the plus side, there weren't many rats in the shop. On the minus side, it reeked of toxic stuff. And, if there were any ghosts on the ship, they'd be hanging out in the shop and engine room.

I did find an old milk crate, a few screwdrivers, and a hammer, slightly bent. Eight fancy candles. Some wire and an axe with a partially splintered handle. And a few partially used rolls of heavy tape.

I dumped all my findings into the plastic milk crate

and hauled it back to the cabin. The suitcases and towels needed pick-up. I'd have to be quick. The sun balanced on the horizon, like a penny on a table. I had about four minutes before everything went dark.

24

THE SUITCASES AND TOWELS REQUIRED a second trip. I picked my disposable flashlight out of the milk crate, just in case the sun sneaked away before I could get back and set up.

On the way down to collect the suitcases, I cut through the library to the center of the ship. The other staircase needed investigation. As I walked through, my big rubber boot stepped on a book and slipped. Like the book was a cartoon banana peel.

I cursed loudly. My butt hurt like I'd been kicked by a kangaroo. I snicked on the disposable flashlight, and shone it around the floor as I waited for my hiney to recover. The weak beam shone on each title, like a wannabe spotlight on a Broadway star.

Two Against the Ice

Call of the Wild

The Long Exile

Manual of Arctic Survival and Useful Eskimo Words

US Army Survival Manual

Life in the Arctic

Arctic Animals

A bunch of books had authors' names larger than the titles.

HARLAN COBEN

JOHN D. MACDONALD

STEPHEN KING
CLIVE CUSSLER
TOM CLANCY
JONATHON KELLERMAN
MICHAEL CONNOLLY

I sighed and sat for a moment as the butt pain ebbed. Books. Normally not something I'd be interested in. But now, well...everything was different, wasn't it?

Observation: When you don't have TV, the internet, or rum, excitement changes. Aren't books television before television was invented? Maybe my tush was trying to tell me something.

These books might come in handy. I did have a lot of time on my hands.

A lot of the titles reflected Arctic or Antarctic themes. Lots of novels involving ships.

As the flashlight beam wavered, I set the light on the survival guide again. A plain yellow cover with black printing. The main title read The US Army Survival Guide FM 21-76.

I peeled open the cover and scanned the table of contents. "Firemaking and Cooking, 41–45" it read. I read it again, just to be sure I'd read what I thought I'd read. I crabbed myself back across the floor until my back rested on the front of a couch. I found section 41 and began to read.

There were several pictures of ways to cook on an open fire.

"I could make supper," I said to myself. The book fit in my coat pocket, along with another couple of books. The rest of them I re-shelved. Just got to try to remember: I put the books in the library. Ha ha.

I returned to my feet. Felt like a charlie horse. I walked through the ache to get my legs working again. I zigzagged into the midship lobby. I followed the spiral staircase down to the lower deck and returned to the engine room for my second load of loot. A quick snack of flour and sugar, just to keep my strength up.

The light inside the ship, which had been nostalgic orange, grayed suddenly. I burst up the stairs as the ship went dark. Dropped a book on the way up. Ah, well. Tomorrow, right?

By the time I was done, the day had been eaten away. I got a chance to put a few things away in my cabin, but the dark stopped me cold. Sun set. Thirst rise. I pulled a bottle of water up beside me.

Observation: Electricity. Power means light. Light would let me stay up all night and work. Or read. No power, no light means no work.

I sipped a bottle of water on the bed, contemplating the day. I drank it until it was gone. About then, I'd realized what I'd done.

How stupid can you be? I asked myself.

I'd finished my last bottle of water.

25

JUST THE THOUGHT OF HAVING no water made me thirsty. But in the absolute dark, this was not a time for a search. Tonight there were stars, but starlight alone is not enough to look for things.

As if on cue, a big old moon bubbled up from the sea like fart in a bathtub. The light was thick enough to throw shadow: moon shadow! Maybe I could look around. I returned to the bar, and scoured the entire area again for water. I fished the entire area for something that might work.

I should have been working on a water supply today. Typical darn teen, right? Not doing what he's supposed to do. Crutch in hand, I decided to take on the small kitchen again. Rats must have night vision, because they were out in numbers I've never seen before. The rats scurried in every direction. Not a bottle anywhere.

I went back to the bar. In a fit of desperation, I tried the pop wand behind the bar. The pop syrup wouldn't dispense. I pushed the carbonated water button, and it gasped, spat, and began to flow. I lifted the wand to my mouth and poured the fizzy water straight into my mouth, a little at a time. The pressure and flow seemed pretty good. Thirst slaked.

In the early moonlight, I returned to my room and loaded part of my bottle collection, then took it up to the bar. From the room I recovered nine empty water bottles. I'd also found one of the bigger water bottles. Plus the empty booze bottles. I had a good-sized water bottle collection now. I poured the carbonated water into the bottles and capped each one. I left the big bottle empty. The wand seemed to have good pressure. It was probably safest where it was. There'd be more water for another day.

On the way back to my room, I didn't even need the flashlight. I thought I'd sleep until the new light of morning and start over then. So I lay down and bundled up. But my stomach was having none of that. It was in Cirque du Soleil mode. Felt like an elephant was jumping a gas-powered unicycle through a flaming ring. If I translated what my stomach just said, it was roughly this: Party time.

Good point, I thought. With a night light like the moon, maybe I don't have to go to bed right away.

26

T HE FLASHLIGHT HELPED ME LOCATE, find, and consider my food supply. Downed a three-quarter cup of flour and sugar mixed. And the white sugar high lead to an idea.

Popcorn.

I grabbed the handle of the popcorn kernel jug and the broken axe. Yep. From the night table drawer, my lighter. I think you can guess what my plan might be.

I scanned my collection of junk. What other things would I need to get this party going? Oven mitts. A pot. I took a large, deep pot and dropped all the party supplies into the bottom, then trucked it out of my cabin, heading aft. I took an outside set of stairs up a deck to the big open deck next to the pool.

In the middle of the green paint of the observation deck, I chose a spot in the middle of the big yellow H. I set down my things, and with the flashlight headed downstairs into the dining room.

After a short search, I took a couple of broken dining room chairs and drag-hauled them up the stairs. The axe made pretty short work of them. I cracked them into manageable splinters.

I got a cardboard box from the deck and collected a bunch of paper garbage I found inside a deck trunk. I piled a mixture of wood furniture, garbage, and box, and attempted to light the box. It refused the flame. I held the flame to the splinters of the leg of a chair. The flame swung through the smaller fibers as if tasting them, but, disgusted by the flavor, the flame quit. Finally I tried the lighter flame on the ball of newspaper sitting on the top of the heap. It ignited willingly and burned quickly until the flame extinguished. Charred pieces of newspaper, fringed with orange ember, rose into the air—once the fringe darkened, they lowered themselves over the side of the ship into the sea.

Apparently I suck at making fires.

I piled more garbage on top of the wood and lit it with my lighter. The flame caught and grew large, but once again the paper burned and flew out to sea in black, ember-fringed leaves. The flame quit, leaving a whiff of smoke and the unburnt wood behind. Strike two.

I tried to recall the section I'd read from the book earlier in the day.

"Is this a test?" I asked aloud, as if I was talking to a teacher. "This is a test. Open book test."

I patted my coat pocket. I still had the survival guide. The moonlight was bright, but not bright enough to read by. Under the sorry beam of my flashlight I found the section on fire-making and re-read it, then tucked the book back into my pocket.

I leaned back on my hands and sat for a minute or two, looking over the pile of stuff for a few minutes. Finally, I rolled forward on to my knees.

"Right ingredients. Wrong order," I announced to myself, as though I had miraculously become some kind of expert on fires. "Yah, stupid kid. Put the easiest to burn on the bottom, hardest to burn on the top. Fire burns UP, moron." There I am, talking to myself like a stepdad again.

So I pulled the fire pile apart. I found some more basic paper with a few file folders. Bunched it up and put it down first. I put the cardboard box on top of that, after I tore it into strips. From the chair remains, I took the smaller splinters and laid them down and put the bigger pieces on top of that.

Took out the survival guide and flashlight and inspected the diagram on page 77 again, comparing it with what I had just done. Good enough for the girls I go with. That saying came from boyfriend number eighteen (I'm totally guessing the number here). Name was Marston, Martin, Marshal, something like that.

I struck a flame with the lighter. The sea breeze made the flame dance and roast the side of my thumb before it began to lick up the sides of the balled paper. The flame cut through the paper quickly and through most of the garbage. Bright orange tongues tasted the shredded cardboard. The cardboard seemed to take a while to be convinced. Finally, it agreed to burn, and passed the flame upward into the small splinters of chair wood.

As chair bits began to roast in the flame, the air turned rancid with a sour shellac-smelling smoke. Observation: Apparently, it's not a good idea to burn painted wood, or inhale the fumes of said wood.

So sue me.

It smelled bad enough that I ducked to let the smoke roll over my head. The chair wood seemed to need convincing, too. Eventually, the finish began to blister, blacken, and burn. Before long, a small crackling fire sparked into the evening air.

For the first time since I'd come aboard, I grinned. A small triumph, right. I could feel the heat of success spread through my body. I can't remember the last time I grinned like this. I raised my right hand and slapped it with my left. Selfie high-five. My accomplishment warmed me nearly as much as the growing heat of the flames.

The heat felt so fine. Almost the same feeling as a good hot shower.

My stomach churned again, which reminded me to stop staring at those hypnotic flames and continue with my supper prep. Today, my stomach dreamt of hot dogs, loaded with fixins, floating like canoes on root beer rivers. Focus. Once the flames dug through the smaller pieces of wood, I set in some larger pieces. Small to big, the book said. I'm summarizing.

Though it was a tiny fire, the smoke gave way to flame and vapor as it roared and fed ferociously. At one point, the fire was almost too hot to approach, so I let the flame eat enough wood to settle to ember.

The pot I'd brought was a huge restaurant pot, probably two feet deep and two feet across, with a brown-and black-stained bottom. I dumped the supplies onto the deck to make way for the cooking of popcorn. I opened the new tub of popcorn kernels and poured maybe a cup into the deep metal pot. The kernels pinged as they danced on the pot's bottom.

My little fire aged quickly. The fresh wood was now mottled with ash as the fire moved deeper into the wood. I'd set the legs of the chair aside. They were the biggest and would last longest. I lay them into the flame. My little fire began to smoke and sputter. The flames floundered. I feared that I might have killed the whole effort.

Then the flame revived, one small tongue at a time. Like the fire was tasting the wood, trying it before it committed. Then, the smoke disappeared again, as the flame rolled high into the North Atlantic sky.

"Oven mitts, where did you go?" I couldn't see where I'd put them. Behind me. One on each hand, I held the pot over the flame and shook it. I wasn't much of a cook, but who can't cook popcorn? The popcorn jangled as it bounced in the pot. I swirled the bottom of the pot over the flame. Nothing happened. The popcorn was probably old.

Then a single kernel popped. The single kernel became the occasional one. One popped and sent a small hot shower of un-popped kernels flying onto the deck of the ship. One hit my wrist and rolled into my oven mitt. Hot as the fire itself. I nearly dropped the pot.

Like the fire, the popcorn took a while to decide what it was going to do. In the end, it decided to pop, nearly all at once. Popped butterfly and mushroom flakes shot from the pot, too, landing in the fire, on the deck. A few reluctant kernels hesitated, until finally they, too, exploded in chorus.

The popping began to taper away. Something smelled like it was beginning to burn. So I pulled the pot out of the fire and set it on the deck beside me for a few moments to cool. While I waited, I stoked the fire with the remains of the chairs, including the cushions.

The fire choked for a few moments, and slowly began to eat everything I'd fed it. It wasn't a pleasant campfire smell—the finish on the chairs, the chair fabric ,and the stuffing smelled like burning plastic. Like a house fire, or a garbage fire. But it wasn't like I was going to sing Kumby-yah and cry or anything. Let's face it, I don't even have a guitar. If I did, I'd probably use it for kindling.

I tapped the outside of the pot with my fingers to test for temperature. The pot was cool enough to touch. Dinner was served! One of those beers would have made a perfect accompaniment, but they were long-finished, so I uncapped a bottle of the carbonated water I scored from the fountain machine at the bar.

A happy burn rose from my gut, up my chest. I felt a grin split wide open. A gurgle built in my throat, which became a laugh. I threw my head back and let 'er rip.

Weird kind of laugh. I'd laughed a lot of different kinds of laughs, but this was a first. Obviously the situation is not funny in any way. But I laughed myself sick, almost. So there you go.

"Yes! I did it!" I bragged to the night sky. "Supper time!" I would have asked myself to dance, but I was so hungry.

Feast time. I sat cross legged, on the metal deck, which was now warm because of the fire. I set the pot in my lap, and my bottle beside my right knee.

OK. It wasn't movie-great popcorn. No butter. No movie. No sticky floor and seat. No annoying tall guy with big hair blocking the view. But you know the saying: Beggars can't be choosers. The triumph of the moment gave the popcorn a fantastic taste to this boy who hadn't really eaten for four days. I wanted to bury my head in the pot. I wanted to shove handfuls into my food-hole. But that popcorn was so valuable, I needed every morsel. Even the burnt ones. So I took little dainty handfuls. My stomach tasted it and began to complain.

"More is on the way," I said. "So shut your mouth." Several hundred small handfuls later, and the popcorn was nearly done. A deep swig of warm water washed everything down.

I didn't have a movie, but I did have entertainment. A popped flake had shot out of the pot, and as I ate I watched it dance on the deck some feet away. A whiff of ocean breeze waltzed the flake away from the fire. As it reached the ring of shadow surrounding the fire, a young fist of fur streaked across the deck, snatched the whirling flake, and stuffed it in its mouth.

I scanned the wreath of shadow, and several rats lingered, like a bunch of shy teenagers, waiting for someone to ask them to dance.

I know exactly how that feels. I am the classic wallflower. I think of the last time I went to a school dance. From what I've told you about my life, you can likely guess how popular I am. Somehow, though, I always ended up at the school dances. I guess 'cause my best friend usually went. You know my best friend, by now, don't you? Some well-adjusted humans would dance in the middle of the school gym. And me, with a few others, would stand like rats on the outside edges looking in.

Once in a while, I'd get brave enough to steal from the shadows into the ring of light, but it had ended in failure so many times. So many bad, awkward, awful stories. I had learned my lesson. Stay in the shadows. That's how my whole life has felt. Like I wasn't invited to the party.

Like I wasn't welcome. Maybe that's why I liked drinking so much. It helped me forget all that stuff.

As I watched, several rats approached the one who'd scored the flake of popcorn. As I watched, they surrounded and attacked him. One of the larger rats climbed on top of the young creature, and with his teeth, he tore open the smaller one's throat.

The young creature somehow managed to squeal, but it was in vain. The blood and exposed flesh invited a frenzy. Rats swarmed over the body while his heart still beat. They tore at him, carving bites for their own suppers out of the poor creature's ebbing life. If I thought I'd been overly paranoid about the rats, this demonstration set me straight.

"Ewww. Dudes," I said. "Chill, man. That's just not cool." My hipster warning had no effect on the bloody buffet brawl. Maybe it would help if I had a beard. I felt my chin. Something was growing there. I should check in a mirror and see what's going on.

I took a final gulp of carbonated water. I checked the pot for any remaining edible bits. Dead soldiers rolled around the pot bottom. I swirled them around, which made the pot jangle like an alarm.

The sound scattered the moiling mass of rats. A bloody pool of scrap bone and fur remained. The carcass had been gnawed to bone, its eyes plucked out, much of the flesh devoured.

The fire seemed hungry too. It burned through the chair remains quickly. Now it burned low, embers glowing as the ocean breeze blew. I began dropping supplies into the empty pot. And once the fire was too weak to cast warmth, I took to my feet and followed the moonlit deck to my cabin.

On impulse I tried my phone. Not like I'd get a signal, out here, wherever here might be. It booted up, and then, as soon as it started properly, shut down. Big tease.

My stomach wasn't full, but it had something to work on. For the first night since I'd been on this tub, my stomach shut up. It focused instead on getting to work to digest the popcorn supper I'd just made.

I'm not on the observation deck, so I'm on the wrong deck to make this comment, I will anyhow. Observation: It's much easier to sleep when you have something in your stomach.

27

SOMETIME IN THE NIGHT, I awoke. I'd been thrown out of bed by the boat as it pitched. I think. I was asleep at the time, so "thrown" may be a bit dramatic. I may have rolled off the bed onto the floor. But it wouldn't have happened without the help of the ship.

I could hear the objects in my cabin, rolling and sliding around the cabin interior, demolition-derby style. It was pitch black. I could hear the howl of wind, and pound of the sea. I pawed around trying to find the edge of my bed. But the ship bucked and rolled and my face found the edge of the bed first. I climbed back on, and once the ship settled down for a moment or two, I tested my nose with my hand. Some leaking liquid. Probably blood.

I dabbed a little on my tongue. Blood, for sure.

I felt for the disposable flashlight I left on my nightstand. Don't know why I bothered. Of course, the flashlight had spilled onto the floor long ago. It skated around the floor with a lot of other stuff, smashing around like a un-reffed hockey game. Good thing the furniture was bolted to the floor. I backed my body up into a corner, where the bed met two cabin walls, and braced myself.

A gale shrieked through the ship's rigging. The sea smashed and hissed. The night was dark as ink.

The boat flailed in all directions.

"Rock and roll," I yelled.

The rolls were far more violent than the rocks. The rolls felt as though the entire ship was going to capsize. The ship was rolling from port to starboard. It rocked me head to toe.

The port side lifted the pillow end of my bed until it felt as though I was standing. The mattress felt like it would toboggan off the bed frame. Then, the ship rolled back the opposite way, dropping my head down, and flipping my legs toward the sky.

My bed was bolted to the floor against two walls. One wall just behind my pillow. So until I figured out what was going on, I got a good head slam into the metal wall. Saw stars. The only light I saw that night. Maybe this is what it felt like to be a mosquito on my mom when one of my stepdads beat her.

The ship shunted though the waves and the motion started to change. The huge waves battered the bow slowly, turning the ship broadside to the waves. The rocking motion became awkward and lumpy as a rolling motion began to grow. The waves must have been monster-sized to make the boat move like this. The speed of the boat's turn increased until it felt as though it were sideways to the storm surge. The bed began to rise, foot first, until it felt as though I was nearly standing on my head. The ship groaned and I could hear clunks and thunks elsewhere in the ship. Then the Russian beast rolled violently the opposite direction, nearly bucking me off the bed. To finish it all off, the wave crest broke on the side of the boat, smashing the boat senseless and throwing me nearly across the cabin. There was a long loud snake hiss as a fringe of spray and foam spit down on the hull.

The ship crested the wave top and jerked in the opposite direction, sliding into the neighboring trough, I'd guess. I was on my back on the cabin floor when the next move slid me back between the two single beds, along with my collection of stuff.

The ship paused for a moment. It had decided to take a small break. Relax. Maybe light a cigarette. I crab-walked backwards until the back of my head hit the cabin wall next to my bed. A quick roll and I was back in my bed. The ship complained: The groans of a battered hull, and from somewhere a sound of water trickling, dripping. The amplified smell of salt and seaweed. All of this in a darkness as thick as used oil. Black, blind, and sticky.

The ship rolled through the bottom of the trough and began a climb up the next wave. The foot of the bed lifted my feet to the sky. I could picture the wave closing like fingers over the ship, spinning and shaking it before letting the boat go, then the whole process began again. Sort of an eternal carnival ride from hell.

The motion reminded me of bed spins after a night of heavy drinking. Except this was far worse. Without alcohol, I couldn't pass out. Plus, I actually had to cling to my bed, so falling asleep was absolutely out of the question.

And, without light, it was impossible to do anything but hang on. The lack of light also meant I couldn't see to keep myself oriented. Before long, nausea churned my stomach. I didn't dare get out of bed, much less leave the cabin.

After about the 15th wave, my skin was hot and damp. My precious supper, my hard work, wanted to leave through the front door, if you know what I mean. I couldn't do anything except feel it arrive and open the door when it asked to be let out.

I spewed a fountain of vomit into the air above me, as the ship's motion pulled my head down and pushed my feet up high, and then forced me through a shower of vomit as the ship shoved my face up and threw my feet down.

Despite being soaked in popcorn-flecked puke, I

couldn't manage to do anything but cling to the bed as the sea continued to toss the ship around. Like a boomerang, a few minutes later the nausea returned and I heaved whatever was left in my stomach. Puking again. Fortunately, I am good at it. Olympic hurler.

Good thing Sailor isn't here.

I puked myself far beyond empty. I was parched, starved, and filthy, but the Lyubov Orlova wouldn't let me do anything about it. I couldn't even safely move to another location. The surges seemed to swallow the entire ship sometimes.

I thought of the square hole in the front deck. The ship must be taking on water, lots of it. No power to run the pumps to get rid of it. The more water it takes on, the worse the ship behaves, which means the more water it takes on. Reminds me of me when I drink. This dreadful Russian might just sink. Worst thought: I couldn't even make it to a lifeboat, if my life depended on it. And it might.

28

CLUTCHED THE BED FOR HOURS, waiting for a little morning light so I might be able to change things up.

My hands and legs got cramps several times. They were stiff with a muscle ache and exhaustion from gripping the sides of the bed. I held myself in place when the ship got the crap kicked out of it. I rested when it rested.

My face was sticky and foul with vomit, the rest of my body a temple of pain. I held on through the storm until the first light broke. A weak gray light rimmed the porthole. Not much to see by, but an encouragement that morning was on the way.

29

THE GROWING LIGHT SLOWLY REVEALED a destroyed cabin. The tub of flour had tipped and rolled around in the room until the lid came off. It tumbled and rolled, dumping my tiny supply of flour over all over the room. Same with the sugar. I watched the popcorn container skid from wall to wall in the bedroom. But the threaded lid had held through the tempest. The rice had tipped out of its container, but fortunately it was in a sealed sack, which had belly-flopped out of its container. The sack lay like a body on the floor, sliding just a little with the motion of the ship. Water bottles, pots, tools, and supplies jangled and roiled in a stew as the ship bucked.

Once the light was strong enough, I took to my feet. They quavered a little. Robbed of its supper, my stomach matched the violence of the sea. My mouth was puckered and parched as a grandmother's kiss with her false teeth out. Don't know why I just said that. Bit weird.

I waited until the ship hit the next tiny calm between waves, then leapt from the bed and groped for a dog-eared armchair, bolted to the floor. Took me a couple of seconds. I lifted my feet to let the stew of debris swarm and mash around the foot of the chair. For a few moments I rocked with the boat, catching my breath and trying to think.

I sat and waited as the ship battered and rolled, lifted and dropped into another short calm. When everything settled for a moment, I hopped to my feet. Out the cabin door, I burst to the wooden railing along the covered promenade deck. The cabin door swung shut behind me. I instantly went from a comfortable temperature in the cabin, to ice. On the positive side, I couldn't smell myself any longer.

I clung to the railing and knelt on the deck, while the ship bucked through its sequence again before settling in the trough between waves. I stood up and glanced out the deck windows. Snow white, white with snow. This was a winter storm. Raging seas and another blinding January blizzard. I think it's still January. My semi-pickled mind makes it almost impossible to say for sure.

I dashed for the doors leading to the inside of the ship. Not a good day to hang on the open deck.

The ship started to heave again before I made it to the forward lounge. I'm not exactly a track star, okay? When I say "dashed" or "sprinted," it's all relative. I knelt by the spiral staircase and clung to the stairway railing. Everywhere was a sound of large objects scraping across the deck, colliding, sliding around, bashing, and smashing. The scream of rats. The groans of the ship grew much louder. The ship's motion caused me to pivot into the stairs, tore the railing from my grip, and tossed me from the stairs onto the deck carpeting several feet away. Then a brief stillness.

As the ship dropped into the trough between the waves, I sprinted forward, through the doors and into the forward lounge. This, upon reflection, was not a good choice.

The ship began to elevate again. The closest thing I could find was a lounge table, fixed to the floor. As I hung on to the table, a river of debris—cushions, cans, cups, rats, and garbage—streamed down on me. Several tables away the carcass of the TV smashed and spun through fixed furniture, spitting shards of plastic and glass until it slammed into the far wall.

As the ship topped the wave, the squall of debris changed direction and slammed back toward me. The motion swung my body around to face the debris. The TV bashed a dance between the fixed bits of furniture and lurched toward me. It was an old-school TV. Huge and heavy. The plastic and glass hulk spun somewhat gracefully, like Michael Jackson, before plowing into a table, not like Michael Jackson. The tabletop tore off the base and shot like a giant Frisbee over my head.

I imagined me holding onto that tabletop and flying across the room like that. I don't want to have to set my own bones. Or fix my own teeth.

Still, I wasn't about to let go. I'd literally cartwheel across the room if I did. And I'm not a gymnast. So, I clung to the tabletop. The TV veered left. Might miss me. Then back right, straight toward me. Nope. Perfect aim. As the TV was about to strike my table, I let go, and flew across the room into another table behind me, which caught my lower rib cage. The top of the table I'd been holding flipped up and off its base like a bottle cap off a beer bottle.

Excruciating pain fireballed through my chest as I took my next breath. Then the ship slid into a calm. I climbed to my feet during the calm, and looked for refuge. With the flow of stuff in the room, I couldn't see safety anywhere. I gripped another table and the TV shoved and spun its way across the room, leaving the table bent on its moorings.

The next lull allowed me to retreat to the hallway. Waiting for the quiet seconds between waves, I made my way to the library, where I could nurse my pain. A few books skidded over the floor like crabs. But there were no large pieces of furniture and debris slamming around the room.

I picked a corner seat on the inside wall of the library, facing the sea. Even with the light, there wasn't much to see. Fists of cold gray sea water boiled over the deck and clobbered the library windows. The water turned the windows black, and withdrew in green rivers. Once the water withdrew, the blizzard pounded the window. Once in a while, in a calm moment, a dark wall of water loomed out of the blizzard and smacked the ship.

My seat bucked and rose, twisted and dropped. I swallowed deeply, trying to swallow the growing nausea as it fought its way up my throat again. I doubled over to heave, but there was nothing left. My stomach pumped in and out like an accordion. The tabletop hit to the ribs amped the pain to a delightful new level. I nearly passed out. Let me say, I'd almost rather have been doing my own home dentistry with pliers and a hammer.

This felt like being strapped to a mechanical bull, stuck in full rodeo mode, for hours.

My grip weakened because of the pain, which allowed the ship to pick me up and throw me across the room. Fortunately, I ended up shoulder-rolling into a couch on the other side of the room. Then a short lull between waves, and I climbed back into my seat, aching and exhausted. Really, really tired of riding the storm.

Please stop, I breathed. Please. I begged the storm, like I begged my stepdad.

But the sea would not relent. In a fog of fatigue, I again loosened my hold on the seat and again bounced off my seat, my body flying around the room like a drunken frog. Pain. Pain. Pain. Ridiculous, hilarious, stupendous amounts of pain. Like a full-body massage given by a sumo wrestler using a sledge hammer.

Without a clock, there was no way to know how long I sat there. The motion made it literally impossible to do anything but cling to my seat. And even that only sometimes. As the day wore on, the storm's force seemed to subside a little. The books skidded less violently. The smash and jingle of the ship lessened, too.

No fire today. I won't be eating, I realized. Though I'm on the wrong deck again, insight strikes. Observation: Would have been smart to make extra food. Although it would probably just be in the garbage-debris stew now if I had.

As the storm calmed, I noticed my thirst. It was always the first to cry out, like a hungry baby. Babies don't care what's going on, just scream for what they want.

The storm had forced me into the workout of my life, and I needed a drink. Water, specifically. In the shifting cabin, I found my feet and followed the motion of the ship and the floor to the bar. The bottles stowed on the bar shelves were fine, but clinked back and forth rhythmically, keeping time with the ship's rock.

Behind the bar, I knelt on the floor. I kept a hand on a polished metal railing on the bar's edge. I took a hold of the drink dispenser wand, threw my head back, held the wand over my mouth, and pushed the carbonated water button. Just small shots so I didn't waste anything. Mmmmm. Warm, sour-tasting water.

The water renewed my body awareness. Sheer exhaustion. Every muscle ached. My hands throbbed, exhausted by clinging to the ship. Every breath hurt. I probably broke a rib or two. I replaced the drink dispenser wand in its holster.

A couple of bottles had rolled in behind the bar, and threw themselves around. I ousted them from the bar area. Which left a good clear space of floor beneath my feet.

I let go of the railing and lay in a heap on the floor. I needed sleep now, even more than food. The daylight was beginning to fade.

Back to my room, I thought. Sleep, glorious sleep. I was almost salivating for it, like I was thinking of a juicy steak. The ship pitched and rolled. The last light of day; I needed to return to my room. I used my well-practiced run-and-cling strategy to return to my room.

Out the starboard doors into the covered promenade corridor. The bitter bite of the winter storm nipped at my cheeks and fingers. Snow and sea water washing constantly over the ship had coated the outside in a layer of ice, and spiked the edges with icicles. The covered deck was mostly protected, though the sea had smashed through somewhere and had flowed and frozen on the decking to the stern.

I stopped outside the door to think things through one last time before sleep.

The ship's motion had dampened, but it was still moving far too violently to chance a campfire. Food was out of the question. The storm also seemed to have cleared out the rats somehow. Who knew where they had holed up to weather the storm? I'd heard rat screams and squeaks, but hadn't seen a critter through the entire storm.

The gray cotton sky blackened with the stain of night.

"Better get in," I muttered to myself. "Looks like it's going to be another dark one tonight." The storm clouds choked out any moonlight.

As I opened the door, the smell of vomit reached my nose. Normally it would have brought on more nausea, but I was too tired, and too empty. I wasn't interested in finding a new cabin to sleep in just yet. Plus, I hadn't made a reservation. Bad joke. It had to be bad so I wouldn't be tempted to laugh. It would hurt too much.

Instead, I stripped the bedding off my vomit bed, balled it up, and chucked it out onto the deck to deal with later. I chose the bed opposite the one I'd thrown up on, and laid down, waiting for dark. As long as I lay with my legs and arms spread wide, I didn't roll out of bed.

Though tired beyond words, it was a difficult job to get to sleep. My ribs jolted me with electric shocks of pain unless I lay perfectly still. To be fair, I tried to lie perfectly still—if only the ship hadn't jump around like an over-caffeinated leaping lemur.

My head pounded like a cat-sized rat trapped in a gerbil ball. Body aches. The smaller aches collected themselves together to form a larger, unionized ache, one that took over entirely. I felt as though I'd been severely beaten. To top it off, my stomach begged for food and drink. But it was night. And dark like a dark, dark darkness. How's that for a metaphor? So dark, your eyeballs starve, too. I held my hand in front of my face. Couldn't see a hint of it.

I believe I eventually slid into an uneasy sleep, because a couple of hours passed more quickly than I can explain. But I woke up often. Pain, hunger, or general jitters.

~

AFTER MIDNIGHT, I COULD HEAR things smashing in the kitchen, and the sound of a slurred, angry voice tearing into my mother. Dad was home. Stepdad, technically. I slipped out from under the sheets, and slid under the bed frame.

"You stupid cow," Murray screamed.

"Murray, leave me alone. Ow!" she screamed. "Stop it." The loud smashes became softer as 32-year-old Murray McMood turned from the furniture and fixtures to my mom's body. My six-year-old hands trembled. Tears skidded sideways, rolled over my nose, and leapt into the soft gray fur of the dust bunnies under the bed.

My mom wailed as the beating continued. The wails quieted to moans, finally fading to silence.

The sound of my stepdad's heavy footsteps came down the hall, and my door flew open, the door knob punching through the drywall.

"Sean, you brat," my stepdad declared. "I'm gonna give you some." He kicked the bed, lifting it from its feet and smashing it to the floor. I wet my pajamas and crowded against the wall, hoping for some kind of escape. My stepdad pawed the top of the mattress, looking for me.

"Where are you, you little crapper?" Murray screamed in a white-hot rage. "You come when I call." He booted the bed again, but this time his toe caught the edge of the frame wrong, so he roared in pain. He hopped back and turned to the wall, threw a fist through the drywall. Murray stomped out of the room into the living room, flopped into the tattered recliner, and turned on the TV. Jerry Springer's talk show blared through the house.

I lay there cold, in urine-soaked PJs, afraid to move. Drowning with guilt for not helping my mom. Finally I fell into an uneasy sleep.

∿

I AWOKE YELLING, CROWDED AGAINST the beige paneling of the cabin wall. It took me a few moments to shake off the dream and realize I was safe. Ha, ha. Not safe at all. Probably dying slowly, right?

I did check my pants. Dreams where you wet your own pants are scarier than most.

Funny to say out loud: I like this ship much, much more than any of my family, my mom, and the dad of the day. I'll take this cheap cruise ship vacation over home any day. Even with the crap service and the pathetic menu selection. As weird as it is to say, my life has probably improved.

My mothership.

The boat was still. All was quiet. Eerie compared with the storm-inspired furniture maraca. I opened my eyes, and the cabin portholes glowed like green eyes. Green. What the...? I blinked a bunch of times. Still green. A raw hunger/thirst chewed at my belly.

I threw off the bedclothes. The cold slapped me awake instantly. Freezing. I could see my own breath glow in a green cloud. Through the starboard windows, I checked out the green light. Just in case it was an alien abduction or something. I've heard bad things about their probes and bedside manner.

I'm crimped with serious pain. Like I'm sixteen with the body of a senior citizen. I was only beginning to recover from the beating the storm and ship had given me. The pain had congealed in my limbs as I slept. Stiff and robotic, I could barely walk.

The sky pulsed with rows of green clouds. Bright green. They rolled and wrinkled, waved, broke, and re-joined in sort of a dance, maybe. The moon must have been frustrated by the storm cloud and had left the sky.

"Cool," I muttered. Not aliens, hence safe to step outside. You have to remember, I hadn't seen a televi-sion or a screen of any kind for a while, except the dead one hurling toward me in the forward lounge during the storm. So, a boiling green sky was like a lost episode of The Walking Dead. No aliens, just zombies. I also had no friends. Long before I ended up on this ship I had started talking to myself. Have you noticed?

I stepped out of the cabin door to study the sky through the windows of the promenade corridor. Wide awake. I could hear the green display crackle. I gazed through the windows until my stomach decided to groan like a bloat-ed accordion. Idea: supper.

Back to the cabin. Nightstand: lighter. The flashlight. No idea where it ended up, so I thumbed a flame out of the lighter and began to search for the flashlight. Found my popping pot first. Two carbonated waters that I'd bot-tled earlier. Had a small drink from one before I threw them into the pot.

My disposable flashlight had somehow scuttled be-hind the defunct toilet in bathroom. It still worked, too! The flashlight's weak orange glow helped me find the last couple things I needed to make supper. The axe. I tried to step around the large beach of spilled sugar and flour poured over the floor. I might have to eat it sometime. The tub of popcorn I found battered, but otherwise fine.

"A double batch tonight," I promised myself. And I'll save half, just in case.

A spare pea-green blanket served as an extra coat as I carried supplies out of the cabin. Forward to the set of stairs leading up a deck. Then toward the stern to the aft observation deck. I took it slow. The entire deck was coated in a thick sheet of ice.

In the green evening light, the ship actually looked like a decorated green gingerbread house. Everything, I mean everything, had been coated with a heavy layer of ice, two inches thick. The edge of all flat surfaces was fringed with icicles and green as the sky. Seriously weird and beautiful. But deadly. I realized I could easily skate right off the edge of the ship into the freaking Atlantic.

A couple of times I paused and took a seat on the benches bolted to the deck. The sky seemed alive with green. The light snaked back and forth, pitching and rolling. It crackled and snapped as it danced.

"Woah," I announced. "I don't know what you're doing," I said to the sky, "but I like it." The sky somehow provided more than light, almost a presence, a friendship. Like I said, I was lonely. And desperate. Hey, if the sky is willing to talk to me, I'm going to talk back.

On the aft observation deck, I set down the pot and supplies. The pot and axe skated gently back and forth in place on the ice-covered deck, marking the ship's motion. Once I was sure they wouldn't skid off the deck, I slithered my way to the dining room in search of paper and chairs for firewood. When I opened the door into the dining area, a host of rats ceased their work, looked at me, as though surprised I was still around, and scrambled out of view.

The rats are probably starved, like me. Couldn't get anything to eat in the storm. We're all fighting the same battle.

I hefted the axe, ready to chop if the rats decided to eat my face.

The dining room was a tumble of furniture. The storm had thrown everything around in a drunken rage—chairs, a few tables, smashed dishes, and garbage. A bunch of chairs had been splintered during the storm, which made my job easier. I just had to pick up the bits. Got to be smart about this, right? I've learned two things about fires, so far. Small, medium, large. And an armload of wood.

I found a battered cardboard box and dumped my load into it. A quick skid out the door and I rejoined my fire supplies. A mischief of rats backed into a circle around the supplies on the deck, like it was time to play a kindergarten game. Maybe Ring Around the Rosie?

"Dudes. Get out of here. Very dangerous. Do not, I repeat, do not play with fire." My words made them scatter, scrabbling over the ice surface for cover. Once they realized the deck was a skating rink, they turned and careened frantically in what they may have hoped was a safe direction. But in a few cases, their attempted course changes didn't matter. Three or four slipped under the railing and off the edge of the ship. They rat-screamed as they plunged off the edge, the eerie cries fading as they belly-flopped into a hungry ocean.

I spent a little time building the fire, following the steps that had worked the last time. Paper at the bottom. Shredded cardboard box next, then splinters and small sticks of furniture next. I lit the fire, and in no time, the warm orange tongues licked the sky. Green, meet orange. You're like opposites, but I've always been told opposites attract. Fire, meet sky. Look at me, matchmaker for the elements.

From the box, I found a seat cushion stripped of its legs and back. This I used to keep my butt warm. Ingenious, I thought. I poked at the fire for a while, making sure it grew properly. The fire had a little trouble as it melted through the sheet of ice to the decking below. It hissed and blathered as it turned the ice to water to steam.

Once the fire was hot, but not a wicked flame, I poured a couple cups of popcorn into the pot and shuffled it over the fire. Soon kernels cracked and expanded to fill the pot. I slid the pot off the fire when the popping slowed. As I set it down, the pot hissed and melted through the slushed deck ice beside me. Anticipation twisted another groan from my stomach.

The fluffy white flakes tasted as good as anything I'd ever eaten. Turns out, when you're starving, flavor isn't a deal at all. I threw caution to the green wind and abandoned the dainty handful strategy of my first popcorn supper. After stuffing my face for a few minutes, I turned again to the snaking, green sky. From where I sat, orange arms of fire waved over the green light. I shivered at the beauty and the wonderful feeling of a full stomach. A brave rat scrambled across the ice close enough to collect a couple of wayward flakes and retreat to the shadows. I could see the glow of eyes at the edge of the ring of firelight.

A small patch of cold wet soaked through the seat of my pants. The fire had melted the ice in a ring around the fire pit. The water had mostly stayed there and slowly soaked through my cushion. I carefully got up from my spot to stand. I had eaten both batches of popcorn and was still feeling extravagant. I chucked the dead soldiers and burnt stuff toward the rats.

First the rats freaked, suspecting an attack. So they backed away. Once they realized it was not an attack they mobbed toward my offering. There was a scrum. The creatures brawled in a heap, squealing and screaming over the popcorn remnants.

At the end of it all, another two rats lay bleeding on the ice, life leaving them quickly. I glimpsed the injured bodies for just a second, before the rats swarmed over them to feast on warm remains. Once they'd devoured the carcasses, they fought each other to lick the blood off the ice.

"That's disgusting!" I yelled. Apparently, I prefer being gusted. Ha ha. At the sound of my voice, the rats scattered. A couple more skated over the edge of the ship. When they realized I wasn't going to move, the surviving rats returned to finish their feast.

The green sky continued to shimmer and move above, and the fire died down a little. I stoked it with a little more wood. Another batch. I dropped another cup of popcorn kernels into the pot and rolled them on the bottom of the pot over the fire. The kernels blossomed into another pot of white fluff. I pulled the pot off the fire. The food was good, but I could hardly keep my eyes off that sky. I downed two bottles of water. The first one, the one I'd already started, I nipped tiny sips of quickly. The second one I lingered over.

The fizz had flattened. I did have a couple handfuls of popcorn flakes left over, but stopped myself from eating them.

"I might need this later," I reminded myself out loud. What had we just learned? Rough seas mean we can't cook. Are you taking notes? When I say "we," you're with me now, aren't you, reader? I imagine you somewhere on this old tub. Least I hope you are. This is how these stupid words make me feel better. They're like footprints in the snow, ones we share. I go first, and you're right behind me. So this food is for the both of us.

So, I left the last of the popcorn in the pot, set the supplies on the popcorn, and skated back to my accommodations. Tomorrow I'll complain to the crew about the dangerous ice on deck. I left the fire smoldering on deck. It'll burn itself out. And, I'm full enough that I'll sleep like a baby. Hopefully better than a baby, actually. They don't sleep that well sometimes.

A knot of rats rumbled outside my cabin door, trying to get inside. Some pawed and scrabbled through the vomited bedclothes rumpled outside of the cabin.

"Why are you here?" I yelled. "No rats allowed." My voice sent them helter-skelter every which way.

Then I remembered.

30

ATS' NOSES ARE BETTER THAN their eyes. "Flour and sugar." Well, and vomit. One last rat emerged from the tuft of bedclothes on the deck, chewing something. "Dude, you like recycled popcorn?" The beast seemed confused, looked around for his friends, and, finding himself alone, beelined aft.

The door seemed okay when I inspected it. Good: It was still latched. Bad: They'd scratched their way through the varnish of the bottom door panel. There were some bite marks there. If I had left them alone for any longer, they'd have managed to get through the door. No sawdust. I guess they were actually eating their way through the wood. Then my first-class cabin would be like any other on this craptastic cruise.

I opened the door, stepped inside, and set everything down. Then I placed my gum-booted foot on something soft that shrieked. A rat, at least one, had followed me through the door!

There'd be no sleeping with that creature in the room. No rat sleepovers allowed.

Plan A: Open the cabin door and scare the beast out of the room. Flaw: Not going to leave the door open with all this food on the floor. I'll end up with 50 more in here.

Plan B: Kill the rat. Flaw: It's going to be gross. And there might be more than one. Fumbled for the flashlight, which I'd left in my popcorn pot. With the flashlight beam, then my spear-crutch. Time to hunt.

Holding the crutch's handgrip like a spear in my right hand, and the flashlight in my left, I returned to where I'd stepped on the rat. I began to cross the floor, weaving the beam to make sure I covered every inch of floor space with the flashlight. The floor was a small beach of flour and sugar. And that's where I found the rat, head buried in flour. Eating like a homeless person at a restaurant dumpster, its body frosted white by the flour. Like a giant, four-legged croissant. The rat studied the flashlight beam, but it refused to stop eating. I totally understood. Hunger does that to you.

I thrust the crutch at the creature, hitting it square in the back. I could feel something snap as the crutch landed. Probably the rat's spine. I watched the creature attempt to flee. Its front legs worked fine. But not its hind ones. So it began to pull itself through the flour with its front paws, while its hind ones dragged behind uselessly. Like me, it knew the game was over and offered a forlorn squeal.

A huge pang of guilt exploded in my gut. How awful to be a rat, I thought. No one cares if you live or die.

I should be picking on something my own size, right?

My guilt made me rethink Plan B. But I'd already taken the best of its life. It wasn't fair to let it live now. Plus, I hadn't been able to locate any rat-sized crutches. Better finish the job. I held the crutch poised above the squirming creature for a few seconds.

If I don't kill this rat, I'll have rats in here until I'm rescued or die. "Sorry, rat. It's you or me. And it's not going to be me today."

I brought the crutch down quickly on the rat's head, crushing it flat. Blood, brains, teeth and tongue mashed into the white flour. The front paws twitched in the flashlight as the rat's reflexes made their last protest.

An incredible sadness stormed my good mood. Sure, it's a rat. Sure, it'd eat my face off if I let it, but life is life, right? I guess you have to sink pretty low to feel compassion for rats. Dude. It's terrible. I haven't even been drinking. I guess in a way, I feel like one of them.

Once I'd mourned, I scoured the rest of the room for any more rats. Fortunately, I couldn't scare up any more.

I double checked the door of my cabin—I made sure that it was latched, and I locked it for good measure. In the bathroom, I could hear the sound of scrabbling echo up the toilet, the toilet sort of amplifying the sound. I had the heebie-jeebies, as my mom would say. That's sort of a jittery paranoia, in case you didn't know. Just in case, I balled a filthy towel and wedged it into the toilet bowl. For the sink drain, I found a used washcloth to do the same. It seemed too small for a rat, but I wanted to be sure. The shower drain was already blocked with a fine-meshed grate.

As an extra measure of safety, I swept the room with the flashlight again.

The mess was impressive. The storm had blenderized my teenage-slob décor. "I've got to clean this up," I announced. "Or move cabins." No rats. I carefully stowed the pot in thecloset door, shut in behind a slice of plywood. The pot could move a little, but it was held in place. but the sides of the drawer would hold the pot in place if the seas grew heavy again.

In that pot waited a load of popcorn. Tomorrow's dinner. The thought made me grin. I'd get a badge for sure if I were a Boy Scout.

Then a small seed of thought popped into my head: The rats will smell the popcorn. Which means they'll be back. Maybe even tonight. The thought brought to mind another idea—a towel against the bottom of the door. The towel didn't do much, except it made me feel better, so I guess it did its job. I felt secure enough to sleep. I could tell because the pure adrenaline from my rat hunting faded like a drunken party memory.

I lay awake for a while. I could still see some of the green glow on the rim of the porthole. The green sky-snakes slowly danced out of light. By the time the green disappeared, I had checked out of reality, under a heap of blankets and sheets, probably snoring like a two-stroke dirt bike.

31

HEN I AWOKE, IT WAS long after first light. Thick yellow beams of light poured through portholes and windows. At the door, a constant quiet scratching. In an instant, it all came back. I threw back the heap of blankets, took my crutch in hand and prowled through the cabin, looking for rats I'd missed, or some that had found a way in while I slept.

The rats were either well-hidden or none had made it in during the night. I went to the door of the cabin and knocked on it, and the rat mob on the other side of the door cleared away like pigs at a bacon convention. Ooh. Bad metaphor. I'm instantly hungry. I'm tempted to write the word "bacon" down on a sheet of paper and try frying it for supper.

Still armed with my crutch, I cracked the door open. No creatures sought entrance, so I threw open the door and stepped onto the promenade deck. Some of the bolder rats sat on their haunches and studied me. What I had heard as rats' scratching might actually have been rats' eating. The rat crew had scratched away a substantial amount of door paneling. Still, I saw no wood chips or sawdust on the ground. Talk about high fiber. If I let them continue, it wouldn't be long before they added my cabin to part of the rat territory. I'd have no place to sleep. I had to be vigilant. And unsentimental.

Though it was brisk, the weather had warmed enough to begin melting the ice. The deck now dripped and gurgled as the ice melted. The boat still looked as though it were decorated like a birthday cake. White this time.

The ship looked beautiful, like she was wearing a beautiful gown to the Oscars, or the Russian equivalent. All of Lyubov Orlova's blemishes, her scabs and pimples, and missing equipment, all dressed in wedding whites.

"You're beautiful, Lyubov!" I wolf-whistled. She'd dressed up, just for little old me.

I turned to survey the cabin. The bright light made clear the storm's destruction. Today's job was to rat-proof the cabin and clean up the spilled sugar, flour, and barf. I left the cabin door open and fetched my bowl of popcorn. My breakfast.

As I ate, I did some sloppy math based on how much I'd eaten and how many meals I thought I'd get out of the remaining popcorn. At two meals a day, there was less than a week's worth of popcorn, I think. Rice, I had a few pounds. But I had no idea how to cook it. I'd only had it in a restaurant a few times.

Note to self: Look for a cookbook in the library. Every library has a cookbook, right?

The puke was an easy clean. I closed the cabin door, balled the puke-soaked bedclothes, walked them down the covered promenade hallway, onto the aft decking. Up the stairs to the after observation deck. I tossed the whole set into the nearly empty outdoor swimming pool. There were lots more sheets and blankets where those came from. Then back to the cabin. The rats were back. Sure enough, they were eating my door. Desperate, if you ask me. Not much of a future in door eating. If you want an open door, I've been told, get a good education.

"Go to college," I yelled. Not many seemed to be positive about post-secondary education. They took to the hills.

"Cleanup day," I chirruped. With the rats gone, I decided to prop the cabin door open with the clear plastic jug of popcorn. The ugly job was sending the dead rat to the morgue, and notifying next of kin. Just kidding. My cell phone doesn't work.

I ended up sliding the carcass onto the head of my axe and tossing the remains onto the promenade deck. It lay there like a lumpy, football-shaped welcome mat. But I had second thoughts. These rats are desperate enough to eat it. The carcass would bring them back to my door. So I loaded it onto the axe head again and walked it down the promenade deck to the end of the covered decking and heaved it into the sea.

"Sorry, and God rest your sad, furry soul. I commit your body to the deep." I watched as the carcass wafted like a sheet of paper and settled gently on the sea. Hopefully, that rat wouldn't be reincarnated and come back as my next stepdad.

Focus: cabin cleanup. Back at the cabin I realized I shouldn't have left the door open. That's just asking for a party. Fortunately, I didn't find anyone inside. Instead, I scooped up the rat-splat flour and put it in a box for disposal later. No flour and sugar left to eat now. Got to get rid of it, because I don't want to help the rats at all.

The rice was still in its burlap bag. I lifted the rice bag and smelled it. It had a flat smell of grain through the bag. If I could smell it, the rats could too. The smell, to them, would be like Michael Bublé crooning to middle-aged moms. There'd be a swooning crowd soon. Not good. So I placed the bag in its plastic tub. The lid sealed the smell away from the cabin. With all of my food safely stowed, I was good to go.

That left me the problem of the carpet. The sugar and flour were ground in, and there was no way of cleaning it up. There was a strong barf patch in the carpet beside the bed. No way of getting rid of it..

With a kitchen knife, I worked a small hole through the teal blue carpet. I should have ditched it long ago. Worn. Stained. Stink of mold. I flipped the sharp edge up, and cut and tore around the carpet patch out. Glued to the decking. In most places the glue released the carpet easily. The glue was tired, like the rest of the ship. In a few places, it took some pretty stiff work to get it away from the floor. After some work, I pulled the trouble spots into the promenade hallway, rolled the carpet up, and got ready to haul it to the swimming pool on the back deck.

Once I closed the cabin door, I began hauling everything to the swimming pool on the aft observation deck. By the time I'd arrived to throw the first piece of carpet into the pool, there were rats treading scum water at the pool bottom.

Woah! The storm had deepened the pool by a couple of feet. Some had made it onto a small island formed by the ball of bedsheets. No palm tree. The islanders scrounged through the fabric folds looking for goodies.

The island was tiny, though. A vicious fight for a piece of turf. So some were treading water frantically. Some weren't so lucky. A few more furry hunks stewing in the muck.

I tossed in the carpet. The putrid stuff slammed down beside the island of rats as they ate. At first they squealed. The carpet settled into the pool scum. In a couple of places it poked above the water to add to the islands of stuff. The doomed rats moved onto the carpet islands and began to attack the flour and sugar stuck in the fibers. I could see another rat or two being torn apart by the others in the frenzy.

Like filthy, furry sharks. "Would you attack me?" I asked. None of the rats seemed to notice the question. Instead, I frowned briefly as I guessed at the answer.

Back to the cabin I returned, and found another platoon of rats working on the cabin door. They backed off as soon as I strode through the rear door toward the cabin. For a moment I was confused.

But then I remembered: the popcorn.

So I tried to think of something that would scare them away for good.

"Justin Bieber!" I yelled.

They backed away, but only just out of reach. "Uh.

Miley Cyrus?" One of the bigger rats blinked. The fact that neither name scared them may suggest some of the reasons why we weren't getting along.

It was lunchtime anyway. I opened the cabin door, went inside, closed the door safely behind me, and pulled the popcorn pot out of the open drawer. A bottle of water, too.

"Honey, I'm going out for lunch," I yelled.

Technically, I was thinking of a picnic. Popcorn in hand, I knocked on the cabin door and swung it open. The rats studded the top of the promenade deck. I was careful to shut the door behind me as I began to move sternward, eating as I went. I dropped the occasional popcorn flake to get the snarl of beasts to follow, which they did. As I reached the aft door to the covered promenade hallway, I turned to push the door open with my butt. Parading behind me came the rat horde. I turned and lunged at the rats, who scattered quickly, but didn't bother to try and hide themselves the way they had when I'd first come aboard. Almost as in-your-face as an army of door-to-door salespeople. But I knew how to lose them all.

32

TURNED AND EXITED THE COVER of the promenade deck hallway, and took a set of stairs up to the aft observation deck. Then up to the captain's deck, and up to the funnel. Up the metal rung ladder welded to the back, to the funnel's top.

"Ah. Monsieur, your table is ready."

I was hoping that rats don't do ladders. So I studied the side of the funnel for a minute. A few had followed me up the stairs, but they seemed stymied by the metal rung ladder. I flicked a flake toward them, like Jimmy

Hendrix throwing a guitar pick into the throng. I focused on the popcorn. I heard the scream as the scrum of rats negotiated below.

Time to focus on lunch. Just because I had nothing to do, and couldn't waste a flake, I thought I'd eat one at a time. I couldn't afford to eat like I'd eat at the movies, sort of slapping a huge mitt of the stuff at my mouth and hoping that fifty percent went in. Each piece was too precious. I sipped a little water.

No butter, which sucked. But the sun was thick and warm, like butter, a little warmer than the heat-stealing breeze. The popcorn tasted like heaven.

The sea, in the bright sunlight was a cold gray-green. I thought about my rescue. It had been four, maybe five days already, though it was hard to say for sure. It should have happened by now, shouldn't it? I'd called my mom. Had she been listening?

The popcorn might carry me through. The rice. What would happen if I ran out of food? What would I eat? How much carbonated water was in the pop dispenser? I had at least a week of food. Impossible to say about the water.

I ate slowly. Nip some water. Then fourteen flakes of popcorn (count them).

I'll need another food source, soon. Fish? Seaweed? I'd need equipment. I needed to explore the boat again. The thought was a little frightening. A rat rebellion seemed inevitable. I felt like a steak on two legs, walking around a ship of carnivores. Rats eat door wood and each other. Not a refined palate. So, there's a good chance I am delicious.

I needed a serious shower. Would rats consider a lack of cleanliness a turn-off or a marinade?

Much, much later, I finished the popcorn. There were a few burnt flakes and dead soldiers in the bottom of the pot. Instead of throwing to the rats, I poured the remains down one of the smaller stacks sticking out the top of the funnel. The kernels jangled and pinged into the bowels of the ship. I wiped the pot out with my hand.

Another idea. Inspired in part by the ship's funnel. Gonna get rid of the smell of food in my room. Off the funnel deck, down the stairs, into the covered hallway to the cabin. Rats loitered outside the cabin door, though they didn't seem to be working on the door with the same fervor they had earlier.

I shooed them from the door and shut myself inside. The pot I placed on the decking in a spot where the carpet had been stripped from the floor. I balled up a few sheets of that foolscap paper I've got. I dropped the paper balls in the bottom of the pot and lit them. Smoke oozed from the pot and slowly filled the room with a campfire smell. I let the smoke infuse the room in the hope that the smoke smell would pave over the food smell. Cabin clean. Now me.

I kicked off my boot and shoe. My feet, especially my left—the one in the boot—reeked like an aged French goat cheese. I had found some discarded socks when I cruised the boat last time. I'll collect a few and start doing laundry, maybe. At this moment, the rest of my odors slowly made themselves known, a disgusting mob of stinks. My smell gathered an ugly strength. I felt a-streel. My greasy head was all mops and brooms.

It was time for a hygiene moment. But drinking water was far too valuable to use as bathwater.

I thought a moment. Then it hit me: I'm floating on a huge ocean. Duh.

33

A T THE END OF A long rope, I attached a blue plastic bucket with a sturdy metal handle. From the lower quarterdeck, I dropped the bucket into the ocean and whipped the rope until the bucket lay on its side and took on water. Hoist. Woah. Heavy.

Up on the deck, I poured it into my big pot. Cold. Cold as a math test in January. I snagged a couple more buckets. Then I waddled the pot up to my campfire spot on the aft observation deck.

I struck a new fire and dropped the pot into the middle of the fresh coals. While I waited for the water to heat, I gathered and organized wooden chair and table bits into different stacks: small, medium, and large. In a battered cardboard box, I gathered paper garbage.

Just to be fancy, I dragged one of the good chairs out and set it next to the fire.

The pot began to send up whispers of steam. Warm enough, I thought. Didn't want to burn too much wood. I had no idea how much I'd need, right?

I left the pot in the fire and stripped down. The water was lukewarm, but it felt good. I used a new hotel soap and a washcloth I'd found. I had a small stained towel to dry with. Head to toe soap. Head to toe rinse. I was careful and kept the bath water clean.

Then I dunked my clothes in the pot water. Soaped them up. Dropped them back in the pot, and set them out to tan on the chair, next to the fire, until they dried. I built up the fire a little. It's cold when you stand naked on the deck, even on a sunny day on the North Atlantic.

With my kind of luck, this is when the rescue helicopter and TV crews would show up. "Channel 5 reporting on that missing boy. Oh, Lordy, can you guys see that back in the studio?"

"Absolutely, Ken. He's naked as a jaybird." Whatever a jaybird is.

"It looks like he's doing some kind of weird initiation rite. He seems to be wearing one rubber boot and one running shoe."

"An absolute nut job, Ken. We've got a psychiatrist here to comment on what she thinks she's seeing."

I put a blanket over myself, just in case the helicopter actually showed up. I roasted a few key items like my gonch and socks. An item at a time, I began to put myself back together. All clothes were clean, though damp.

While I was at it, I took a kitchen knife and stabbed a couple of new holes in my belt. I'm losing some of my waistline. Pants won't stay on.

I got to say, I felt pretty good. Pretty fine. Clean is a fantastic feeling. No wonder all those people laugh and party in detergent ads.

I dumped the dirty bath/laundry water and wiped out the pot. Time for popcorn. With the remains of the fire, I cooked up another double batch of popcorn. Then I was good to go.

I decided to take my supper in the library. I have a few good meals of popcorn left. Then I got to figure rice. Water, I don't know how that's going to work. So, I pulled the fire apart. That way I can conserve wood. It started to complain, mostly moving from flame to smudge smoke.

In the library, I sat in front of the bookshelves and browsed while I palmed a few popcorn flakes at a time. Most of the books were novels. If I get a little time, I'll dig into them. No cookbooks though. There were a bunch of Arctic survival manuals. Which reminded me of the book I'd already found: The US Army Survival Manual 21-76. I don't understand the numbers in the title, but it had a bunch of survival techniques. It looked like a book mostly designed for surviving on land, but I figure, survival is survival, right?

When I'd gone through all the books, and eaten my supper, I went back to my room. I poured the rest of the popcorn into a sealed tub. No smell, right? Out of the nightstand drawer, I pulled the Survival Guide. There was just enough light to illuminate the pages. First page, I struck gold. Here's what it says:

"You can remain alive anywhere in the world when you keep your wits. This is a major lesson in survival. Remember that nature and the elements are neither your friend nor your enemy—they are actually disinterested. Instead, it is your determination to live and your ability to make nature work for you that are the deciding factors."

I say, true. I'd also add, that nature and the elements are a better parent than the ones I've actually had.

That's what I've done, I exalted. I kept my wits. I started out without them. In fact, my lack of wits led me here. But I've managed to keep my head.

Panic thought: I'd forgotten to check on the ship's water level.

34

MY BEST REASON TO LOSE my head: The ship is slowly sinking. I checked the square hole on the foredeck, and the little puddle that jerked around at the bottom is now a lot deeper. A lot. I should have checked on that earlier. I got carried away by a fit of cleanliness. Another storm or two and the ship's a goner, I think.

Second best reason to lose my head: This is probably my fifth day at sea. I thought for sure I'd be rescued by now. Maybe they didn't know I was on this thing, but I can't believe they'd let a tub this size float around on the ocean. And what if I hit something?

I had been totally thinking of abandoning my writing. It would be a little lame to be missing for a couple of days and write a thing this dramatic. But after five days, there's a good chance I'm going to be here a lot longer. Which means my chances of dying are rising. My original melodramatic note may not be that far off the mark.

So, I'm spending more time on my story, just in case it survives and I don't. I suppose it's kind of like a lifejacket. I'll put my life into this story, and let her drift. Someone will find it, assuming the ship doesn't sink. That way part of me survives. When they read it, these words kind of bring me back to life, don't they? Weird that a bunch of letters can actually contain flesh and blood. Anyhow, I was a little behind on writing it, until now. I realize this story might be important. So, I'm caught up. I even used the dictionary a couple of times. Can you tell?

Here's today's discovery: Survival Guide, page 161: an amazing section on killing and eating animals. You'll never guess what it included. You can't, I'd bet. And, I hope you never have to rely on its advice.

35

THE MANUAL READS "BOTH RATS and mice are palatable meat." How disgusting. I have to admit I felt a little sick to my stomach with the thought. The manual provided a diagram with some kind of general varmint with little dotted lines to indicate how someone would gut and skin said varmint.

Here's the general idea: To gut an animal, you slice little doors into the animal's belly. It's a lot like the dissecting I did in Biology this year. You open the doors, and turn the animal over. The guts fall out, except where they attach.

Then you rip the guts out. Guess what? You can eat rat heart, lungs, liver, brain and tongue. You're supposed to save the blood, which is a good source of salt, apparently. This is not making me feel hungry here. You save the fat, maybe to use as butter, I don't know. Apparently, you can cook and eat the head. Mmmm. Crispy rat head. No thank you.

You hack out the plumbing leading to the throat and butthole. No kidding. Once the guts are gone, you get rid of the fur. You make little cuts around the legs of the rat, around its neck, and around its junk. Then you basically peel the skin off. Eeesh. Then you make a stew. The book recommends you boil the furless, gutless carcass with the rat's liver and some dandelion leaves, to make a stew. Boil for ten minutes. Ten minutes will kill all bacteria and parasites. If it comes down to eating rats, this is what I will need to do. A shiver rolled up my spine. Rat stew for supper?

The survival guide reminded me of my food problem. I've got to see what I can eat before I run out of options.

I'd better check out the bigger kitchen more carefully. I gotta find other things to eat. The popcorn won't last. Even if I figured out what to do with the rice, there's only ten pounds of it. The flour has been spoiled by the rats, as has the sugar. I don't know why I'm keeping them, but they're tubbed, and sealed, and in the cabin. But if it's a choice between disgusting flour and boiled rats, I might want to eat tainted flour, right? I guess I could get desperate enough. God, I hope I get rescued soon.

Before I could catch myself, I was fantasizing. Finding boxes of Doritos, a cart of hot dogs, and cases of beer. The idea caused my stomach to groan with pleasure. Then I told it the truth. It wasn't getting any of it. That news through it into a gastronomic tantrum.

There was enough light left to check out the downstairs kitchen. I should take a good look. Maybe I won't have to try roast rat.

I smell good, generally, except for my boot, which I can smell as I sit here. The boot needs to be rinsed and dried. Next time I do laundry, I guess. My flashlight. A few empty water bottles. A candle, and my lighter, and my crutch. The rats weren't outside the door any longer. I hoped that meant that my clean up and campfire smell had been effective.

When I went upstairs to the bar, the rats scattered as I walked behind the counter to reload the water bottles. The dispenser coughed and belched a little air while I filled them. I wonder if that means it's running out. Better find a new water source soon. Maybe in the big kitchen.

The bottom decks were a lot creepier. Seriously. The afternoon light was strong, which made me feel a little better. So instead of using the outside stairs, I took the spiral staircase in the midship lobby and circled down two decks. Rats scattered down the hall as I walked. It felt as though they were getting used to me. Probably not a good sign.

On the lower deck, there were two separate hallways, one on either side of the ship. The hallway on the left waited in gloom. In the right hallway, light shone through the cracks in the cabin doors. Of course, I chose the right hallway. I opened a cabin door on that lower deck.

The whole hallway glowed orange. At the hallway's end, I found the door to the big kitchen. Right underneath the dining room. The popcorn and stuff, I had found in the smaller kitchen just off of the dining room, but I hadn't searched this one well. I had been too freaked on my first search to do a good job.

The first thing was rats. But you're getting the idea. They're everywhere and always lurking right? So just assume wherever I go, they'll be there. The next was kitchen supplies. The pots I had were good, but I might need more. If I got a good rain, for example, I might want to collect water. I might need to boil rats. The kitchen had been stripped, but the battered and bent stuff had been left behind. Only things worthy of scrap had been left. Maybe that's why I'm on this ship. In a weird way, I kinda belong here. I'm garage sale material.

There were a couple of huge pots, so I put the stuff I wanted to keep in the pots and put it near the door on the way out. Lots of stuff like metal spoons, potato mashers, tongs, that kind of thing. I found another lighter and a large box half full of stick matches. More firepower. A set of screwdrivers and knives. No water. But a few more empties. I think I'm going to hang on to those. If I find enough, I'll fill them all up with carbonated water until it runs out. That way I'll know how much water I've got.

I found four plastic tubs. Small amounts of sugar and flour. Salt. Not much. But the tubs are great, because they keep the smell of things inside. Might be handy for something. My stack of stuff was getting pretty huge. It was going to take me a few trips to get it up to the cabin, but good stuff.

At the back of the kitchen was this large white metal shed. I'd guess it was a walk-in fridge. The ship had been sitting for a couple of years without power. I thought of my fridge. It got pretty disgusting after a couple of weeks. The milk goes chunky. The cheddar begins to turn green and white. Slime grows on cold cuts. Give a fridge a couple of years, it'd be a zombie paradise. Rats, I'm not sure about, but if there was rotten food in there, and there was a way in, the place would be a rat restaurant.

The fridge latch was a bit odd. A button on the end of a long rod. It took me a minute to figure out how to open the door. Not much different than a fence gate. As I considered the latch, a circle of rats formed around me, maybe ten feet away in every direction. It was like I was opening a Christmas present for all of us.

I almost forgot. I had my crutch, flashlight, and a lighter, the matches and a couple candles. You have to be prepared, right? It was hard to hold everything and open the fridge door at the same time. So I chose the crutch, and got ready to stab anything that might come at me. I pushed the button in gently. The latch clanked open and the door opened slowly.

It opened easily. As the door seal cracked open, there was a rush of air, rank, like a nuclear fart. Suddenly the whole place reeked. The door swung open wide on its own. The rats rushed in closer. Inside, rat-free. Which was good news.

"Stop," I yelled. The rats stopped instantly—except one, who seemed mesmerized by the smell. He got the end of my crutch in the stomach, and hard. He flopped around on the floor like an ocean-starved fish to get away from me.

Once he floundered out of reach, he was attacked by his kind.

They balled up and rolled around in a squealing mob. The injured one tried to get up. At first it seemed like they were wrestling. Then there was some blood, like they were nipping the weak one. The nips turned into chomps, and suddenly there was blood everywhere, and then bone, and then not even bone.

Sometimes in the ball, they get confused. They bite blindly, I guess. So another one sometimes goes down with the injured one. One or two rats accidentally bite the wrong one, and before you know it, there's an extra meal for dinner.

This time, the beast who's being eaten looked at me for a moment as the rest devoured his body. He was overwhelmed, yet knew what's happening. For the few seconds we connected, his eyes looked surprised, helpless, then pained. Finally, lifeless. Then they ate his face and eyes.

The fridge's stench felt like a punch in the nose: putrid,

pungent, and powerful. I stepped across the threshold and pulled the door closed behind me, to keep the rats out. The smell was brutal, but if there was any food in here, I wanted to find it before the rats did.

I turned on my flashlight and the orange beam warmed up the room a little. I set the crutch by the door. I didn't think I'd need it.

The fridge was crowded with stuff. There were boxes of produce completely molded. Who knows what it was?

The fridge shambles were kind of disgusting in some places. But sometimes it was sort of past disgusting, the way a skeleton is just less creepy than a rotting corpse.

Like these apples I found. At least I think they were apples. They'd shriveled into sort of giant brown prunes. There were some old grapes that had shriveled into raisins, on the stem. There was a stack of boxes marked "lettuce," the box bottoms lined with black feathery rot.

There were some rotting things like meat. Long gone. Shriveled and black. It looked like long huge scabs. There were a few packaged cold cuts, which just looked as though they were dried, but otherwise they looked okay. The "best before" dates were from August and September, three years ago. No mold or anything. Just expired. The color looked a bit off; preservatives, I'd guess. I opened a package and it smelled like a cadaver. Not going to touch the stuff.

I found a couple of green blocks of stuff. From the shape, I inferred it was cheese. Entirely green, still in plastic.

If I'd been at home, I would have been disgusted, I think. I remember avoiding bananas because they were slightly bruised. I wasn't sure about any of this stuff, but beggars can't be choosers, can they? I took a chance, and hoped it wouldn't make me sick later. If it stays down, I win. If it comes up, I lose.

A few tiny wheels of cheese, coated with a red waxy

coating. I grabbed a small one. I found the tab and pulled. It peeled pretty easily. The cheese seemed clear of mold. I waved the block under my nose. It stunk, but a cheesy stink.

I pinched a bit out with my fingers, and put it on my tongue. A funky flavor, but otherwise it seemed okay. I tried a little more, taking a good bite out of the block. Not bad. Even tasty. It felt heavy in my throat compared to the popcorn.

My flashlight's beam wavered from yellow to orange, to a dull yellow, to black. I shook it. It offered me a precious orange glow before it faded to a final blackness.

Darker than a cow's gut.

In the utter dark, I stepped towards the door—at least I thought it was the door. As I did, I tripped. Out of my hands flew the hunk of cheese. My elbow landed in a mush of rot. My flashlight flew and clattered across the floor somewhere in front of me.

There I was, the devil to pay and no pitch hot, as my mom would say.

36

THE DARKNESS IN THE FRIDGE was that same mad-making darkness I'd experienced a few nights before. It was like my eyes were thirsty for light, trying to drink it in from somewhere, but there was no shadow or color anywhere. They almost hurt as they tried to find something to do with themselves. I found a clear spot on the floor and sat down.

After my eyes struggled for a while, I closed them. It was easier. The fridge numbed the noise, too. It was hard to hear anything. My ears were thirsty, too, striking out to find sound somewhere.

Sitting there with nothing to do, I understood that the ship was never quiet. There was always noise. The sound of the sea, the creaks and groans. The moan of the wind. But in the fridge, dead quiet.

From my stomach, I could feel panic radiate up into my throat. I wanted to throw a full-on fit. I told myself there were no rats in here. I said it over and over, which seemed to help. That was the big bonus of being trapped in a walk-in fridge.

I think I was sitting, facing the door. As I sat there, my ears found a quiet sound. It was actually to my left. It was a quiet scratching sound. The sound itself was muted but it was clear enough.

I rolled forward onto my knees. I could feel a box of something directly in front of me, so I twisted to the left, towards the scratching sound.

The path toward the sound jagged through towers of rotting boxes. But I eventually got to what I thought was the door. I felt the wall and located a gap. Soft rubber filled the space—like the edge of a door. I followed the rubber up with my hand, which lead me to my feet. On my tiptoes, I could feel the rubber turn right and cross the top of the door.

So I ran my hand down the inside of the door where the latch should be. The inside was smooth metal, with the odd scab of food, or something, fixed to the surface. I couldn't find the latch. I ran my hand across in the opposite direction thinking I'd missed the latch somehow. But I couldn't find it that way either.

I could feel the panic boil up. "Maybe the latch is on the door frame," I said to myself. My left hand, which I kept on the rubber gap on the door, I moved to the left. My right hand I kept on the rubber while my left stroked the metal looking for some kind latch mechanism, door handle or something.

Nothing. I littered the air with a few choice words.

Checked again, more carefully. Absolutely nothing. The door didn't seem to open from the inside. The panic gave way to an explosion of anger and I groped away from the door until my hands found a box. I picked the box up and hurled it across the fridge.

But I stopped when I realized my flashlight, or the candles and matches, might have been in that box. My tantrum would mess up the room, and I'd have a dickens of a time finding my matches and candles. In short, I'd be screwed.

Once my freakout finished, I felt like taking a nap. I'd been trapped places like this before. One of my stepdads, Warren, used to do this to me, when I was younger and we still lived with him. He'd lock me in the garden shed sometimes because he was mad at me. Sometimes just because. Sometimes I was dressed. Sometimes I was in my PJs. One time I was just in my underwear.

The first few times it was horrible. But, I dare you to believe it, I learned to like it. One reason: My stepdad never locked himself in with me. The trouble was now outside the shed, so I knew I'd be fine for a while. A few times he'd lock me in overnight. It was always bad news for my mom, though. My mom would let me out, usually. She looked like hell. Purple eyes. Fat lip. A couple of times, a missing tooth.

The shed wasn't as dark as the fridge on the ship, though. The shed had cracks that let light in. This had no cracks. But no rats, either. They wouldn't be scratching their way through this door and eating my face. I supposed I should be panicking. Instead, I felt like lying down and sleeping, which is what I used to do in the shed.

I fell asleep. For how long, I have no idea. It might have been the next day, or two days, two hours, or two minutes. All I know is that I slept.

When I awoke, the seas were heavier again. I could feel the boat rock. But something had changed.

I touched the door. The door faced the back of the ship, which meant the walls on my right and left were port and starboard, respectively. My back faced the bow. I closed my eyes to follow the boat's movement as best I could. It seemed to be rocking from the door of the fridge to the wall behind me. I waited a couple of minutes and studied the motion, ignoring the hint of nausea.

In the last storm, the boat waffled broadside to the waves, so the ship rolled violently side to side. That's the way a ship without engines hits the waves. In these seas, it was front to back, steady as church-going girlfriend. At least I assumed it was front to back. Hard to tell in the complete dark. I don't know what to say except to say that a boat should move that way if it had a working engine in it—or maybe if it was being towed.

That's what got me looking for a way out again. I had to find out what was going on. I didn't want to miss my own rescue, if that was what was happening. I had to get out of this box. Now.

37

CRAWLED THROUGH THE MAZE OF boxes on the floor, away from the door, to where I felt like I'd been standing before I tripped. I found a few things on the floor. The remains of something, probably from the box I'd hurled across the room earlier. I got to where I think I began, and I replayed my fall again in my mind. I'd had the candle and matches in my left hand when I stumbled forward, and the flashlight in my right. The dead flashlight was obviously less important than the candle and matches, so I went for a search on my left.

First I crawled from the crutch to the door. I couldn't feel anything on the floor. I found part of the cheese wheel

I'd been eating, brushed off a couple of chunky bits, and snacked on it right there. There was a narrow path to my left through stacks of things. I checked the floor that way. I put my hands in a few things on that floor, but couldn't find what I was looking for. Back to the crutch, my home base in the fridge.

To my left, I found a stack of boxes probably waist high. The top of the uppermost box was open, which meant the candle and matches could have ended up inside. So I gingerly began to grope through the contents. I guessed it might have been lettuce, maybe. The outsides felt dry and leafy, and the leaves felt rather large and dried. As I pawed through the box, I broke one of the dried things open, and this ooze ended up on my fingers, which I scraped off on the box edge.

Nothing in that box. I groped the rest of the stack to see if they had openings. Sometimes boxes are open, sort of, to let air get at things, yet make things stackable. I couldn't feel any opening where a box of matches or a candle could get in. This was like looking for good grammar in a Bush speech.

To the stack next to it, toward the door. I put my hands through unnamable stuff. No point in cleaning my hands off until I'd found my candle and matches. The boxes were all produce, I'd guess. Soft and mushy. Creamy mush sometimes. Lots of brittle and dead. The occasional prickle. No matches and candle.

It was starting to get tricky in there. The seas were getting pretty heavy. I was on my feet in the middle of the fridge mess. I hoped I could keep my cheese down.

The next stack was short, and the top of the boxes was pleated closed. I dropped to my knees and felt the spaces between the stacks I'd checked already. I couldn't find anything but odd bits of debris. Another cheese wheel! I stuffed it into my pocket. I might need it.

My search from hell continued. I remember once I

went to this haunted house for Halloween. For part of it, they'd blindfold you and make you put your hands in things. They told me I was in a house from hell. I remember they made me put my hand in a bowl of spaghetti and told me it was earthworms. That kind of thing. That's what this was like, except there was no one to guide what you touched, and the blindfold was permanent.

As I went through another stack of produce boxes, my fingers scuffed what felt like the strike pad of a matchbox. I pinched the edges and pulled it up. The matches! In the pitching seas. I was careful this time. It'd be pretty easy to lose them and die. I pinched a few matches out of the box and slid them into my pocket, and made sure the box was closed. From the matches in my pocket I brought one up and struck it on the side of the box. An orange flame coughed to life on the end of the match. My eyes quit working for a second as they adjusted to the bright light. The door was just to my left, and as the match glowed, I couldn't see a latch on the inside of the door.

I set the box of matches down carefully so I could find them again, and shifted the burning match to my left hand, and pulled a new match out of my pocket. Just as the first was singeing my fingertips, I lit the next one, and blew the old one out and dropped it on the floor. Carefully. Last thing I need is to light one of these boxes on fire and end up roasting to death. I inspected the side of the door to the left of the frame. There didn't seem to be a latch release there, either.

I lit another match and moved right. The inside of the door was smooth; I couldn't find anything on the right either. I lit another match and moved left again. It was smooth. Maybe this door didn't open from the inside. But that would be stupid, right? How did this door open from the inside?

I dropped the match, and as I did so, I noticed a pedal device on the floor, partially covered by a flap of cardboard. A foot pedal? Made sense, maybe. I crushed the cardboard into the corner and out of the way and stomped the pedal to the floor.

The door released with a gasp. A strangled gray light tumbled through the opening. A sight for starved eyes, I can tell you.

Immediately, there were rats. One tried to break through the opening, but I let him have it with my boot and he flew across the kitchen. The rest backed away. The door wanted to swing wide as the bow dropped down the side of another wave.

I figured the fridge might be an awesome spot to hide from rats, now that I know how to open the door—so I kept the rats out of it, caught the edge of the door and slammed it shut. I'd come back for my crutch and supplies later.

It was hard to tell whether it was early morning or twilight. The light through the kitchen portholes was weak and gray. The sensations of motion I'd felt in the fridge were right. The boat was plowing bow first through some heavy seas, which meant something was up.

The stuff I'd collected from the kitchen skated back and forth across the kitchen floor like a drunken marching band. The noise was nearly deafening compared to the near silence of the fridge.

I wanted to see if I was being rescued or not. So I sprinted from the kitchen to the set of spiral stairs at midship. The waves set me on my can a few times. I ran up to the bridge deck, through the chartroom into the wheel house. I grabbed the handrail at the base of the ship's dashboard.

The bow nosed into a monstrous wave, which broke over the bow in a thick cloud smashing against the bridge windows. The windows were black with water, the bridge literally under the sea. Then, needling through, the bow broke through the back of the wave. The black retreated in green rivers to reveal an angry ocean. I could see some kind of heavy line extending from the bow of the ship, into the water ahead. I blinked. I had not been drunk for days. So unless I was seeing things, the ship was being towed!

38

T HE SHIP'S BOW FOLLOWED THE next wave up to the crest, and broke through, and as it did, I could see a large tug ahead in the distance! I'd been rescued! Well. I'm getting ahead of myself here. I hadn't been rescued, but the ship had been found, at least.

I don't know how long I stood on the bridge. Debris in the chartroom clattered around like beans in a maraca. I held the silver hand rail for dear life. This was pretty intense sea. And it seemed to be escalating. Like my mom as she drank.

At the bottom of the trough, the wave crests towered over the ship like New York skyscrapers. The fronts of the waves were an angry gray, laced with collars of rabid white foam. The tug that pulled us was smaller, and a few hundred meters in front. It seemed to glow. Hull painted sky blue, to match the bridge, and the rest of the topsides white. As the tug broke through the crest of a wave, she flashed a brown-orange hull heel, before she bobbed into a trough out of sight. When we crested one wave, I could catch glimpses of her pulling hard, until she shot over the advancing wave crest and disappeared.

After a while, balancing on the bridge turned into a good workout. But there would be no rescue in these seas. There's no way the tug could pull alongside. Plus, it would be impossible to signal the tug. The easiest way would have been to light a fire on the deck, which wasn't possible. Or I could have screamed and waved at them from the deck, but a walk on the open deck would be suicide at this point.

My watch, then, was pointless. I could stand in the bridge getting a workout trying to keep on my feet, or I could go lie in my cabin on my bed. Besides, my tongue felt like sandpaper. I needed a good drink of water. As the ship crested another wave, I ran for the spiral stairs. Down two floors, and then sat on the floor holding on to the railing while the ship broached the next crest. Then a scoot through the doors into the covered promenade hallway. I ran along the outside edge of the hallway, running my hand along the handrail. The surge began to pull the ship upwards, towards the next wave top. Before it peaked, I threw open the cabin door and dove onto the bed.

The fridge had been reasonably warm, probably because it was so well insulated that it kept in the warmth of the decaying food. The cabin was a fridge by comparison, so I kicked off my footwear and heaped myself in blankets.

The beds had been designed for this sort of a rocking motion, so it was less difficult to stay in bed. Plus, this storm didn't seem as violent as the last one I'd lived through.

The cabin had fared much better in this storm than the last. There were only a couple of things rolling across the floor, and the supplies hadn't broken loose again. Not that it mattered, because I'd been rescued. To be accurate: nearly rescued.

"Sailor, I'll be home to do your litterbox, soon, buddy."

I was tempted to read a little, but the light was poor. So I waited. Indulging lustful thoughts of Big Mac meals, deep-fried chicken, and bottomless cups of Coke.

When I woke again, it was dark and angry. It took me a moment to figure out where I was. Not the fridge, thank God. I lay there as the sea boomed and hissed and smacked the ship around.

39

THE WEATHER SEEMED TO WORSEN. It hadn't gotten as bad as the first storm I'd been in, but it was pretty bad. It was much better in my cabin, because I'd stowed things so they wouldn't fly around. The things rattled and thumped in place, but at least they weren't bashing around the room. And I wouldn't have to clean everything up.

Once again, it was hard to stay in bed. I rolled side to side as the ship climbed the waves and dove into the troughs. I was dog tired and wanted to sleep, but unless I grabbed the bedside from time to time, the storm would roll me onto the floor. For hours, as the night wore on, I lay clinging to the bed.

Sometime in the middle of the night, something changed. Again.

40

FOR THE ENTIRE DAY AND night, as I'd been towed, I'd been rocked side to side. Now, as I lay there, I felt my head rise, then drop as my feet lifted. That meant the boat wasn't attacking the waves with the bow. Now it waffled broadside. In these kinds of seas, bad news.

I felt sick to my stomach. It wasn't the throw of the ship that turned my stomach. It was the suspicion that the tug was no longer attached.

If the tow rope had snapped, the status of my rescue

would be in question again. It was way too rough for another ship to snug alongside this ship. I waited for the early light to arrive so I could suss the situation. The predawn gray slowly broke over the boat. I waited until the light was strong enough to see by.

As the boat lifted the head of my bed, I readied myself for another expedition, to check on my rescue status. The ship leveled out at the top of the wave before it dropped into the trough. I dashed out the cabin door, slamming it behind me, then through the double doors into the midship lobby. I'd hoped to make the spiral stairs, but I didn't quite, so I grabbed a metal handhold bolted to the wall just inside the double doors and knelt while the wave crest punched the starboard side. The ship shuddered before it slid into the gutter between the waves.

Then I ran up the stairs two decks through the chartroom, into the bridge. I tripped and fell as the boat shunted over the crown of another wave. But I found my feet and dove into the bridge and grabbed hold of the chrome railing under the bridge controls.

The windows clouded with green and white froth of a wave. A small stream of water slid through the starboard bridge door and over the carpet. I stood and waited while the wave water melted away into some kind of view. Another wall of water on the way. First observation: The ship was broadside to the waves. Which meant the tow had been lost. Or the tug had lost power.

But given what I know of tugboats, I'd guess the tow line was lost.

Second observation: The tow line, which looked like a black shoelace from the bridge, was out of view, or gone. I wasn't sure which. The froth of another wave smashed the starboard and coated the bridge windows for a few moments. As it cleared the decks I looked again.

If the tug was there, it should be in front of the ship. Right there. I wouldn't lose sight of it in the waves. I could see nothing. The black lines would hold tight from the bow into the waves. If the tug was still towing me. I scanned like I was hunting for hooch at home. No lines in sight.

Another wave crest washed over bow and smashed the bridge while I waited. Yes, the tow line was gone. There was no tug in sight.

It didn't necessarily mean that I'd been abandoned, of course. It just might mean that the line broke and they were waiting for calmer sea before attaching another tow. Surely, they wouldn't leave me to drift on the wide ocean, would they?

I stood there for a while, holding to the railing, riding the ship like a surfboard under my feet. I had to be sure I was seeing what I thought I was. Waves clouded and drained from the bridge windows like tears. Kinda felt like the ship might be crying. Flailing, staggering in a surly sea. And there was nothing to wipe the tears away, except a good punch of sea water and more tears.

Dear mothership, would you like a tissue?

41

CAN'T TELL YOU HOW LOW I felt. I, like this old Russian tub, shed a few tears. To taste hope and have it taken away again nearly killed me. Like finding out the next stepdad is as bad or worse than the last one. It lays you low.

I caught myself standing on the bridge looking out on the sea. I don't know what I was hoping to find. But there I stood, staring out the windows, for how long, I couldn't say. My arms began to ache which sorta woke me up. No point, really. I might as well go back to bed. If I'm going to be rescued, I'll be rescued after this storm fades.

I made the return trip to the cabin, kicked off my shoes and hunkered down under my heap of linen and blankets. The day darkened into night. The waves backed off a little, but not that much. A tug wouldn't try an approach at night in these seas, I thought. Too dangerous. "I just want to go to sleep," I yelled at the storm. "You win, OK?"

Hungry and thirsty, I sipped a bottle of water and scarfed a few handfuls of popcorn.

So I thought I'd close my eyes for a few minutes. I awoke a long time later. It was day. Couldn't tell you what day it was, mind you. Just that it was day. The sea had settled a lot, though the ship was still rocking. I was starving again. And thirsty. Put my runner and boot back on.

I think there was more cheese in the fridge, wasn't there? Plus, I had to go get my loot from the kitchen that the storm had tantrumed all over the place. But first to the foredeck, to see what was going on with the tug and my rescue.

I walked out the cabin door and toward the bow. The sea had settled enough that nothing was going to wash over the deck, like happened in yesterday's storm. At least I think it was yesterday. The deck had largely dried. I found a spot where a couple of six-inch ropes had been thrown over a bollard on the deck, and looped through a rope hole in the bow. One of the lines had sawed itself through on the edge of the decking and the rope braid had splayed open in a nest of curls like Al Yankovic's hair.

The other line had held, but the length of it fed out the deck hole and dropped straight into the water below. They'd probably lost the one line and decided to cut the other. As the ship bobbed in place, I scanned the horizon before the ship to see if the tug lurked anywhere. It had to be somewhere close by. The seas were calm enough they could pull alongside.

I checked the square hole in the deck. The water level

had risen another few feet. I needed to take a look in the engine room. It must be completely sloshed.

I walked to the observation deck, and up the stairs to the funnel, to the 360-degree view up top.

I checked every compass degree carefully. No sign of it. My heart dropped. It wanted to drop earlier, but I kept telling myself that the tug wouldn't abandon me. I didn't think anyone would let this old hunk of junk just float away.

It can't be legal, can it? Wow. I can't tell you how many times I'd been hassled for littering on the school grounds. Leaving a chip bag to blow in the wind. How could letting a ship float away be legal? An ultimate littering moment. It was irresponsible. Even if they didn't know I was on board, they shouldn't have left Lyubov to drift either.

I sat on the cold steel plate at the top of the stack for a long time. I wasn't being thoughtful. I was so overwhelmed with what I saw—or, rather, what I didn't see—I had no energy left to move. Instant depression. Loneliness. Terror. Deep sadness. Each emotion sat like a bag of wet sand on my chest.

And I cried. I'd felt alone often. Let's face it; I wasn't Mr. Popular. I had no human friends. Zero. Not one I could even think of. Except alcohol. My one buddy, who depended on me entirely, was a cat. And I'd let him down because I chose a drink instead of him. Even on land I was lonely. But it was another kind of loneliness than this.

I can't describe the feeling sitting atop the ship. No land, no ship in any direction. The sea gray with white fringe, calming after a rage. No one to give a damn whether you live or die. Not the kind of lonely when you're in a crowd and no one will talk to you. Not the kind of lonely when you live in a house with people you're allegedly related to who make you hate life. This was the kind of lonely a pioneer must have felt, pulling a buggy onto a plain so vast he couldn't see the end of it. Away from any-thing that made me feel safe: telephones, iPods, hospitals, malls, and traffic. A kind of loneliness that made me want to talk to myself.

I'd felt like crying before, but I'd often block it out, because of what it might mean to the people around me. Like stepdad eighteen, just before he left a couple of months back, he got me cornered in the kitchen and let me have it. He shouldn't have been able to beat me, because he was a bumbling fat drunk. But the fact that he was three hundred and fifty pounds was a big advantage. How does someone who weighs 125 land a punch on a three hundred fifty-pound cushion with any force? It was like punching a bean bag chair.

Once he'd trapped me between the fridge and the far wall, hemmed in by his huge gut, it was all over. He put the hurt on me. I wanted to cry after he'd pounded me into near blackness, but he'd beat me beyond tears. The only way to keep your dignity in situations like that is defiance. I defied him, and defied him. Which is stupid, really. It just made him more and more angry. He wanted to see me cry. It felt like if I cried, I would lose. He just wanted to see a tear. But I wouldn't give that jerk the satisfaction. Eventually he just got tired of raising his fat arms and quit. "Stupid porker," I blurted out, as I left the apartment and went and found a place to cry by myself.

Tears came easily when I started to let them out. There were enough that I wondered if I should cry over a bowl and drink them later. They'd also taste good on popcorn. I cried a long while, too. Maybe I was getting rid of all the cries I should have had along the way. I tasted one tear. That wasn't fresh water leaking out my eyes. Definitely sea water.

As the day began to dim, my sandpaper tongue re-minded me I needed to refill my water bottle collection. I needed them topped up in case of another storm, plus

I needed a good drink myself. Plus, I needed to find out how much water I had left. It was either a popcorn supper, or if I braved the dim bowels of the ship, I could get another wheel of cheese. Something to think about.

Digging through the fridge again was mighty tempting. Cheese would make a great appetizer before a good bonfire, popcorn, and a bottle of water. On second thought, forget the cheese. I didn't feel like going into the bowels of the beast so soon after escaping.

I went down to the cabin, took my collection of water bottles up to the bar, and began loading the bottles with carbonated water. I filled four bottles and most of a fifth before the dispenser began to hack like one of my mother's coughing fits.

I held it to the bottle until the dispenser head began to sputter, then gasp, before it quit altogether. Four and half bottles. Another problem to solve later. I delivered them to the cabin, then took a bottle and my popcorn supplies, including the axe, and headed to the aft observation deck.

The sky determined to stay grim. As the evening light began to leave the sky, the gray blackened. I took the axe into the dining room and hacked apart a few more chairs. There was a table top now decapitated from its legs. I took the legs and smashed the crap out of the top, without doing much but ruining the finish. I hauled it all out to the black smudge on the deck, and set up the fire.

A flick from the lighter and the fire leapt through the wood. I made two batches of the good stuff, and ate them both. After a few minutes, the heat from the fire spread over the metal decking and heated the deck under my seat.

My mind kept jumping to thoughts of fast food, hamburgers specifically. French fries. Soft serve ice cream dipped in chocolate. Endless, refillable cups of root beer. The sky shared my sorrow, it seemed. The gray darkened into some kind of weather. Day decided to leave, which left me with the fire on the deck.

Behind me, a row of rat eyes glowed like shiny dimes hovering in the dark. I threw the remains of the popcorn into the fire. Flash of insight: I don't have my flashlight. It's busted. It's one of those nights that's an all-consuming darkness. Once I'm away from this fire, I'll be groping.

The weather turned out to be precipitation. And the storm sent samples as if, perhaps, I was at one of those restaurants where you get to whiff and taste the wine and decide if you want to keep it. A flake or two of snow sparked against my cheek. "Take it back," I said to the waiter. The clouds seemed to slowly break open, like a soup thickening into stew.

I drank down the water, enjoying the heat for a few moments. Some of the flakes fried and bubbled on the decking close to the fire. The storm decided to take it to the next level, and swooped down on the deck with an avalanche of white. I packed up everything and made for the cabin. A few feet into my journey, the sky broke open. So difficult to see. And slick as the bottle, as my mom would say. I was left with a blind grope to the cabin. Took me forever, FOREVER, to get back to the cabin. I have no idea whether I let some lucky rat into my room or not. Didn't even care.

Though the snow was thick and heavy as a first date, the sea was calm. I dropped the pot somewhere in the cabin and fumbled into bed, under my lovely heap of bedding.

I had to face this possibility: The rescue might not happen. It might be up to me to figure out a way out of this mess. I might be completely and utterly alone. Again, death is less of a joke than it was.

42

AWOKE LATER AND THERE WAS light. I assumed it was morning. Snow still fell. Don't feel like getting up today.

It seemed to take all my energy just to scratch another tick in my notebook for another day. I lay around for another long time. Until the mood to move hit me.

Up to the bridge for a look around. It was impossible to see the sky for the falling snow. It looked like I was now the captain of a giant floating vanilla cake. Cake. How I wish. I stepped out the bridge doors onto the deck to serve me up a slice. It was heavy and slushy on the underside. I took a bite.

Not cake, I thought, as the slush slaked down my throat and chin. Water. This is water. This is a gift.

Then, a face-palm. Duh. I should have figured this a long time ago. That fish took a long time to land.

I scooted down to the cabin, pulled out my big pots, and hauled them through the rear promenade deck doors to the open deck. I packed them to the brim with snow. I punched the snow in with my fist to make sure I got as much in as possible. Then I stowed the pots in the cabin.

It would be nice to have an army of pots for this situation. I needed anything that would hold water. There were a few left in the kitchen, some I had left behind.

Thinking of the kitchen jangled my memory a little. The kitchen. My crutch. My crutch was in the fridge. My recently scavenged supplies were scattered throughout the kitchen. I'd lost my flashlight. My matches were still downstairs. The snow storm did offer a little white light. It would be dim, but enough.

I took the axe down the spiral stairs and into the bowels of the beast. Many of the cabin doors had closed themselves in the storm. So I went down the hall swinging the axe like a golf club, smashing the thin wood paneling out of the middles of the doors. "Let there be light," I yelled. The hallway began to glow a cool white as the snow-strangled light broke through. The paneling would be excellent kindling, too.

About halfway down the hallway, smashing doors out of the port cabin, I found a knit sailor's cap. I'm not sure how I missed it in my first search. It had a nice piece of rat crap perched lightly on the rolled knit side. Whatever. Head, meet hat. Hat, head.

I made it back to the kitchen.

The stuff I'd found I'd originally stored in some big pots. Of course, the storm had thrown my finds all over. So I had to start all over again. I relocated lots of it—most of it, I think. I found the important stuff, including another few pots and things that could hold water. One of those long-necked lighters. Rats were making way for me as I moved around the kitchen. Honestly, I can't say that the axe helped scare them. Do rats know what an axe can do?

I had to get down on hands and knees a few times because my stuff had slid under tables and equipment. At the end of one stainless steel counter, bolted to the floor stood a giant, ancient mixer. The mixer sat on a stand a few inches off the ground. I could see another long-necked lighter lying up against the wall underneath. I used the axe handle to finagle the lighter to the close edge of the mixer stand. I reached underneath, to grab it, and something ripped into my pinky finger!

I pulled my hand away instantly and looked under the mixer stand. A rat sat next to the lighter, glaring back at me. My finger gushed. I slid the axe handle under the mixer stand and swung it at the little vermin. I'm sure he wished he hadn't tried to eat my finger. By the time I was done, I had to wipe off the axe handle with a kitchen rag I found on the floor nearby.

I fished out the lighter, which was now streaked with

blood, and wiped it down too. I turned around on my knees to find a circle of rats closing around the smell of blood. Lunch time.

To my feet. I didn't want to be on the floor if I had to take on a mischief of starving rats.

A couple of rats dared to pass too close so I used my booted foot to let them know what I thought of their bravado. One flipped end over end like a football into the wall and cartwheeled to the floor. He seemed dazed but he had no time to feel sorry for himself. The horde set upon him in a moment.

The lighter I tossed into a big pot, with my collection of things. Then, I backed away with one of the big pots in my left hand and the axe in my right.

I thought the rats might follow me because of the blood, but once I'd cleared away from the mixer, they swarmed underneath the mixer stand and attacked the rat carcass in a squealing throng.

The pot I dropped off at the kitchen door, where my other supplies were waiting. While the rats rumbled over food, it seemed like a good time to clear out the fridge. I took the lighter and made my way over.

My finger, where the rat had bitten it, hurt like hell. Another saying that doesn't quite make sense. It seemed pretty red, too. I'd probably have to go up to the clinic and scrounge for some disinfectant. I had a few bandages in my cabin. I checked and the scrag of rats rolled around the kitchen floor. It seemed safe to leave the fridge door open for a few moments while I retrieved my crutch and found that wheel of cheese. I had to be quick so the smell of the rotten food wouldn't draw the critters back. I grabbed my crutch. I looked quickly for the flashlight, but couldn't find it. It might not be a big loss—the battery didn't have much left to give. The matches were where I'd left them. And I found the wheel of cheese that I had left behind. It was stored in a round wooden container.

As I pulled it out into the light, I could read the label: French Brie.

I got the door closed before anything went inside, I think. The tumble of rats had moved from the mixer across the floor, still in a fur tornado. They moved toward my stuff near the kitchen door—a blur of squeals and fur. I stomped on the floor with my crutch to get their attention. They stopped and looked at me. Wide, juicy rivers of blood followed the rats across the floor. By the time the bite-fest was done, there were another three carcasses. The group dispersed into the kitchen for a few seconds, and turned back to pick clean the trail of rat meat they'd left behind. One rat dragged a fur-covered drumstick into a hole in the wall.

Though the mischief of rats had backed away, a couple of rats still lingered over a pile of rags, which had been dragged out from somewhere. In the middle of the salad of filth, I could hear a chorus of tiny squeaks. I stepped toward the sound, and a couple of rats stepped back, each with a tiny squealing baby rat in its mouth. The baby rats didn't have a chance.

The adult rats moved away from me as I moved closer, eating the babies greedily. The tiny squeaks stopped as they chewed and swallowed most of the bodies. One rat crunched through a baby's tiny brain. A warm lunch with built-in gravy.

They weren't newborn rats. Already their little bodies had grown the first fuzz of fur. Like Justin Bieber if he tried to grow a moustache. Of course, there must be rats being born all over the ship. It made sense. Yet, this was the first time I'd actually seen pups. You'd think with all of the rats being born, this would be a common sight.

There were at least four loads of stuff I had to take up. I divided the stuff as evenly as I could. The first load included the cheese, which if left behind, would soon be gone. As I lifted the pot, and prepared to leave, another little nest of soiled kitchen rags squeaked weakly. I set everything down again and bent over the rags. An adult rat had claimed whatever was inside.

The rags looked suddenly like a filthy flower, and in the middle of that flower was a tiny, helpless baby rat, squeaking frantically. Maybe because its eyes weren't opened, and it couldn't figure out what was going on. It was probably yelling for its mom, but mom had either turned on it, abandoned it, or been murdered. And it the kitchen was cold. I reached into the rags, and took out the fragile sack of life. Fuzzy. Pink. Confused. The size of my thumb.

By rights, I should have hurled the thing across the room, or left it there for its kind to eat. It'd just grow up to be a bedeviled, fur-bearing son of a cod catcher. But looking at that sorry creature in the white light of a snow storm, I couldn't do either. Just like when I found Sailor. It brought a lump to my throat and for a few seconds I had to beat down an urge to cry.

I found Sailor. Someone in our building had literally thrown him away. I lugged a couple of bags of garbage out to the dumpster behind our building. I flipped back the plastic lid and tossed the bags inside. For some reason, I thought I heard a squeak. A meow. Something-kind-of-living sound. I looked inside the dumpster, and I heard the sound again. Buried deep. I thought maybe the critter had fallen inside.

I pulled half of the crap out of that dumpster, and I couldn't find the beast. I pulled the rest of it out. Still couldn't find it. By now I was covered with goo and garbage juice.

Started tossing the bags back in, and then one of them meowed. He was in a full-sized black garbage bag by himself. The top of the bag had been double-knotted to keep him there. I tore the bag open and let the cat out onto a grass strip behind the dumpster while I tossed everything back into the trash.

He followed me upstairs. Mom was so stoned she didn't notice. When she complained a couple of days later, I lied and told her she had said I could keep him. Somehow the story hit her right and she let him stay, long as she didn't have to take care of him. "I ain't no good at taken care of nothing." Her exact words. And truer words were never spoken.

I looked at the still-feasting ring of rats in a blood-rage search for food. I couldn't let the little guy go. I checked. I think it's a guy. He has a little nub between his hind legs. I found the sailor's toque, which I'd stowed in one of the pots, and cradled the little guy in there.

I looked for a place to put him, so he'd be safe. The pots were all too dangerous. The other utensils and things I'd collected could easily roll around and smash him to death.

So I put the sailor's toque, with the rat in it, on my head. I could feel the creature struggle feebly under the knit for a few seconds. A tiny wriggling tumor. Then he either died or decided this was a good place to hang out, because he quieted down. I wasn't going to check until I got all this stuff back to the cabin. Four loads back to the cabin. The four new pots I collected I took outside one at a time, scrubbed with one snowball, rinsed with a second one, then filled to the brim with snow. Each got packed back to my cabin for safe storage.

The rat bite on my forefinger needed some attention, but my stomach screamed for food. I was starved. I wrapped my finger in a mostly clean paper napkin, one that I'd scammed from the kitchen.

I'd kill for a Google search on the subject of raising rats. I bet there's a video or two. Sadly, without the internet, the rat's life was in much greater danger.

The cheese I decided to eat in the library. Even through the packaging it smelled strong, which would bring the rats. I didn't want them near my cabin.

Up to the library I went, with my last few bottles of carbonated water and my wheel of cheese. I picked the couch overlooking the sea and opened the plastic cheese packaging. The cheese had a skin on it, marbled brown and white. In a couple of spots, puddles of mold. With the odd moldy scab in a few places. The mold didn't bother me too much. At home, our cheese always seemed to get moldy.

I cut off the bits of mold I found. Inside the wheel the cheese seemed creamy and white. I dug in. It was delicious. I ate until I felt full, truly full. I sipped the carbonated water.

Even with the fancy food, I'd been dropping weight, quickly. I slipped my belt off, and cut a couple of new holes. Cinched her up tight.

As I ate, a small crowd of rats gathered around to watch me eat. They came as close as they dared, just out of range of my feet. They watched me eat like I was the most interesting show they'd ever seen, which may have been possible. I could start my own TV network. The Eating Network. Popular with the hipster rat crowd.

As I ate, the lump under my hat stirred. I finished my meal and removed my hat. I think the smell of cheese woke up my new pet.

I tore some of the moldy cheese skin into tiny bits and tried to slip them into the baby rat's mouth. Too big. I pulled them away and tore those into miniscule crumbs. I flipped the wriggling beast onto his back and shoved the tiny crumbs into his mouth. He fought every single mouthful, squeaking and writhing like a break-dancing earthworm.

Then he seemed to change its mind about the cheese bits. The rat nibbled at first, then chomped the cheese bits down and squeaked for more (at least I think that's what he was doing). I fed him a steady stream until he belched,

I think. He chewed on my finger a little. "Careful, dude. Don't bite the hand that feeds you." His attitude reminds me of Sailor, too.

For his drink, I headed outside, and brought in a small snowball. I turned the little guy onto his feet on the table next to the snowball, next to a slush puddle of snow. I pushed his nose into the drink. He sputtered and choked, but then seemed to catch on.

His eyes seemed locked closed. His fur had begun to come in, sandy brown. Lots of his pink flesh still showed. I saved the bits of cheese rind for him. Another murderous thought: I should have thrown him into the pack of rats who watched me. But, today I'm not going to give him to this hairy horde. I found a plastic Walmart bag and wrapped up the cheese rind for later. This little blind creature schlepped around on the table top, drunkenly, through the snow puddle.

"Dude, you need drinking lessons," I told him. "You don't dance in water, you drink it. And remember, you drink first and then get drunk." The thing sniffed around, and seemed to snort a little water up its nose, which brought on a small fit.

"You look like a Dennis to me," I announced. Don't know where the idea came from. The name had appeared to me instantly. "Hello, Dennis," I greeted him. Of course, he didn't reply. "Sup, Dennis?" A full stomach made Dennis stagger. He reeled around the tabletop. I used my hands to keep him up on the table. After a minute, he crapped on the wood finish. Then he started shivering. "Back in the hat," I declared. I wrapped him in the knitted cap, and fit the cap over my head. He seemed to worm around a little before laying still.

This whole episode inspired me to swear to write a children's book after I'm rescued. I'll call it The Rat in the Hat. Original, don't you think? Dennis nibbled on my head, as if to protest.

From the library I went up to the clinic, and looked around until I found some small sample-size tubes of antiseptic cream. I scrounged a bandage from the drawer in the examination table and a bottle of hydrogen peroxide. Apparently, it's not good to use as an antiseptic any longer. Like I can be picky. I poured a few batches of peroxide on the gash and let it foam. Cleaned it off and repeated that until the foam response settled down a little. Then I gooped up my finger, and wrapped it in the bandage.

Since the cheese had filled me up, with the remaining light I decided to try cooking rice, so if my first attempt failed I wouldn't sob with hunger. The popcorn supply would end soon. I've heard rice is kind of like pasta. You boil it, basically. I was also tired of boring popcorn, so I decided to boil this stuff in sea water. The boiling will purify the water and the salt will flavor the rice.

I know. I'm so gourmet.

Since I hadn't tried making this stuff before, I decided to try a small batch. I'd use the popcorn for my meals and attempt a small batch of rice or two as a supplement. And, hell or high water, I'd have to eat it.

The sea water I managed to get by lowering my blue bucket on a rope and filling my pot. I hauled enough water up that I could make a potful, which I did. The rice basically ended up being white, salty mush.

White, salty, delicious mush. What made it great was the fact that it was far heavier than the popcorn I'd been eating. I'd just eaten cheese, and the rice topped me up entirely. The snarling dogs of hunger vanished for a while. Popcorn seemed to disappear as soon as I ate it, so I had been feeling hungry nearly constantly.

First try was a resounding success. Now that I'm good with making rice, I've got a few more days of food.

43

A FEW DAYS LATER, DENNIS OPENED his eyes.

"Dude," I exclaimed. "Welcome to the world of sight. If you'd told me today was the day, I'd have dressed up." You'd laugh if I told you how I'd spent hours chopping grains of rice in half and feeding them to Dennis. I'd found a used syringe to squirt water into his mouth, too. Labor of love, I tell you. If I'd had anything better to do, I would have done it.

You'll probably notice that the story jumped a few days here. That's me feeding the rat instead of writing down the exciting details of my adventure. I know. You want to know what happened. I'll tell you what happened. Dennis happened.

I wiped off his mouth with my hand and he nipped the tip of my finger. "Ouch, damn you, Dennis." He shrank and shivered at the tone of my voice. I'm going to chalk the nippiness up to teething. Babies teethe, don't they? He'd better be grateful when he's older. He'd better empty the dishwasher without me having to ask.

As the days passed, I began to set myself up as if I might not be rescued for some time. So I boiled the snow water I'd collected. I put the boiled water into a battered 100-cup coffee maker I'd found in the kitchen. It worked well as a water dispenser, even if the water ended up tasting like stale coffee. Kind of tasty actually, like I'd bought a coffee from a gas station.

The rest of the pots of water I boiled and poured into my extensive bottle collection. Any bottle with a cap, I filled with water. At the end of it all, I still had a half a pot of water, which I used first. Dipped an old ceramic mug into it.

Food supplies were running low. I'd found one last

cheese wheel in the fridge. The rest of the fridge contents were garbage. I finished the popcorn in pretty short order. It wasn't hard to do, because I needed to eat at least a huge potful in order to get a meal in my belly. Even though I was careful with the rice, it seemed to go pretty quickly. It was now less than a week after my first cooking attempt, and it was almost all gone. Since this could go on for a while, I needed to find another food source.

In the afternoons I'd been reading books. Mostly because I was bored, I'd also been going through my copy of the US Army Survival Manual. Wouldn't you know it, in one of the sections, there's a food source inventory. Basically, I'm supposed to do inventory of the environment and determine what I have most of and use that, if possible, as a source of food.

Remember what I told you the book recommends I eat for the next little while? That's right, rats.

There's a section on how to catch a rat. Which, in my case, shouldn't be a problem.

I think I also told you about how to butcher a rat, a short procedure on page 161. It's quite disgusting. The book gives a short section on how to take the fur off. How to cut the belly open and scrape the guts out. How to remove the fur. The book recommends hanging on to most of the guts and the head, which can be eaten, if I'm desperate.

I read it out loud to Dennis, who was wandering around on the table, eating some of the rice bits I'd left for him. His eyes were open now, and he was covered in a decent carpet of fur. He looked at me as if to say, "You've got to be kidding."

"Fair enough, dude," I said as though he'd spoken aloud. "Heads and guts are off limits." The carcass needs to be boiled for ten minutes, and the book suggests the carcass of a rat or a mouse be boiled with dandelion leaves, which are in short supply on this ship. There were

some spices in the downstairs kitchen. I'd left them behind because I have no idea what to do with them.

Once I got down to a couple pounds of rice, I knew it
was time to try boiled rat. I wanted to try it before I ran
out of rice. I'm sure I may not eat the first one or two that
I cook. I'd like to sort it out before I'm utterly forced to
eat rat meat. Besides, it might be kind of good on rice, like
some kind of sushi.

I'd run out of water in a couple of pots, so I lashed a
few pots to the deck up on top of the funnel. Lashed them
because if we caught another storm, it'd be goodbye pots.
I left them out there to catch the rain or snow, whatever
fell from the sky.

Today, I thought I'd have my meal in the middle of
the morning. I was so damn hungry I could hardly stand
it. Dennis had grown to a size where he was sloppy in my
hat. He leaned over the side of my head and chewed on
my ear. "Ow, you jerk." I tested my ear with my fingers.
He'd drawn blood. I was still hoping he'd get through the
biting phase. "My ears aren't cookies. Okay?" He leaned
over and chomped on my ear again. I don't think he liked
it when I was doing a lot of work. My motion threw him
around, which made it hard to sleep, I'd guess. Teenagers. Thank God we have no video games.

"Listen, Dennis," I roared. "I'm learning to kill and eat
rats. You wanna be first?"

I had spent a long time chopping up chairs and stuff
in the dining room for firewood, so I only needed to go
up and get everything ready. The day was gray, like most
days. The seas were heavier, but stuff stayed mostly in
place.

People's fates are like the fates of ships! Or so it said
on a bulletin board inside the ship lounge. The whole bulletin board was devoted to the life of the actress Lyubov
Petrovna Orlova, for whom the ship was named. She was
a Russian film star who could sing, a Russian version of

Judy Garland. She won the Stalin Prize. She even had a planet named after her. Her name literally means "eagle's love." A little ironic, I think, now that her namesake is loaded with rats. Another document I found in the lounge mentioned that she was an alcoholic, too. Apparently, she nearly lost everything to drink. Someone confronted her, and she stopped. Cold turkey.

"What do you have to say about that, Dennis?" I asked. Dennis was sleeping in my hat. He rolled over when I mentioned his name.

I watched a small black sliver thread its way across the horizon. A fresh hope blew in my chest for a while, until the object slipped over the horizon and out of sight. The fresh breeze blew sour.

I set up for a fire in my regular place on the aft observation deck. I grabbed a pot of seawater from the lower aft deck. Pulled out my good chair, brought out all my utensils and started the fire. Flames leapt into the air with just a short flick from the lighter. It's amazing what practice can do to one's fire-making skills. "You see that, Dennis?" Of course, he didn't. The freak was asleep. "I'm practically an arsonist."

As the fire burned, I nestled the pot of seawater in the coals and waited for it to boil. Once it had boiled I dumped in a tub of rice. In a few moments, the smell of the boiling rice doubled the crowd of watching rats.

"Honestly, Dennis, if this is how it feels to be a celebrity," I complained. "Just so you all know, I'm not Lyubov Orlova. I don't do autographs." The pot came out and onto the deck beside my chair for a while to cool. The rat ring around me stared longingly at the pot. Dennis stirred from his sleep, trying to shake his way out of the sailor's cap. I brought him out to my lap, where he sat and joined the rest of us as we stared at the pot. He'd grown from the size of my thumb to half the size of my hand.

The rice was actually just a white porridge after my

cooking job. I know I'm cooking it too much. I pinched a little glob of the white paste and held it out on my forefinger for Dennis. "Supper time, dude." He moved in instantly and took a few bites and finished it. I gave him another couple until he slowed down a little. He'd get a drink when I got back to the cabin. "Back you go, Dennis." I dropped the sailor toque over him, and picked him up and placed him on my head. He objected a little. I could feel him mouth around my scalp, looking for a place to sink his teeth. "Don't do it," I warned. Instead, he took a tiny, cute rat crap on my head. Least I think he did. Thank goodness I hadn't given him anything to drink. He eventually settled and went to sleep.

My hat barely covered him anymore. "No more hat rides, Fatty," I told him. The weather was warm enough that I could live without the hat, too. I still wore my coat around often. It had a huge inside pocket. I tucked the furry jerk into it, with a little paper.

I took my spoon and shoveled the rice paste into my mouth. I finally hit my limit with only a little left over. Can I tell you how good a full stomach feels? It's amazing. The extra rice went into a plastic container with a lid.

Back in the cabin, I put Dennis gently into the rice pot. The pot was deep enough to work as a cage. Plus there'd still be stuff left in there, and he'd finish it off. He was my pre-wash cycle. Sure enough, as soon as I put him in there, he set to work on the pot, on a project to lick the entire thing clean.

It was good to leave him in the pot, because I didn't want him around for my next task. The US Army Survival Manual was next to my bed. I retrieved it. From my collection of kitchen stuff, I pulled a large carving knife. The crutch was in my closet. I think you can guess what I'm about to do.

44

ENNIS WAS SCRATCHING AROUND THE pot when I closed the cabin door. I couldn't be sure of the best spot to hunt rats, but I seemed to get closest to them in the kitchen on the main deck. Plus, the walk-in fridge had bait, if I needed any.

The kitchen was a party of rats when I arrived. Squabbles and activity all through the equipment and space. One of the kitchen corners was open and free from equipment. That's where I decided to set my trap. I went to the walk-in fridge, grabbed a little rotten goo of some kind, tossed the goo in the corner and backed away. Within seconds, several rats were fighting over the rot. I moved in with my crutch held like a spear. The rats didn't seem to notice. With the soft rubber crutch tip missing, I held a spear of sorts, the tip a sharp circle of metal tubing. Then I thrust the crutch end into the swarm, and felt it crush and snap as it landed. As the mob suddenly dispersed, I found myself with one rat with a crushed head and another with what looked like a broken back leg. I took the end of the crutch to the one with the broken back leg and ended up smashing the crutch metal through its haunches.

It lay there cowering, immobile. I took the end of the crutch and mashed its head into the floor. Pink brain squeezed through the split skull. An eye popped out of its socket, still attached to the retinal cord. The rats around me were salivating at the sight, thinking I'd just made lunch for them all. Instead, I picked both beasts up by their tails and walked out of the kitchen, leaving a trail of blood dripping from them as I left. The horde of rats closed in behind me to lick the trail clean behind me.

I went back to the cabin and put the two dead rats in a covered pot while I got together the things I needed for my first butchery session. The survival manual. A couple of knives. Both were pretty sharp. A big one for chopping and a small one. A piece of a broken cutting board. Dennis had fallen asleep in the bottom of his pot. I left him there. I lugged everything up to the aft observation deck. The morning fire still smoldered a little. I fetched a few more sticks and poked it back into flame.

A rat was hunched on my chair nibbling away at the cushion. I must have spilled a little rice. It cleared out as I approached.

45

WARNING: THE NEXT BIT IS going to be disgusting. I opened my book to page 161 and began to follow the instructions. Step one: Bleed the animal by cutting its throat. Done. That happened as I walked here from the kitchen. Step two: Place the carcass belly up and split the hide from throat to tail, cutting around sexual organs. Eeesh. I held the carcass down on the cutting board, and took my big knife and poked the throat. The tip didn't want to go in. I guess the knife wasn't as sharp as I thought it was. I jammed it through the skin. Air wheezed through the little hole I cut. I brought the knife-tip down the furry belly, making sure the tip stayed buried beneath the skin. The further down I ran the knife, the more the cut opened like a zipper on a winter coat. Inside, the pale gleam of organs and tubing. This rat happened to be a boy, so I cut to the right of his junk as I made my way to the tail. Then I cut around the other side of his piece.

Wait. I was reading the section on large game. This book is not clear. I screwed this one up. Apparently, for smaller animals, you just cut an opening across the midpoint of the back. The book has a little picture of a squirrel. It reads, "Insert two fingers under the hide on both sides of the cut and pull both pieces off." I'm supposed to stick my fingers into the cut and pull the skin off like its clothing. I'll try it anyhow. I rolled the rat I was working on to its belly and cut a ring around where the belt would go. Then I stuck my fingers in and pulled.

According to the diagram, it's easy. Not so in real life. The skin does peel off like clothing, but not without a fight, and splatters of moisture and blood. And a horrible sucking sound. The cut down the belly dropped some of the entrails through, like the gooey insides of some sick piñata. Though the skin came off, I had to cut a few parts where the fur stuck to bone and cartilage. The front was easy. I just chopped off the guy's head. Around the business end, I had to cut the tail off, along with some of the hind end. The anus was a bit of a trick that I didn't want to deal with.

The carcass, without skin and fur, was red and streaked with little bits of white. I chucked a few of the remains into the fire, where they hissed and stunk for a few moments before they were overpowered by flame sizzled to ash. With the small knife, I tried to do the next step which was to pull out the organs and intestines and stuff. Lots of it was out already.

The book said I could keep the heart and the liver for eating. No thanks. I looked at the liver to see if there were worms or anything living in it, like the book says. It seemed fine. I chucked it into the fire, too. I had to scrape and cut the back end to get the rest of the guts out. The smoke from the fire now carried a general meat smell. Though it wasn't exactly a smell that would make you walk into a restaurant and buy a burger, it smelled like heaven to me.

A couple of intestinal tubes oozed some goo. I was careful to keep the ooze away from the rest of the carcass. Apparently, it can "taint" the meat. I rolled the carcass onto its side and axed off the rat feet and scraped away the odd patch of fur and skin that still was attached. Voila. Supper.

With the guts gone and the fur, head and feet removed, it looked a lot more like food. Sort of a reddish looking wimpy-sized chicken.

The second carcass was easier to prepare. Like with fire-starting, experience helps. Within a few minutes I had a big meal, ready for cooking. Not that it was time to eat. I had to store these two critters until I could enjoy my feast. I decided to tie a bucket to the flag pole on the aft observation deck. I had a plastic bucket with a lid in the cabin, which I retrieved. I dropped the meat inside and popped on the lid. Then I clipped the bucket handle to the retainer ring assembly, and hauled it up a couple of feet off the railing, cleating the rope in place.

According to the survival guide, most seaweed is edible. So I thought I'd maybe try and catch some from the stern of the main deck. I got down there, and my bucket and rope were still there. I hauled up a bucket of seawater to cook the rats with. That might help with flavor.

As for seaweed, even though it didn't run away from me, it was still a pretty hard thing to catch. The stern of the main deck is the closest to the water I can get on this hulk. Even still, it's another ten or twelve feet to sea level from there. I don't have a net or anything. So I thought about it for a while. It might be one of those things I can only get once in a while, like after a storm.

After the ship gets smashed in a storm, seaweed decorates the deck. There's a lot of it around now, but it's dried like scabs to the ship. I won't eat these scabs. I'd try fresh stuff, though. I would just have to harvest it right afterwards. I'd already had a big feed of rice, so I wouldn't boil that up either. Just meat for supper, then. The seawater I took up to the aft deck and left near my fire for later.

I spent some time up in the cabin. I woke Dennis and

we lounged together on the bed while I read the survival guide's tips for surviving in cold-water sea situations. "Dennis, you don't know how lucky we are." Most of the tips had to do with surviving in a raft or small boat of some kind. "We'd be dead if this boat was a raft." Observation: If you're going to drift alone at sea, a small cruise ship is the way to go.

46

DECIDED TO HAVE SUPPER JUST before the sun went down. I put all my things together, and Dennis in my coat pocket. He's a furry meatball. The fire smoldered a little, hungry for more to eat, so I stoked it a little and it came back to life. I boiled the crap out of those two rats—a lot longer than the ten-minute safety window. I boiled them until the meat peeled away from the bones.

My stomach jumped at the smell. I hoped it'd taste like chicken. I let my fingers tear off a tiny drumstick. I nibbled tentatively. "Hmmm. Salty and gamey." Dennis, like the other rats, stared at the food as I ate. Just so you know, it does taste like sort of a bad grade of chicken. "I don't know, buddy. You may not like this. You're probably related." I offered him a morsel, which he loved. What is the difference between eating the meat raw, like I'd seen other rats do, and eating it butchered and boiled? I may have just turned Dennis into a cannibal.

He didn't seem to complain. Eating two rats together I was almost full. Close, but no cigar. I could have used a huge bowl of ice cream. "Dennis, let me tell you about ice cream," I began. I explained as best I could. He seemed interested for a couple of minutes, and then he passed out on the deck stuffed with the first cooked meat he'd ever had.

"My real dad loved ice cream," I said to Dennis. "I remember mom and me getting into the car on a summer Sunday. We drove to this little convenience store called Moo Moos. I wanted to get some weird ice cream flavor, like tiger or something. But my real dad insisted I only have vanilla. He told me it was the only true ice cream. It's the real one. So I got vanilla, because I didn't want to make him mad. 'Cause he would have beat the rat-raisins out of me." I had to swallow a mouthful of saliva. "It was so creamy." Dennis' eyes were closed. He snored a high-pitched whistle. "Dennis, you furry bastard," I complained, quietly. "That's rude." But what can you expect from a teenage rat?

As twilight fell I began to clean up. I hung the bucket back on the flag pole and cleaned up everything else. The seas had settled, and as the sky darkened, billions of stars took over the sky. "Holy Toledo, Dennis. Have you ever seen so many stars in your life?" Course he hadn't. Just opened his eyes a couple of days ago. Just making conversation.

With the last heat of the fire, I stared at the sky. I could see the haze of the Milky Way, which I hadn't seen except in a science textbook. It's like the stars smoked a little, and the star smoke smudged the sky.

I left the fire and headed up to the funnel. Though there was no moon, the stars were enough to see by. I lay on my back on the funnel top and stared at the sky. Dennis rooted around on my chest.

There were so many stars it bothered my eyes. Cosmic rat eyes staring down on me. If a pair of stars meant one rat, there was a mischief in the sky.

The sky reminded me of driving down a highway at night in a snowstorm. Each flake flies at you, galaxies competing for your attention. It's exhausting.

These skies were similar, except I wasn't moving through the stars. In town, when you look up into a starry sky, you might see a dozen stars on a clear night. You could count them. Here, under this sky, it'd be stupid to try. "Dennis, look at the sky," I ordered.

Stars ask for attention. I've been hit in the head hard enough to see stars. The kind of hit a stepdad throws to get my attention. This is like a clout on the head from the universe. The sky screamed silently at me: Wake up! Pay attention!

The stars moved into my thoughts. Space is trippy to think about. "I'm looking at infinity," I told Dennis. "Nothing and infinity." Observation: You can't count to infinity, but you can glance at it.

"No wonder my eyes are starting to hurt." Dennis seemed unphilosophical at the moment. "You can't get to see infinity often where I'm from," I told him. "Kids don't appreciate nothing these days."

My mind somehow jumped from the sky to a Big Mac. This indicates to me that I'm profoundly shallow. Mysteries of the universe to fast food. Even though I'm burping full.

I relaxed and focused on a faint silver-edged cloud as it drifted. The cloud grew a tail as a jet airliner tracked across the sky. I couldn't see the plane, nor any lights blinking. But the vapor trail glowed a little with sky light.

"Some night we'll have to camp out here," I told Dennis.

At last I returned to the fire, shooed away the rats, put the chair back in the dining room, took my stuff in the big pot and headed to the cabin.

The next few days blurred together. They mostly went the same way, except I finished off the rice. I had already finished the popcorn. I was now exclusively a meat eater. There'd been enough melted snow and a couple of rain storms to keep me in water. My water bottle collection was still nearly full. The rat hunting was keeping me alive at the moment.

One of those days we had a decent storm. I ended up finding a few bits of seaweed—huge floating bulbs with tails and some flat green streamers. I had a boiled stew of seaweed. The book said I could eat it raw, but I wasn't that brave. Or hungry. It tasted all right. The bulb was a bit rubbery, even cooked. The flat green stuff was like eating bitter birthday streamers. But apparently it's all loaded with vitamins, and it fills the stomach.

After the last storm, the ship had taken on a lot of extra water. The engine room was now a disgusting pool room. The water was nearly to the top of the stairs, just inside the engine room. There was enough water that it affected the way the boat moved in the water. In heavy seas, the water below sloshed around below and I could feel it. I figured I was good for another couple of storms, maybe, depending on their size.

Sinking had become certain at this point. The old Russian tub could only take on more water. And the more water she took on, the more water she asked for. Her slow sink reminded me of my own life. Sure, I was fine at any particular moment. But my general lifestyle was taking me down slowly. Only a matter of time.

I had already picked out the best of the lifeboats. It was the only one where the engine and prop had been taken out carefully, without damaging the bottom. I found a couple of pieces of rubber that I cut up with my axe and a kitchen knife. I fit the rubber chunks into the hole.

I was storing most of my water collection in that boat now, just in case. I kept my leftovers there, too. Rats couldn't get inside, which was good. But if I had to launch, I'd have everything with me.

No sign of rescue.

47

AST NIGHT WE HAD A doozy. All hell broke loose. Dennis and I hunkered down. I didn't end up throwing up. I guess I've got my sea legs now. But the boat wallowed in the waves like a four hundred-pound man in a wheelbarrow. The storm cleared about the middle of the afternoon, and by the time I went downstairs, sea water moiled about four feet deep on the lowest deck of cabins.

Rats and garbage floating on a layer of scum.

I immediately checked on the lifeboat. Made sure everything was ship shape. Carried what I thought I could use and decked her out best I could. I'd found enough old lifejackets to save a holy host. I laid them out to make a mattress. It's warm enough out now—I think I'll sleep in the lifeboat.

Full alert. DEFCON 1. Time to freak out.

PART II

48

FOODWISE, I DIDN'T NEED A thing. For the moment there were plenty of rats to eat. I got occasional veggies from the sea. I could keep going like this for a while, at least. Dennis was a nearly full grown bugger now. He was a hefty ball of fur, and lazy as all getout. What else can you expect from a gadabout?

The days started to warm a little, too. It was probably the middle of March, so spring was coming on. Plus, who knows where the boat is drifting? I'd found a book that talked about ocean gyres, and apparently there's one in the North Atlantic. So that would take me to Ireland, maybe. On the other hand, I could be headed to the Caribbean, couldn't I? Next time I see the captain, I'll ask.

One warm, calm afternoon, I was sitting on the funnel top in my T-shirt. All around me stretched the flat disk of sea, a thin thread between the blue-gray sea and blue sky. I was leaning against one of the stacks that rose from the engine room on the lower deck. Dennis had chosen a spot on my lap in the sun to sleep. "You think these engines will ever run again?" I asked him. He opened one eye as I spoke, and closed it slowly. "I didn't think so, either," I replied. We dozed a little. I'd already eaten a couple of boiled rats for breakfast. I had a couple more skinned and ready to go for supper.

When I awoke, I opened my eyes. On the horizon was a black flea riding a white thread between sea and sky. Probably another boat. Small as a wood sliver. My heart raced a little faster. But I pushed my hope into a closet. I'd seen a boat or two pass on the horizon before.

I studied it for the next while. The black outline grew larger, and grayed as it grew closer. A boat, certainly. The gray began to take on color. It looked like a large, dilapidated tug. A battered royal blue, with a black funnel. Its rust-colored prow sliced through the sleepy sea. As it grew closer, I realized she was steaming straight for the ship. There were figures moving about on the bow of the boat. Excitement ballooned and burst in my gut.

"Dennis! We may be saved!" I shouted, and sprang to my feet. That scared him out of sleep, I can tell you. I took Dennis down to the cabin and put him into a little bed I'd made for him. He looked at me oddly and then curled up to sleep.

I ran to the railing on the observation deck. I was absolutely over the top with joy when, as the boat grew closer, it broke for the Orlova's stern. I assumed it was because they wanted to land a person on the boat, and the stern offered the easiest access.

I did notice that the people on deck were all male, sun-worn and sinewy. I stood above them waving like an idiot as they pulled up. Several of them jabbered away in a language I didn't understand. Pointing at me with some confusion. Loose fitting linens. Turbans. The boat looked as though it was going to pull away, but I waved them on and motioned for them to board. The boat backed away.

"No, no, no," I yelled, "don't leave, please don't leave." I waved my hands over my head. "Come aboard," I screamed, in as friendly a scream as I could muster. If they're here to rescue me, why would they pull away?

I streaked down the stairs to the after deck. The crew seemed to hesitate and look back to the tug's bridge for some kind of direction. I stepped through the gap in the railing and motioned for them to approach. One of the men standing on the deck asked me a question, I think, in his language.

"I'm English," I insisted. "Does anyone speak English?" The man who had spoken to me turned to the bridge, and shrugged. For several moments, nothing happened. Then a door opened gently, and a bald fat man pushed a young, rope-thin boy dressed in dirty white clothes onto the deck. The boy blinked to cope with the afternoon sunlight. He took some uncertain steps toward me. He was probably thirteen years old. When he got close enough, the man who'd spoken to me grabbed his wrist and pulled him forward. He said something to the youngster.

"Hello," the young boy said.

"Hello," I replied. "Do you speak English?" I asked. A cloud of confusion crossed his face before he brightened.

"Yes, I speak the English." Mr. Nutman would not be pleased.

"I am looking for a ride home," I said slowly. He tipped his head and squinted. "I need to go home." He didn't seem to understand.

The man beside him spoke a few words to him. The boy squinted as he processed the words.

"Is dis your boat?" he finally asked.

"No, it's not," I said. He seemed to understand and spoke to the man beside him.

"The news, they talk about this boat. It is, how you say?" the boy puzzled for a moment, until the older man brought the back of his hand across the side of the boy's head. "It is lost," he said. "It is free?"

"Do you want the boat?" I asked the boy. He took my sentence and ate it slowly, word by word. Then nodded. "Yes, yes. We want the boat."

"It's not mine," I replied. The boy's face clouded. I don't think he understood. I panicked a little. It seemed to matter a lot that the boat belonged to me. "Yes, the boat is mine," I yelled. The boy smiled and nodded. "I will give it to you, if you'll help me." The boy translated for the man. The man turned to the tug's bridge and nodded, and waved the boat forward. The old tug swung around until her starboard kissed the hull of the Lyubov Orlova. The man and boy on the bow came around the side and boarded through the railing gap for the stern bollard. Several other men followed behind. The tug tied up to the rear of the ship. And a flurry of activity began. Several men on the deck above caught a thinner rope and began hauling it over the deck rail. The thin rope attached to a huge rope, which slowly rose from the deck of the tug toward the deck of the Lyubov Orlova. Once the rope was in the crew's hands, they pulled it forward, toward the bow.

The bald man with the kid grabbed and clenched the kid's right arm roughly, then barked a few words at him.

"Where ... is... the ... beeper?" he asked.

"Beeper?" I asked. The man squeezed the boy's arm until he winced.

"Not beeper," the boy grimaced and shook his head, frustrated. "Uh.... how you say... sensor?"

"Sensor?" I asked, shaking my head.

"The boat sink sensor?" the boy added, frowning with pain.

"I don't know what you're talking about," I replied, and shook my head.

It took several seconds before my message sunk in.

The man grumped and threw the boy's arm down in disgust. The boy rubbed his elbow. There seemed to be an impossible number of boys and men on that little tug. After a few tasks were completed, the entire group seemed to slowly turn to a search. I wandered down to the lower deck, where most of them seemed to be concentrating their efforts. The water submerging the lower deck seemed to bother them some. A small group seemed to discuss the problem.

The others focused their efforts on the upper, outside parts of the ship. They swarmed up around the bridge and funnel, until one of the men gave a shout. Immediately a crowd gathered around him. He was near the port bridge door, staring at a panel on the railing. Word passed through the ship. The boss strode up to the decking. When he arrived the worker began to unbolt a white, football-shaped device, clamped firmly to the railing.

Once removed, the device was passed carefully through a crowd of hands to the boss, who accepted it with a nod. He spoke to the men briefly. When he finished, the men exploded into activity again, resuming their search.

After another half hour, the search ended. The group prepared to tow the ship. I returned to the aft observation deck and watched as several of the boys hauled their collection of belongings onto the ship. There were so many onboard the tug that apparently several had been sent aboard to use the ship as sleeping quarters.

The young kid returned from the ship, with his bedding and extra things. He was looking sort of lost. I met him at the bottom of the stairs.

"Follow me," I said. It took a few seconds to process, but he nodded and followed. I led him up to my cabin.

"You can sleep here," I said. I showed him the pull-out couch, which was in the other room. He set down his things.

Once I settled him, we trundled up to the lifeboat and back to reclaim my old bed. Without the threat of sinking, I knew I'd sleep a little better.

As we toured the room, Dennis awoke and squeaked. The kid freaked out and stepped back. I walked over to Dennis, and he stepped into my hands. The kid seemed horrified.

"This is my friend, Dennis," I announced.

"You have...pet?" he asked.

"Yes, pet." I replied. "His name is Dennis." I stroked Dennis with my hand to demonstrate he was tame.

"Dennis," he repeated. Though when he said it sound-ed more like Denise. He grimaced and nodded, but wouldn't touch Dennis.

Dennis bit my hand as if to advertise his nastiness. "You little jerk," I yelled. I shook my hand to rid myself of the pain and checked it for blood. Nothing serious. I grinned to show it was fine and quickly lifted Dennis back into his nest. I think he bit me because of the way the kid pronounced his name.

"My name is Sean," I said.

"I am Batoor," he replied.

"Batoor," I repeated.

"Batoor," he repeated, putting a stronger emphasis on the second syllable.

"Batoor," I repeated, imitating his pronunciation. He nodded.

"Come," Batoor said. He left the cabin and made his way to the aft observation deck, overlooking the tug.

A few of the men re-boarded the tug once the tow rope had been installed. The tug drifted away from the Orlova's hull. Several men joined us on the aft observa-tion deck, as if some kind of event were going to take place. The boss came out holding the white oval that had been removed from the ship's railing. In his other hand he held an orange buoy with a little antenna on top.

"Sink the ship," Batoor declared.

"Sink the ship?" I asked, suddenly panicked.

Batoor put a hand on my wrist, to calm me. "We...uh... pretend the ship sink," he said.

"Oh," I replied.

"The sensor...," he said. He gestured to me that it would be dropped in the water. "It is EPIRB." Each letter was a linguistic struggle.

"Oh," I replied. He understood that I had no idea.

He struggled to find the right words. "Emergency... Position-Indicating...Response...Beacon." He spoke as though each word cost twenty-five cents, and he had to search for the coins. "When it goes in water, people think ship sink. They stop looking for it."

"Oh," I repeated. "I don't think anyone was looking for it, though."

We watched as the boss and another man worked on preparing the device. They had pulled the cover off the oval object and were looking at a puck-shaped mechanism inside. They replaced the cover. Then they dropped the thing into the water. The orange buoy had a little light on top, which began to blink after a minute or two. The boss gently lowered the buoy into the water in silence. When he turned from the water, he barked an order and the entire group resumed their activity.

The tug pulled slowly alongside the Orlova's port side, two men paced along the railing, paying out the rope that ran along the length of the deck toward the bow. A couple men offloaded a bright red gas-powered pump and several lengths of hose.

Another two men ran the lengths of hose into the ship's gut, while another stood by the pump preparing the engine. The hose connected, a young boy tugged at the pull start until the engine putted to life. A few minutes later, the limp lines thickened with sea water, and began spewing all it had over the side.

"Where are they taking the ship?" I asked Batoor.

"Chittagong," he replied. "To the ship breakers."

"So you aren't here to rescue me?"

Batoor looked at me oddly. "No, we want ship. It is money for us."

"How do I get home?" I asked.

Batoor shrugged. "Maybe you work with us, until we get home. Then you go home. I ask boss man, Samandar."

"Yes, please ask Samandar for me." I looked at him. "Are you from Chittagong?"

Batoor seemed saddened by my question. "I live at Mingora." He frowned. "It is in Swat Valley. It is city in mountains, far away. I come to work on boats to make money for my family. Where do you live?"

"I live in St. John's, Newfoundland."

"Why do you live on this boat?" Batoor asked.

"It was an accident," I replied.

"Accident?" Batoor looked confused.

"Mistake."

"Ah, mistake," Batoor repeated. "So you do not have food?"

"Ummm... Sort of. I eat rats," I announced.

"Rats?"

"Like Dennis."

"You eat Dennis?"

"No, I eat other rats." Batoor squinted at me, confused. "I ran out of other food. So I hunt rats." Batoor probably still didn't understand, but he moved on.

"We eat fish," Batoor said. "And na'an. It is bread."

"Can I eat your food?" I asked.

"I ask Samandar," he replied.

"What language do you speak?"

"Pashto," he replied. "And a bit of Arabic. A little Bengali. A little Khasi."

"And English," I added with a grin. He refused to smile. All business.

"And English," he repeated.

"Wow. That's pretty good. I only speak English."

"I sleep on your boat, and the workers, too."

The ship eased forward as the tow rope tightened and the ship began to move forward.

"So we're going to Chittagong?" I asked.

"Chittagong," Batoor agreed with a nod.

49

THE ARRIVAL OF THE SALVAGERS proved beneficial for my diet. I didn't get much to eat, but what I did get was much better than I was used to. They caught fish and prepared it. They also made fresh na'an every day, and we got fruit, too. It wasn't a lot, but it was so much better. No more rats. The downside was I had to work. A lot. Hard. And long hours. No more lounging with Dennis on the top of the funnel.

We began to work taking apart the ship. We removed toilets and sinks. We unbolted chairs, dressers, cabinets, and TVs from the floors and walls. We dismantled the kitchen entirely. We'd strip this old tub down to bare metal. Mucked each thing off into piles. In each room we collected piles of scrap sorted by type and kind. Recycling on steroids.

The rat population took a beating. As we took the ship to bone, rats had fewer and fewer places to hide. There were countless carcasses every day. Most of them we shoveled over the side and into the drink.

I had to be careful with Dennis. He didn't want to hang with me as I worked all day, so he rested in the cabin. But one wrong step, and he'd be in Davy Jones' Locker, too.

I hoped these people knew the weather and water around here. Because if we were to get a storm, this ship would lob fixture and furniture at us like they were snowballs.

I worked alongside Batoor, for obvious reasons. I thought I was working hard, but it was nothing compared to how Batoor worked. He made me look like a lazy oaf—which, admittedly, I probably was. The boss, Samandar, didn't like me, probably because I wouldn't work as hard as Batoor. Samandar didn't whip me like he whipped the other boys, but he seemed to want to. Even Batoor seemed underwhelmed by my efforts.

After a couple days of towing, I saw land. I never thought I'd be so thankful to see it. As we pulled toward the coast, I called Batoor.

"Is this Chittagong?" I asked. He didn't want to stop working. He was hefting mattresses that had been taken from empty cabins. I was leaning on the upper deck's starboard railing, drooling at the sight.

Batoor stopped long enough to steal a quick glance and shake his head. "This is, how you say in English, Gibraltar. It is Spain."

I must have seemed confused.

"We go through another sea, the Mediterannean, to Egypt."

"Could I get off the boat?" I asked.

"No, no, no," Batoor insisted. "We do not stop."

"Could you ask Samandar for me, please?"

"He will be angry. He will not like this question. He will hit me."

"He will hit you?"

"Samandar is not nice."

I stood there, taking it all in. Batoor, rolled his eyes, probably at my laziness, and worked the twin mattress up a set of stairs. Samandar came up behind me and smacked my head with his open hand. I turned around. He scowled. He pointed at the ship—his way of telling me to get back to work.

"Don't you ballyrag me. Use your words, not your fists," I said to him, rubbing my head with my hand. I picked up my mattress and followed Batoor.

Batoor had finished with the mattresses and was now rolling lengths of steel cable on the deck. Samandar called him over. He snapped a few phrases at him, and Batoor, turned to me with sad eyes and spoke. "If you do not

work harder, the boss says, you cannot share our food."
Batoor looked at Samandar.

"I gave you my ship," I said to Batoor. Batoor translated.

Samandar pouted and shook his head. He barked a few more phrases to Batoor. Batoor's eyes deadened as he took in the last phrase or two. "This ship is mine now. If you do not work, we throw you into the sea."

Samandar stormed off. Batoor looked at me.

"He wouldn't throw me into the ocean," I said. "It's not legal."

"He throw people into the sea before," Batoor said. "They died. If you work, you live."

"That's some crooked, my friend." Batoor looked at me with a quiz in his eyes. I shrugged.

So I began to work harder, and longer. I still couldn't work like Batoor.

The Mediterranean Sea glowed like a jewel. A cheerful blue and green, it reminded me of a swimming pool. The sea so calm and clear it begged for beach towels and swimming trunks. Dolphins visiting. The odd turtle drifted past. Clouds of fish darkening the water, swimming in school formation.

My pants. My belt began to fail. I had to take the leather and cut a few new holes just to keep my pants on. Hardly an ounce of fat on my old belly any longer.

It took a little more than three days to move through the Straits of Gibraltar to Egypt's Mediterranean coast. The days passed quickly. We worked fifteen or sixteen hour days on the boat, fell dead asleep for a few hours, then got back up and did it all over again.

"We journey through this...river...no, not river. I do not know word for this."

"Oh," I said. I thought for a moment. "Canal. The Suez Canal?"

"That is right," he exclaimed. "The Suez Canal. We go

through this canal, from this ocean to another ocean." He pointed to the coast. "This Port Said. We go to Red Sea. Then a few more days, we arrive."

According to Batoor, we had to convoy through at a certain time, with other ships. Our progress began to slow. Men on the back of the tug and the front of the Orlova began to shorten the tow line until it the Orlova's bow towered over the tug's stern. We pulled in closer to the land, and took a place among several ships, all of them waiting to go through the canal.

We anchored and floated for supper and the evening. The next morning we were up early, on deck, and ready as we moved with cluster of ships toward the entrance of the canal. The light breeze had a bit of a bite to it. Fine fingers of mist rose from the sea into the air. In the sky, the odd marshmallow lump of cloud. The horizon was striped with orange and pink. Low rows of buildings on both sides of the canal winked, sometimes with street lights that had not yet gone out, sometimes with an early morning sun reflecting off window glass.

The cluster of ships slowly converged into a long line, just before the entrance to the canal. Then, in a long, slow line, we begin down a river-like strip of water, one which basically runs through the Egyptian desert.

We were expected to work, as usual. So we got to work. I tried to be out on the deck as often as I could. The canal is quite wide, as wide as a large river. I wondered about getting a life jacket and throwing myself into the sea. I could swim to the edge, and then I'd be in Egypt. Maybe I could make my way home from here, I thought. What are Egyptians like? Would they help me?

The desert heat turned the old Russian tub into an oven. This was hot beyond anything I'd ever known. The rest of the crew bore the heat as though it were nothing. At home, if it was a degree warmer than comfortable, we had a cuffer to grouse about the weather.

Miles ahead I could see a bridge, and a few hours later we passed under The road on either side of the canal was propped up on stilts. One tall tower stood on either side, and cables suspended the bridge high over the top of the canal. Samandar came up behind me. He whacked me with a stick on the side of the head. Scared me out of my skin.

I turned around. Samandar looked a little frightened for a second. Honestly, he should be. I'm at least fifty pounds heavier than he is, and I'm a good head taller. "Who knit ya, Chummy? You hit me again, Samandar, by God, I'll put a boot to ya," I yelled. I could hear the words of my drunken mother piping straight through my own lips. Samandar's look of confidence wavered. "It's no wonder your employees never smile."

The morning sun began to gather heat as it rose and burned off the mist. The bank on both sides was beige, the color of sand. Belts of short buildings, like industrial strip malls. Shadows, made by the clouds, crossed the sand and water. For long stretches there was desert on either side. Hotter than a two-dollar rifle. Don't know what that means, exactly, but that's a common way of complaining where I come from.

The Egyptians must have felt like the canal was a highway, for no one seemed to want to live along the banks. Most of the structures on the water, where there were any at all, were commercial and ugly. Ahead of us, the entire trip since we entered the canal, loomed the black shape of a cargo ship's stern. Behind us crawled another cargo ship.

We pulled into a large body of water, which made it look, to me, like we were through the canal and back to the sea. "What's after the canal?" I asked Batoor.

"This is the Great Bitter Lake," he said. "There is more canal up there." He pointed east.

"How many times have you been through the canal?"

"I think, ten times," he said.

"How long have you been working for Samandar?" I asked.

"Two years," he said.

"Does he pay well?"

"He does not pay," Batoor said flatly, with a frown. "If we work, we eat. If we do not, we starve. Or worse."

"He doesn't pay?" I asked. "Seriously?" I looked at Batoor.

"Nothing. He pays nothing," Batoor insisted. "He says he send money to home. He does not, I think."

"So that's slavery," I replied. "You're slaves?"

Batoor's face struggled, as he tried to keep his emotion controlled. He nodded. One tear leaked out of his eye. "I think, you are slave now, too," Batoor announced.

50

TODAY WE WERE TAKING DOORS off hinges, mucking them up to the dining room, and removing door hardware. As the day ended we pulled through the last of the canal.

Batoor was working like the devil beside me, with a screwdriver. "This is the Red Sea," he said while struggling to loosen a hinge. He wouldn't afford himself the luxury of a look at the horizon. "No more Suez Canal." As we pulled into the ocean, the shore fell away on both sides and the boat began to sway, the way it normally did. There was a shout from the tug, and the tug played out the tow rope again, until we were a long way from the ship.

For the next three days, we worked in the engine room, disassembling the equipment, and stripping away anything that could be stripped. I'd had enough, and intense fumes made me dizzy after I'd worked for a while. I think the diesel, oil, and God knows what else vaporized in the heat, which made the engine room noxious. I verged on puking.

"Sorry, Batoor," I announced. "I've got to take a break."

I set my tools down and headed up to the deck. Honestly, the inside of the ship was a kinder place than the outside. We needed refuge from the scorching heat of the day.

The greeny blue ocean was nearly flat, and calm. The heat in the sun was unbearable. In the shade on the deck, it was still intense. I found a little piece of railing shaded by the overhanging lifeboats and relaxed, inhaling the desert air until my head cleared. Batoor had followed me to the deck.

As I stood there, Samandar came up behind me and whacked me with his stick on the side of the head. I turned around. He held the stick at my nose. He spoke to Batoor, who translated to me.

"You are to get back to work."

Samandar whacked the side of my head again. In an instant, I tore the stick out of his hand and pushed him hard. He fell onto his backside. I raised the stick and he cowered. "Coward," I said to him. "Why would you bully a bunch of kids?" Batoor's eyes widened and he vanished, instantly.

I pulled the stick away, just a little. Samandar stood, and from his boot pulled a blade, which he held toward me. I took the stick and smashed his wrist, and the knife fell and skittered across the decking. The hit was hard enough that it made a red mark across the inside of his wrist. He looked at me, terrified. I picked up the knife and tossed it into the ocean.

"What are you, born on a raft? That is some squish." Channeling mother again. "I will throw you and your unclean self into the drink, my friend. Go play out around the door." Mouth agape, he stood back from me. "I've taken out rats bigger than you."

I may be skinny, but I'm a lot taller than Samandar. On the other hand, he'll probably go get bunch of his cronies, come back and put the hurt on me. Guys like him never like a fair fight. I'll have to sleep with one eye open. As my mom would say, "You can't tell the mind of a squid."

51

A COUPLE OF HOURS LATER, THE tugboat gave a couple of short blasts from its horn. It had pulled alongside the ship's stern. I watched Samandar scurry to the back of the ship, still rubbing his wrist. I started to follow when Batoor stopped me. Several other kids followed him onto the deck.

"Do not go. This is for the men only."

"Where are they going?" I asked.

"Two sounds, mean the men stay on the little boat, maybe they have meetings," he said. "Or pirates come." I closed one eye and stared at Batoor.

"Seriously," he said. I had to grin at that one. Batoor was picking up the hipster lingo. Batoor did not grin back.

"Bad to hurt Samandar," he said. "He come back with the other men and you get a beating," he predicted.

"When?" I asked.

"When we are past Somalia," he said. "The Gulf of Aden. They go to the small boat, in case pirates attack. We are near Somalia now. The small boat can go fast." He pointed to the starboard side. "Somalia is there."

With Samandar gone, and the ship filled with kids, the work slowly stopped and the boat relaxed. We stayed out of sight so that men on the tug wouldn't see us. The odd kid kept working, but most stopped. Our first holiday in a while. Batoor and I sat in the shade on the aft deck, looking out at the wake. We would have talked, I'm sure, but with the rest and the quiet, sleep snuck up on both of us.

Some time later, we awoke to some yelling on the decks above us. Batoor seemed to spring out of sleep to the stairs. I followed behind, dopey and slow. He followed the yelling and I followed him, and we collected a group of boys on the observation deck. Two white wakes streaked through the blue sea toward us.

"These are pirates!" Batoor muttered. "We have only a few minutes."

52

THE TUG'S DIESELS HOWLED AND belched black smoke. The boat slewed and heeled up as the captain floored the engines in reverse. One of the men on the tug came out onto the stern. The man pulled the tow line loop from around the stern bollard, and heaved it over the port rail into the drink. He yelled as soon as the line was clear.

The tug roared again, making an escape, leaving us alone on the drink. Batoor looked at me sadly. "We will be attacked. They give us to the pirates, so the tug can escape." The tug, without us, churned away on the port side, using the Orlova's hulk to cover their escape. They were already a good gunshot away. We, on the other hand, were dead in the water.

A number of boys turned toward where Batoor was pointing. Two little motor boats pinched in from opposite ends of the ship, starboard side. The boats were sorry excuses for pirate ships, but they had huge guns mounted in the bow. The pirates fired several warning shots. The slugs pinged off the scabbed metal while our child crew screamed and ducked for cover.

A figure stood behind each gun, nose and mouth covered by a bandana, the head sporting a baseball hat worn brim backward. They let a few more rounds loose on the old tub. Once they rounded the Orlova, they could see the tug making a run for it. One boat lingered around the stern for a second, then broke for the fleeing tug.

The boat on the bow idled for a moment, then joined the pursuit.

"Fantastic," I said. "They left!"

Batoor shook his head. "It is no good. They will come back."

"I've got an idea, Batoor," I said. "Let's get these boys down to the kitchen."

53

WE LISTENED FOR A MOMENT to the fading screams of the pirates' outboard engines. The engine whines were interupted by the bark of heavy gunfire. At the tug. The tug didn't stop. And why would it?

Batoor grabbed my arm and pulled me inside. "It is not safe outside." We found a window on the bridge where we could observe. Fairly soon, the three boats were so distant, it was impossible to tell what was happening.

"They will come for us next," Batoor insisted. "We will all die or they will take us."

"They won't care about this junk heap, will they?"

"They won't take off the boat things. But they take us to their house. I heard of such things. Samandar and the other men tell the pirates we are here. They will want us. We are slaves."

We sat for a few moments in silence. "How many kids are on this ship?" I asked.

"There are ten and five."

I looked at Batoor. "Do you mean fifteen?"

He flashed his five fingers three times.

"Yes, fifteen. We might be able to make it so they don't want to stay long."

As watched, three white wakes began to make their way back toward our ship.

"Let's go," I said to Batoor. "We'll go to the kitchen. Get everyone there." A small group of us headed down, Batoor grabbing kids along the way.

I opened the walk-in fridge. The rotted food still sat inside. I heaved a box of what probably had been meat, and took the remains and tossed them on the floor of the kitchen. "Batoor," I instructed. "Get the boys to empty out this fridge and put the food into the kitchen.

"But the rats," he said. "They will be here then."

"Exactly," I replied. Batoor flashed a grin as he caught on. He yelled at the group in his language, and they began to haul things out of the fridge and throw them onto the kitchen floor. As they began to work, I pulled Batoor aside to explain the plan. Once the work was under way, I went to my cabin and retrieved the flour and sugar. The two tubs I brought down. We poured the contents all over the floor of the kitchen. Rats materialized out of the woodwork.

"Twelve...thirteen...fourteen," I counted. "One missing."

"Where's the other kid?" I asked him. He shrugged.

"I could not find him," he said.

"I'll go look," I said. "Plus, I want to get Dennis."

I headed out on the deck to see where the motor boats were. Two small white boats streaked toward the ship's bow. The tug, not nearly as fast, chugged behind. Lord thunderin' jumpin' that's the head, as me old mudder might say.

From the deck rail, I dove into my cabin. Inside, I found Dennis, sleeping. On the couch next to him, Adar, an 11-year-old boy. Both dead asleep. I shook the young dude's shoulders. He woke into a groggy blear. "Get up," I said. Of course, he didn't understand me. I grabbed his arm and pulled him forward. Once he'd shaken his head free of sleep, I brought a finger to my lips. I pulled him down to the kitchen. Dennis, too, in my hand.

The floor was thick with a tangle of feasting rats, drunk on new rot, rioting and squealing over the putrid food. Dennis, when he smelled the rot, leapt from my hands into the fray.

"Dennis!" I yelled. But there was clearly no way I could get him back. A whine of outboard motors passed us. The boat engines cut to silence when they pulled up to the stern to board the ship.

The rest of the boys had begun to congregate around the walk-in fridge. Batoor looked at me expectantly. "Get everyone into the fridge," I said. "Now." The awful smell had pulled rats from all over the ship into the room. There was a veritable sea of them pouring over the food boxes, devouring everything in sight. Of course, squabbles burst out as rats fought for the food. Squeals of anger and fear from every quarter.

Batoor yelled the instructions in Pashto and the boys picked their way past the rats to the walk-in fridge. The boys lined up around the outside wall of the fridge. I followed them, and once we were all inside, closed the door. Instant utter darkness.

The boys gasped. In my left hand, I held a candle. I fished out my lighter and introduced the flame to the candle wick. I dripped a little wax onto a clean part of the floor and stuck the candle butt into the liquid wax until it hardened. The dim light made it enough to see by, once my eyes had adjusted.

"We must be quiet," I told Batoor.

"I told them," he replied. "They will be quiet. They have heard the same stories I have heard."

With that many smelly bodies in a walk-in freezer, the air turned rank quickly. It was thick with the heat of our bodies and our unwashed smell. The odd person coughed occasionally. But it was OK. The rats were kicking up a decent din outside. Plus, the fridge was well insulated, which dampened any noise we made.

The odd loud noise penetrated the walls of the fridge. There wasn't much they could do to the old ship. She was a sad and sorry pile of scrap. The boys' bedrolls and meager possessions wouldn't be of much interest, nor would my ratty belongings. They'd be looking for us—we were the most valuable thing on board. Fifteen free young slaves. Plus me, makes sixteen.

Batoor leaned into me. "We be slaves. You be a hostage," he said. "You are white."

"Thanks, Batoor," I replied. "That's so comforting."

So we sat quietly. No one had a watch or a phone or anything, so it was impossible to say how much time passed. Once seated and still, most of the boys fell asleep.

There were some loud noises at one point. It sounded to me like one or two of the pirates came into the kitchen area, met the sea of rats, and after freaking out, left in a hurry. They might have fired off one or two shots. Not much noise after that.

I stepped on the floor switch, and the fridge door opened with a quiet gasp. I held the door open a crack. The sky was duckish. No sun, but not utter darkness either. After a long time, I thought I heard an outboard engine roar away. Sounded like one. Could have been two. Batoor was dozing. The ship seemed to return to its old-age groans. If the noises meant anything, they'd be complaints. A senior's list of ailments, maybe.

The other thing I could hear was rat scrabble. Scurrying, digging, fights. and fury of a sea of rats between me and the kitchen door.

I stepped outside the door and let it close silently behind me. The feasting rats cleared a small path for me as I walked. The kitchen door creaked slightly as I pushed it open far enough to get into the cabin hallway. The doors were off all the cabins. The thin remains of light infused the corridor. Couldn't hear a foot, or a voice, or a gun.

54

TIPTOED UP THE HALLWAY TO the spiral staircase. This one staircase tied together all the ship's decks, so I thought I'd listen there. From the lower deck, I couldn't hear a thing. So I slowly stepped up to the main deck, to listen. I couldn't hear anything inside. To the upper deck, I stopped and listened. Nothing.

Suddenly, a drunk-sounding voice broke up the staircase. I dove behind the reception desk and I curled in a ball under the kiosk's counter. The voices grew louder as the men stepped closer and still louder as they began to argue.

It escalated until one of them scattered shot through the lobby. End of argument. Not that different from the way a lot of my stepdads tried to end arguments.

After a sharp-sounding lecture, the men's voices mellowed. One of them laughed and they continued towards the back of the ship into the library. Someone must have told a good joke. And then someone shot out a few library windows.

I lay there for a while until the talking disappeared into the distance. I followed the path they had taken, and walked through the library. The windows gaped like monster mouths, with toothy glass teeth. A couple of bottles lay smashed on the floor. It looked like the men had moved toward the dining room, and out onto the covered stern deck.

I couldn't see anything lurking through the dining room's rear windows. Just to be safe, I hunkered down behind the bar. I tried the soda wand, well, just because I was bored. When I pushed the button it exploded with what sounded like a dry senior-citizen fart.

In a short burst of gunfire, the men shot out the rear dining room windows. The conversation and laughter became clear. At least a half hour later, the voices died. The sound of an outboard motor worked up to a scream moving away from the ship.

The two boats with outboards were gone. If the tug had been pirated, it still could be there. I moved out of my hiding place at the bar, through the confetti of glass shard to the rear of the dining room. The tug should loom and be easy to spot, I thought, as I peered out the windows on the port side. Nothing on that side. Nothing had been tied up behind the ship. I ducked below window level and waddled to the starboard side—nothing on that side either. I took a chance and stepped out onto the rear deck to listen. A quick check over the deck rail, to see if I'd missed a boat.

I stepped up the aft observation deck, one floor above, to confirm the ship was clear. I couldn't find anyone, so I headed down to the kitchen, parted the rat sea, and opened the fridge door. Batoor leapt to his feet as the door swung open. Inside, a groggy group of boys huddled on the floor.

"It's safe now," I told Batoor. "The pirates are gone." I worked with my feet to keep rats out of the fridge, like a hockey player keeping a puck out of the net with a skate.

"What do we do now?" Batoor asked. "There's nothing to do."

"We survive. It's a lot of work to survive," I replied.

The night came on. The moon was full, and the sea glass.

"I don't think we should have a fire tonight," I said. "The pirates may be watching from the shore. It'll take a while until we've drifted far enough away to have a fire again."

"When do you think tugboat return?" Batoor asked.

"You told me the pirates kill or take everyone, didn't you?" I replied.

"Yes," he agreed. "This what the stories say."

"How can you have a story if everyone gets killed?" I asked. Batoor looked at me as though I'd licked the inside of his ear. "The tug came back with them, so I don't think the tug will come back for us. I think the pirates have it. Which means there's a good chance Samanadar and his men are either slaves or dead."

From inside the ship, a Jahan screamed and ran yelling to the aft deck where most of us were sitting enjoying the cool night air. He spoke to Batoor in a shrill tone. Batoor took to his feet immediately.

"There is a pirate still on the ship," he said.

"What?" I yelled. "Back to the fridge," I ordered.

Batoor shook his head. "He is sleeping on one of the floors in a cabin. There are bottles of drinks around him. What do we do?"

"He's probably passed out," I said. Batoor looked at me quizzically. "They were drinking a lot." He shook his head. He didn't understand. "Let's check him out."

The cabin was on the main deck. Batoor followed me with a flashlight and stopped in the hallway. The smell of vomit filled the hall. I went in, and on the floor was a young man, probably Somali, completely bombed out of his mind. He couldn't have been older than fourteen. On the floor beside him lay a large bottle half full of some kind of alchohol. He slept in a pool of vomit, on his back. Very dangerous. "You're lucky to be alive, man. Drunk people can drown in their own vomit."

On the bedframe was a machine gun.

"Batoor," I called. I shone the flashlight into the hall-way for him. When he came in, I passed him the bottle and the machine gun. "He's just a kid," I said. "I don't think he's a big problem."

He came in, and I took the bottle and stood it upright.

"I think we've got to move him, or the rats may harm him," I said. "They'll clean up the puke." The kid was built like Batoor. Skin and bone. He couldn't have weighed eighty pounds, though he looked as tall as me. I grabbed the boy's arms and threw him over my shoulder, and hauled him onto the aft observation deck. There I put him on his side, in case he was sick again. His head rolled around like his neck had snapped. He was so gone. I'd say he was close to alcohol poisoning.

"Shall I call you an ambulance?" I asked him. His head rolled around like a bowling ball. "I take it that means yes." I looked at him grimly. "You're an ambulance."

That, right there, is a quality joke. I suppose it means that one day I'll be a dad.

Batoor brought the gun and the green liquor bottle.

"I think we should hide the gun," I said. "We might need it sometime."

Batoor shook his head. "We throw it into the sea. Guns bring bad things."

"We might need it," I insisted. "The pirates may come back to pick up that kid. I'll go hide it somewhere." Batoor passed me the alcohol and the gun, and I tramped upstairs. I couldn't hide it in my cabin. Everyone would think of looking for it there. The kitchen would be a good place, I thought at first, but I ended up going into the library. The library was still one of my favorite hangouts on the entire ship. The shattered windows had kind of ruined it now, though they let in a nice breeze. I found a couple of shelves that were long enough and still filled with books, and tucked the gun in behind them all.

The bottle, well, let's just say I had a chat with it. I brushed the glass off a cushion and table and sat the bottle down in front of me. I uncapped the bottle and sniffed. No idea what kind of alcohol it was. But a few weeks ago, it wouldn't have mattered.

"I don't know what you are," I told it. "I've been wanting a drink for the last few weeks, and I couldn't find you. Now you show up here. You were even delivered to me. And I don't know what to do." The bottle was half full. Probably enough to get a good buzz going. That buzz would feel so good. I wanted it.

Batoor wandered through the library door. Our eyes met. "I won't get drunk," I said to Batoor. "I just want a little sip." Batoor looked at me, confused. "You know, a little bit."

I took a quick sip. It was strong, and definitely alcohol. That was nearly the last thing I remember.

55

WHEN I AWOKE, I THREW up until the dry heaves had squeezed everything out of me that I had inside, and then some. My head pounded and the room spun. On the floor beside my pool of vomit lay the bottle. And next to that, Batoor—battered, bruised, and either asleep or unconscious.

"Batoor," I yelled. Enough of my memory came back that I remember Batoor trying to take the bottle from me. I started swinging, and must have connected. He lay on the ground with a huge shiner and a fat lip.

I shook him awake. It took a few moments until his eyes fluttered open. When he saw me above him, he flinched and raised his hands to cover his face.

"Oh, Batoor," I exlaimed. "I'm so sorry." The fear in

his face faded a little, once he was out of my reach.

"Did I do that to you?" I asked. He gave a solemn nod, as he tested his lip with his fingers. I was still drunk enough that the tears flowed easily. He saw me starting to weep. "Why you cry?" he asked me, still keeping a healthy distance away.

"I did the same thing to you that my mom and stepdad do to me," I moaned. "I'm the same as them." The sobs turned into another set of dry heaves. I fell to the floor on my knees, until the heaves subsided.

"You are the boss now," he said.

"I am the boss?"

"The boss is the strongest one."

"No!" I said. "That's wrong! That's not right. No one should beat you," I said. "Not your boss, not your mom and dad, not your enemies, or your friends. Especially not your friends. Not me."

"We are friends?" he asked timidly. "You are not the boss?"

"I'm not the boss. I wanted to be your friend, but then I hurt you. I am not the boss. I'm not even your friend when I hurt you."

There was a second bottle next to the Somali.

I remember how it felt to have my dad or stepdad looking at a bottle like I was. Batoor probably had no idea what it meant.

I held the bottle like it was a newborn baby. Everything in me wanted to guzzle the entire thing.

I held it out to Batoor. He stepped forward. Then I pulled it back in. I held it out, and I pulled it back in. Batoor seemed confused.

"Goodbye, friend."

"Goodbye?" Batoor asked. "Where will you go?"

"I was having a little conversation with my old friend." Batoor seemed confused. I grinned and passed him the bottle. "This," I said, "brings bad things. You can chuck this in the sea."

"Chuck?"

"Throw this into the sea for me, please. I'm not sure I can do it." Batoor took the bottle from my hand and hurled it through a smashed window. "Thank you," I said.

"What do we do for food?" Batoor asked. "We ate all the bread tonight. We do not have much water."

"We can eat rats," I said. "I can show you how to gut 'em, skin 'em, and cook 'em."

The new-found freedom didn't sit with all of the boys too well. Several were edgy, unsure of what to do with themselves—nervous, perhaps, as to what might happen next. The evening turned to night, and most of the boys turned in for a good night's sleep.

The next morning, Batoor woke me up. "How do we cook rats?" he asked. "You teach us?"

"Sure," I said. I got up, gathered my supplies, and showed the boys how to hunt rats. We got about twenty rats for our meal. I showed them how to gut and skin them. Then I got a big pot and filled it with sea water and started a fire. We started to boil the meat in the water. We had a small feast.

The Somolian stumbled up from his spot on the ship in a blear. When he found our group, he approached us slowly, unsure of what sort of greeting he'd receive. I offered him a little meat, which we had, and someone passed him some water. No one knew any Somali, and he didn't know any Farsi, Arabic, Pashto, or English.

"I am Batoor."

"IaimBatoor," the Somalian said, pointing to Batoor, saying it as though it were all one word.

Batoor shook his head. "Batoor," he said, tapping his chest.

"Batoor," he repeated. Batoor nodded.

"Sean," I said. Tapping my chest.

"Sean," he repeated.

"Rooble," he said, patting his heart.

"Rooble," Batoor and I repeated. He pointed to the boiled rat meat. I nodded. He dug in.

WATER, WE NOTICED, WAS GOING to be a problem. The boys started rationing what they had. We prepared for rain in case it happened. The Survival Manual didn't offer any tips, except for collecting rainwater. We set up the one repaired lifeboat to catch water.

Hot and dry. The next four days were nothing but heat and blasting light. We ran out of water slowly, one bottle at a time. Chatter dwindled down to nearly nothing. Mouths dried and cracked. Activity slowed to a standstill. Most of us slept. If we moved, we hobbled around like old men. No water, no action. By day we hid in shadows. Nights, we slept out on the deck to get relief from the heat.

Dennis found me sometime that first night. I woke up in the middle of the night to find him hunkered on my chest, asleep. It's a good thing he found me. Honestly, all rats look the same to me. I don't even think I would have noticed if we'd cooked and eaten him. I wouldn't ever tell him that, of course. It would hurt his self-esteem.

I spent a lot of time catching up on my writing. Batoor came in one afternoon and watched me scratch this story onto paper for a while.

"What you write?"

"I am writing the story of what happened."

"In case we die?" Batoor was direct.

"Ah, yes. I guess. Maybe. That way somebody might know what happened to us."

"I write in your book?" he asked.

"Of course," I said. I passed him my pen and scootched over to give him room.

"I write in Pashto," he said. "I write my name."

سلام، امرز مرون بیتور جوادون ید and next to it, in English he wrote "Hello, my name is Batoor Jadoon."

"Now," he said, "your people not forget me."

"No, they will not," I promised.

"We write the names of other boys for your people, too," he said. So he collected each one's name. Here they are:

Bahrawar Lodhi
Droon Tanoli
Adar Atcha
Zgard Qazi
Turan Kharoti
Nang Kundi
Hask Maghdud Khel
Elam Tokhi
Yoon Wur
Alam Shinwari
Helmand Dawar
Izat Unar
Jahan Marwat
Karwan Burki
Rooble Rahim

For the record, these are the names of those of us who struggled to survive. But let it be known that we did the best we could. And if we did die, we died free people.

56

AFTER THE FIFTH DAY, OUR hope ran out. The day beat down on us without pity. We cowered in the ship's bowels until sunset. Then we crawled up to lay on the deck in the moonlight.

The moon was only out for a moment before clouds quietly piled high in the sky. The clouds smothered the moonlight, leaving us in utter darkness. Not the kind of end I pictured us having, but no one gets to choose beginnings or endings, do they? If we did we'd all be Harry Potter.

But then—Forks of lightning spit from sky to sea. White

and hot. A breeze stirred, as though the air had finally awakened.

The odd, fat raindrop whacked against the deck surface. One hit my arm, warm and soft. Then the occasional patter picked up. It reminded me of popcorn popping. Finally, the heavens broke open.

Many of us were too weak to move much. Most lay still, their mouths open, letting the rain splatter into their parched mouths. I was better off than most. I'm not sure why. I was weak, for sure, but I could move around.

A rivulet of water poured over the deck above. I stood underneath and caught it in my mouth, swallowing. The rain brought us all to life slowly. I grabbed a boy and shoved him under the flow I had found, then another boy took his turn. We scrambled to get pots and dishes and anything that would hold water. The deck went from death to a party. It rained heavily for maybe an hour. We drank our fill. We showered. We topped up our water supply. Though we were careful with our water, we had enough to get us through a few more days. And our hope was renewed. If it had rained once, it could rain again.

57

O NE DAY LATER, AFTER A rat feast, I saw a tug pull into the distance. I wasn't sure if I wanted to know what it meant.

Eventually it pulled to the stern of the ship. It was another Bangladeshi scrapper out of Chittagong. Another tug loaded with boys. There was no one on board who spoke English this time, but with Batoor's help, I talked with the ship's captain.

"You can have the ship," I said to the captain. "But the boys and I, we go free." The captain nodded and grinned.

"We've made it ready for scrap. But the boys and I go home. And we need some food and water," I insisted. "Do we have a deal?"

The captain spoke to Batoor. I don't know how you agree on a deal in Bangladesh, so I extended my hand. He took it and shook it. His hand was as limp as a dead rat. "Deal," I said.

The captain spoke to his crew, and a few men disapppeared and returned with bread-making supplies and a small battered stove, which they handed to us. A swarthy man passed us a couple huge plastic jugs of drinking water.

I stood on the bow as the line between us and the tug tightened into a nearly straight line. The tug stained against the pull of the rope. The water boiled white at the back of the tug, the engine raged and thick black exhaust bloomed from the funnel. The rope creaked as the tug struggled to pull us into motion.

The boys were so excited by the bread-making supplies that they got to work right away. Before long, hot na'an was being passed around the ranks. I ended up getting a few pieces. Fresh na'an tastes amazing.

The next few days were leisurely. We had a few things to do to prepare to leave the boat, but most of the work was already done.

"We are close now," Batoor announced. We had been chatting on the bow, one evening, when Batoor had noticed a smell. "I can smell it." I sniffed the air. But whatever whiff he picked up elluded me. "They wait until tide is high. Then, they push the ship up on beach. Then the tide goes out, and we get off."

"And you will be able to go home," I said. Batoor tried to smile.

"Maybe," he said. The older the crab, the harder the claws, as my dear mom might say.

"For sure," I replied. "The captain and I made an

agreement."

"Maybe," he insisted.

58

I T WAS EVENING WHEN THE hulks of beached ships first became visible. Chittagong geography was flat, so the ships stood out easily. Many of the metal hulks lay on their sides. The bridges and funnels pitched at dangerous angles, like a drunk and wonky downtown.

Batoor was right—there was a smell. It was loud enough now, I could smell it. The smell of oil, metal, and decay. With septic undertones. And sort of a flat rusty odor, almost like the taste of blood. "The cutting torches make that smell," Batoor told me. The orange spray of sparks feathered through the poisoned purple night as the workers cut through the hulks. The occasional sounds of yelling. The clank of pounding hammers, the zing of saws chewing through metal.

As we waited, I noticed bugs. We'd not had any insects for our entire voyage. But here, flies and mosquitos clouded the deck and began to invade the ship like flies taking over a carcass. We started swatting the critters as we waited.

The tug shortened the line while we were still offshore. We floated a couple of hours before two more tugs joined us.

On the beach, in a narrow space between two old hulks, a bonfire sprang to life. "We go there," Batoor announced, pointing toward the bonfire. "That is our place."

The final resting place of Lyubov Orlova. Her cemetery plot. She would float free no longer. She was ending life as a boat, but she'd be recycled as a thousand other things, I supposed. Cutlery. Barbeques. Toilet flush levers. High-rise beams. Paper clips. Who knows. Death to the old. Birth to the new.

The tug that had towed us took a place on the port side. The other small tug chugged around the stern to the starboard side. The big tug nosed up to the stern. The low throttle rumble jumped to a roar as the tugs began to push. The calm water boiled behind each. The old tub waffled for a moment, but then began to follow the push to the beach. We began to gather some serious speed. And as we did so, the tugs' engine roar turned to a scream.

We were going fast enough that my shoulder-length hair blew out of my face, which is impressively fast for a boat without engines. The tugs on either side made sure our nose aimed for the bonfire. The bow of the old tub pointed straight into the gap. One final jump in the tug engines wail made it impossible to talk.

The engines quieted. "I was on the shore or on a tug," Batoor said. "I was never on a ship when it was pushed in." He ran from the aft observation deck to the bow. I followed him, jogging. We watched as the bow headed toward the bonfire. Once we were close enough, the tugs on either side dropped away, and the tug from behind pushed as hard as she could.

As we pulled into our spot, it was easy to see, suddenly, that Lyubov Orlova was a small ship. We were being pushed between two old container ships. Both were easily twice as long and twice the height of our little ship. It looked to me like we were closing in on the left side of the opening, too much to the port side.

A young boy ran toward the ship and shouted up to us. Immediately, all of my shipmates except Rooble hunkered down on the decking Batoor, too.

"We go into shore," he yelled at me. "The ship stop quickly. We fall down when the ship meets the beach."

Right. Momentum. Talk about sloppy safety practices.

I quickly sat with a solid steel wall to my back. I made sure there was nothing heavy behind me, and sat down.

Too late I realized Rooble was still standing on the deck. He watched us but seemed confused. When the boat hit the sand, he was slung forward like a he'd been belly bucked by a four hundred-pound sumo wrestler. I ended up being pushed back against the wall, and my head whipped back just enough to whack the steel wall.

I could hear the debris inside the boat smash and tinkle around inside. A plastic cooler flew off the top deck and tumbled its way forward up the decking.

The great old ship's hull began to shudder as she rode up on the beach sand. She began to lean to the right, to starboard. It felt suddenly as if the whole beast was going to roll right over. But she held. Our momentum carried us in a fair ways, and she ground to a halt.

We would have debarked, as they say. But despite being on shore, we were still surrounded by water. I assume they pushed us up on the beach at high tide. So, as Batoor had explained earlier, we'd wait until low tide to get off the tub.

I slept my last night on the boat. I didn't sleep well. One, I was excited to be on land. Two, the boat wasn't rocking, which just felt weird. I ended up pacing the deck until morning.

Early in a hot, sweaty morning, a sour-looking man came onto the boat and motioned for us to follow. He spoke to the boys.

"It is time to go," Batoor translated to me. "We must get off the boat."

I got a few things from my cabin that I wanted to take with me. Dennis, of course, I wanted to come along. My phone, which I hadn't used for a while. Someone hooked up a gangway to the deck door. And then we all decended into Chittagong water, debris, and knee-deep mud.

We slogged our way to firm ground where we were

met by the captain of the tug, and his boss, I think.

"Thank you for the tow," I said the captain. "It's good to be on land." Batoor translated. The men wouldn't move. I wasn't sure why, so I attempted to step around the guys and be on my way. The captain of the ship grabbed my arm and snarled at me.

I had no idea what he was saying. I looked at Batoor. He wouldn't meet my eyes.

"The man says you now work for him. He is the boss man."

"That's not the deal we made," I said. Batoor translated. The captain let go of my arm and backhanded Batoor across the face. He fell on his tea kettle in the mud. The captain spoke. "We are now his slaves," Batoor said, whining. The boys stood in a tight group behind him. "This is bad like Justin Bieber," he said. I would have laughed, if we weren't in a serious brine.

I never paid much attention in Social Studies class. But I'm pretty sure it's illegal to keep kids for slaves, even in this country.

Stupid me. Stupid promises. I shouldn't make deals when I don't know anything about these countries. I've always assumed the entire world is like my own.

59

DEA. "I'VE GOT TO GET something off the ship," I said. The captain jumped when I turned to walk back to our old tub, but he let me do it. I trudged back, with my belongings and Dennis shoved into the pockets of my coat, which I wore. One running shoe in my hand. My boot worked, though I had to work hard to keep the mud from pulling it off me. Up the gangway into the library.

From behind the row of books, I took out the old AK-

47. I didn't know how it worked. I didn't know if it had bullets. But it looked badass enough that it would scare them half to death.

I dumped the gun into a frazzled black plastic garbage bag and walked down the gangway. I rejoined the group. I took a moment to organize myself. The running shoe on my muddy bare foot. The bag in my right hand. I'm ready for the big reveal.

I tore the bag off the gun and pointed at them.

"You ugly mothers," I demanded. "Keep your end of the bargain. We got you the boat. We stripped it all for you. You're going to let us go, or I'm going to use this." The men raised their hands and backed away. I stepped up to the captain and gave him a full backhand. He staggered back and touched his lip with his fingers. "That's for hitting my friend." I followed up by pointing the gun at him. "Let us out, please." Batoor translated.

The man spoke and backed up the beach through the debris. "He says he will take us to the gate," Batoor said.

Rooble looked wide-eyed at the weapon. The gun's presence had surprised almost everyone. Rooble stepped up beside me. With the gun still pointed at the captain and the boss, he shifted my grip on the weapon so I was holding it properly.

The group of boys grabbed their things and moved up the beach. The clouds of insects didn't even register. Pure adreneline. We moved through the towering ship skeletons, bits and bones of old ships. Old steel carcasses, ships' skin and bone. And people crawling like rats over the remains.

The boss eventually led us to a guarded, barbed wire–topped chainlink gate. The gate was guarded by two men who looked armed. The boss spoke a few sentences to the guards who turned to see me holding the gun. Their eyes widened with panic.

Batoor stepped beside me. "He ordered the guards to

open the gate," he said. "We're going to make it out of the yard." I kept the weapon trained on the boss. He stepped up to huge padlock that connected two ends of the gate to keep them from opening.

"Guns, please," I asked. "On the ground in front of them." Batoor translated. They seemed to hesitate. "Now," I yelled. Batoor didn't need to translate. One of the guards blinked heavily. They both unholstered their weapons and set them on the ground. Actually, to be fair, one looked like a cap gun. Rooble quickly picked up both.

The guards swung open one of the gates wide. I stepped through, to the far side of the gate and turned around so everyone was in front of the gun. The entire group stepped through to freedom.

"Now, everyone inside the gate," I ordered. The men backed through the gate. "The guards, too," I ordered. They backed through the gate. "Now lock it." They locked the gate. "Give me the key." I took the key and threw it into the brush across the road. That'll keep 'em busy for a while.

"Let's go," I said. We marched away from the gate as if we knew where we were going. We walked up the treed road from the ship-breaking yard until the road met a highway. The street sign read Dhaka-Chittagong Highway, in English. "Batoor," I called.

"Yes, Sean?" he replied.

"I have no idea where we should go or what we should do. I think you should be the boss, now."

"I don't know what to do either," he said.

"Let's have a meeting," I suggested. We wandered part way up a highway. On the far side was a row of abandoned commercial buildings. We found a deserted warehouse with a dirt parking lot behind, and Batoor signaled the boys to go in for a meeting. The entire meeting was in Pashto, so I had no idea what was going on. Rooble and I sat together. While the others talked, Rooble mimed a lesson on the rifle. He left the strap around my shoulder but showed me how to grip it, how to remove the magazine, and how when I'm aiming to tuck the gun into my shoulder. I'll be glad to leave this thing behind somewhere.

He pulled the magazine out, and with a grin, showed me the inside. It was empty. The gun had no bullets.

60

AFTER SEVERAL MINUTES OF DISCUSSION, Batoor turned to me. "We think we go south to Chittagong. There are many people there. We hard to find. Our homes are in different places. So we decide what to do when we are there. We are close to Bhatari. Turan said he once went in a truck to Chittagong. It is a long walk."

So we walked. A commercial strip followed the highway. Buildings and sidestreets meant we could keep off the main highway while we walked. We walked in silence. I think we didn't talk much because we didn't have much hope. I think everyone expected we would be picked up and either thrown back into the ship-breaking yard or taken to jail.

I did have one sliver of hope. Slavery is illegal here, I think. The rules just aren't enforced. So cops don't bust the ship-breaking operations, but they don't help them either. Unless cops are corrupt, which is possible. I mean it happens in North America. It must happen here, right? But this is me making a sober guess, which is pretty much worthless.

"We drop it," Batoor said, pointing to the gun. "It is trouble."

"Let's keep it until we're sure we're fine," I said. "I'll cover it up." The streets were strewn with garbage, so it was pretty easy to find another bag for the gun. Even in the bag, it looked gun-like, so I balled up some old newspaper and stuffed the bag until it looked like a small guitar. Everybody leaves a guy with a guitar alone. Batoor seemed satisfied once I was done, and we trudged on.

Of course, we were starving. And we hadn't brought any water with us. So the walk seemed to take forever. By now we'd been out of the gate for well over an hour. As we walked south, the industrial development around the highway began to broaden slowly into a city.

I had kept my winter coat. It was loaded with pockets so it kinda worked like a backpackjust because it was a handy thing to hold stuff. Plus, in this kind of heat, it didn't matter whether you had one on or not. Either way, you'd sweat.

I checked on Dennis, sliding my hand into my pocket. He chomped on my finger with all he had.

"Ow!" I complained. "Dennis, you flea-bitten varmit. I'll roast you for supper, I swear."

Batoor heard me and grinned.

By the time we got to Chittagong it was early afternoon. We had no money for anything, which meant we had no way to buy food. The boys started to grumble about their stomachs. Who could blame them. If this adventure taught me one thing it's that the stomach is king.

The other big question, of course, was now that we were here, and free, what did we do next? Chittagong was a dirty, busy place. Dirty is a relative term, of course. My own personal hygiene was a protective shield at this point. Now that we were here, there was no way our ship-breaking slave drivers would find us. There were just too many people.

We found a place in a busy square and sat down for another meeting.

"These boys are Pakistani, like me," Batoor said. "I do not understand what we do now. It is too far to walk, and dangerous."

"What else can we do?"

"We can steal money and food, and then get a train ticket," he said. "But that is dangerous, too."

A weak breeze made the palm leaves wave gently. The breeze was welcome. We sat in silence for some time. "How much are train tickets to Pakistan?" I asked.

"I don't know," he replied. "We find out." So the group of us trudged to the train station. The train station was a long, large, three-story red brick building. The street level was a line of archways leading to the building's insides. The columns supporting the arches were entirely papered with posters and advertisements. My eyes were hungry to read, but the language was written in lines and curls I couldn't process at all. I waited as Batoor asked a few questions and came back.

"Cost 80 tak to get to Dhaka," he said.

"80 tak?"

"That is the name of money in Bangladesh. Money is tak. In America, it is dollar."

"80 tak?" I asked again. "80 bucks, sorry dollars? Is that a lot of money?" I asked.

"Yes," he said, sadly. "Better working on the ships. Then we have food."

"Batoor," I chided. "How can you say that? Those men were cruel jerks."

"It is too hard to change," he said. "Maybe we go back today, the ship yard take us back."

"No," I asserted. "You're not going back. We will find a way to get home."

"The boys are sad," he said.

"It is not easy to be free," I told him. "It means you have to find your own food. You must make your own decisions. You must live with what happens. This is what freedom means. It doesn't mean everything's easy. It just means no one's telling you what to do. You are your own boss man."

"Freedom is hard, then," Batoor concluded.

"Freedom is hard. Especially when you have no money. But it is better than being a slave."

"We go to market," Batoor said. "We find food there." The group seemed extremely low, as we made our way to the market. On the way, we passed an advertisement for a phone just like mine. The sign was inscrutable, but the number was clear. 30,000.

"Batoor, what does this sign say?"

"Phone is 30,000 tak."

"30,000 dollars?"

"Yes," he looked longingly at the image.

"And, a train ticket is 80 tak?"

"Yes," he confirmed.

"Then, I might have an idea." I pulled my phone out of my pocket and showed it to him. "What if I sold my phone?"

He gaped at the phone in my hand. He'd never seen it. "It needs to be charged, but it's nearly new. Could we sell it for 12,500 tak?" Batoor picked up the phone and inspected it. As he did so, the rest of the boys gathered around to ooh and ah.

"Plus, we might be able to sell this," I said to him. As he looked over at me, I patted the bagged gun. "It's got to be worth another 10,000 tak, at least." He grinned and nodded. "We might even be able to buy some food."

"Which store is that?" I asked, pointing to the sign. "We should go there and try and sell it."

Batoor spoke with the gang. They dispersed for a few minutes. One by one they returned. Adar waved us off our seats to follow. He led us to the phone store.

At the door, an armed guard. He didn't want to let Batoor and me in, probably because I smelled like one of Donald Trump's farts. I flashed my phone, and he reluctantly stepped aside. Batoor and I stepped inside. At the counter a snotty clerk looked down at the two of us.

"Do you speak English?" I asked.

He smiled, but seemed completely confused. He looked at Batoor.

"I want to sell my phone," I said, placing it on the glass case before me. Batoor translated.

The clerk looked at me, surpised I had a phone, and confused. I looked at Batoor, who translated.

The clerk nodded and spoke to Batoor. He picked up the phone and inspected it. He spoke to Batoor.

"He says you stole this phone. He will call the police."

I snatched the phone out of the clerk's hands. "Call them, please." I said. Batoor muttered a few words. The clerk backed off a little.

"He asks if you know the phone security code."

"Let me have a charge cord," I asked. Now Batoor was confused. Neither could understand what I was saying. I walked over to a display unit, and grabbed the charge cord and shook the package at the clerk. "Charge cord," I said to Batoor. He shrugged.

The clerk seemed to know what I was talking about. He disappeared behind a curtain and returned with a cord. I plugged my phone in and waited for a couple of minutes until the power kicked in. I booted it up, and waited until the phone asked for my security password. I punched it in and the phone's interface popped up, ready for my next command.

Almost instantly, I got a notice about data roaming charges. I cleared the message. And my phone chugged away. A little green line shot across the top of the screen. Then the message "Text sent."

"It's my phone," I said to the clerk. "I know the password."

Batoor seemed to understand and said something to the clerk.

The clerk seemed satisfied. "Do you want to buy my

phone?" I asked the clerk, through Batoor.

The clerk shrugged. He replied to Batoor. Batoor grew angry and snapped back.

"What did he say, Batoor?"

"He said he'd give us 1,000 tak. I told him we're not idiots."

"Good man," I replied.

The two began a heckle that I couldn't follow. After about five minutes or so, Batoor turned to me. "He says he can give us 9,000 tak. But that is not enough. We must go. You must frown because you are unhappy." I frowned. Batoor matched my frown.

"But where else are we going to sell?" I asked him. "This is the only place we can sell, isn't it?"

"We go," Batoor said sternly. He pointed to the door. I obeyed, unplugged the phone and followed him. Just as we got to the door. The clerk called out.

Batoor smirked, but broke the smirk into an angry look before turning around. The clerk spoke a couple of sentences to him. Batoor shook his head and replied. There were a couple more shots back and forth.

"You must frown again after I tell you what he said. Do not be happy, or he will change his mind." He looked at me and I nodded. "He says he will give us 14,300 tak," Batoor said.

I bent my mouth into the best frown I could. "That will be OK."

Batoor and I returned to the glass case and set the phone down. The man behind the counter reached for it, but Batoor covered it with his hand.

The clerk went behind the curtain and returned a few minutes later with a small pile of colorful bills. He counted them out for Batoor and me. Though I hadn't seen the currency before, I tried to track all the amounts I saw. As best as I could keep up, it hit in the range of what we'd asked. The clerk reluctantly set the last bill on the stack and smoothed the stack of bills with his hand. I pulled the phone from under Batoor's hand, removed the SIM card, and placed the phone back under his hand. Batoor uncovered the phone, and covered the stack of money. The man snatched the phone off the counter and began to examine it.

Batoor passed the money to me, and we left.

Once we were out on the street and far enough away from the store, Batoor's face widened into a huge grin. "This is good for you," he said.

"Let's go buy some train tickets," I said. "If we have anything left over, we can get some food."

The group had a little party over the news of the money, and we made our way to the train terminal to buy a ticket for each of us. Most of the boys wanted tickets for long trips out of Bangladesh into northern Pakistan. But they were surprisingly cheap.

"Where would you like to go, sir?" a ticket seller asked me in English.

"I need to find a Canadian embassy," I replied. The teller nodded and disappeared.

"You need to go to Dhaka," he said. "First class?"

"Cheapest, please."

"Second class, general?" he asked. I nodded. "That will be 80 tak," he said.

"Two, please," I asked. Rooble needed an embassy, too.

Seventeen train tickets ended up being just a little over 1500 tak. So we had plenty of money for food. And food was cheap, too. We returned to the market and worked our way through the stalls buying food—food for the trip, and food to eat at the moment.

I bought an ice-cold bottle of Coke. It cost a fortune. Eighteen tak. As I held it in my hand, I cried. I bawled. I don't know why. I guess there were quite a few times when I thought I'd never have another taste of the things

I love. Just holding that bottle made me realize I had survived. Not all the way survived, but survived enough, thus far.

The cola's fizz seemed to burn my tongue, like millions of microscopic rats loose in my mouth. It felt like they rampaged over my tongue and down my gullet. I'm going to call it delicious.

Batoor hunched over a loaded plate. "Kha ishtya walare." It's Pashto. It means "enjoy your food." Batoor spit a mouth of rice in Droon's ear, a giant grin plastered between his earlobes.

Batoor helped me order a lamb dish, I think he called it kalia. Then some meatball things he called kofta. My eyes and nose leaked as I took it in. Hot, spicy hot. But delicious? I nearly passed out because of the flavor. The only flavor I'd had in the months at sea, if I counted right, was salt.

It was more or less a party. We ate like cows after a lemon-juice cleanse. We spent more on food than on train tickets. We all got something to tide us over on our trips home. I picked a stack of na'an and a couple of bottles of water.

"What a scoff," Batoor said, after he belched his satisfaction.

I laughed until tears streamed down my face. Batoor looked at me daffy.

"You talk Newfie some bit good," I said.

He nodded. "You teached me." I could hear the sound of Mr. Nutman sobbing.

Then, back to the train station. We found a set of benches. Our entire group was heading to first to Dhaka, where Rooble and I'd get off. The rest of the group continued on into Pakistan. There was a train at 2300 hours, or 11 p.m. It made its way to Dhaka and dropped us off there at 0635 the following morning. That meant we had a place to sleep while we traveled.

The old, tired-looking train sat on the rails waiting for passengers. In the dull electric lights of the trainyard, I could see the train was painted steel blue, lumpy with thick coats of paint. We boarded the train as it sat on a bare track. There was no orderly way to get on. A crowd of us pushed and piled into a rail car that was far too small for any of us. There were chickens and goats in the car with us.

What do you get when you put a hundred people, all their luggage, five small goats, and eight chickens in a train car meant to seat sixty? Not a joke, I can tell you. A huge crowded smell. People on the roof of the rail car set up their luggage like seats and sat on the train roof. We were lucky that the boys were good at pushing their way around. The seventeen of us got a small block of six seats, all together. There was going to be little sleep on this train ride. Did I mention smell?

The train pulled from the station some time later. There were guys standing on the outside of the train, holding onto bars at the train windows. I could hear people on the train's roof. It shambled along the rails clacking and rolling, but its forward motion was agonizingly slow. I guess with people on the roof and hanging off the sides, it wasn't going to be a bullet train, right? Must be why the train ride cost the equivalent of a dollar.

The group of us huddled together almost in a puppy pile to get some sleep.

"Ow, Dennis, you jerk," I complained. He sank his teeth into my finger again. I hadn't bought him a train ticket. I was balled on the floor, with my head against the foot of one of the benches. The interior of the car was lit by two dim bulbs that pulsed brighter and dimmer in time with the engine. When we pulled into a station, they dimmed. When we pulled out they brightened.

The back end of a goat swung around over my head, just as it let go some goat turds on the inside of the train car. It was like one of those candy dispenser machines where you put in a quarter and out comes a handful of Glosettes. This was two handfuls of goat poo dropped onto my stuff, and all over the inside of the train car. The owner, a dark white haired, goateed man, seemed not to care. I shoved the beast out of my space and toward the owner. The chickens flapped around the other end of the car, thank God. They were dropping chicken bombs all over the place, too.

And then it hit me. Dennis. What was I going to do with Dennis? I should have been asleep, and all I could think about was what to do with Dennis.

61

MIGHT BE ABLE TO TAKE him home, I suppose. But then he'd have to be a different kind of pet. He'd have to have his shots, and live in a cage. I could let him go, here, and let him be with his kind. But he was a bit too much of a princess to do well living on his own. Maybe one of the boys would take him to where they lived, like Batoor. No one would take care of him like I would though. Would Batoor put up with his biting? Not likely. What to do?

It felt as though the train stopped every few feet. The crappy speaker mounted somewhere in the car would screech an announcement before every stop. It would rumble on for a while, then more people shoved their way into the car. Sometimes a few left. The constant flow of people coming and going in such crowded conditions meant everybody was constantly jostling. My traveling companions were pretty good sleepers. Used to the crowded conditions, I guess. I couldn't sleep a wink.

Finally, as the first light of dawn lined the horizon,

some of the boys awoke. I have no idea what time it was. Finally, the announcment. The only word I recognized of the hundreds spoken over the speaker: "Dhaka."

When the train finally stopped at the platform in Dhaka in the early morning light, the entire train exploded into a riot. People pushing their way on. People pushing their way off. Off the roof, onto the roof. Bleats of goats. Chicken fluster and call. The roof covering the platform was loaded with people. It served as a second platform for those traveling on the roof. A complete free-for-all.

The mob broke up our group. Somehow we managed to regroup a good distance away. Batoor rounded up the occassional wayward soul.

Once we made our way to the edge of the crowd we were able to move freely toward the main terminal and onto the street. The main terminal was a white modern fluted architecture of arches. Our train, of course, wasn't allowed anywhere near the fancy building. We found a spot where we could meet out of the way.

"Does everyone have his ticket?" I asked. Batoor translated and each of the boys, except Rooble, held his ticket out. "We are all from the Swat Valley area," Batoor said. "We get another train together." Batoor pointed at Rooble and me. "It is only you who go away." I checked my cash reserves. I had almost 6000 tak left. I gave Batoor 5000. He pushed my hand away as I held it out.

"Take it," I insisted. "The embassy should have everything I need. You might need more food or a bus ride or something. You're the boss man now," I told him. "You must make sure they get home."

"They will speak English in there, won't they?" I asked, pointing at the terminal. Batoor nodded. "I guess it's time to say goodbye, then."

I wanted to cry. I really did. But I'd look like a severe loser. So I tried to tuck the emotion away and keep a straight face. Batoor seemed to be trying the same thing.

His lip trembled a little, like mine. We shook hands.

"B'y that was some time," I said, opening my arms wide. Batoor and I embraced, each of us needing three baths to quell the smell. "You are my good friend, Batoor. I will never forget you." I held him for a moment at arm's length. "If you're on Facebook," I continued. He looked at me, confused.

I shook the hands of the other boys.

"Take care, Batoor. Go straight home now." I held Rooble by the arm. The gun in the garbage bag in the other. He knew he was supposed to go with me, but the group of boys were magnetic, and pulled him in. Batoor and I parted slowly, both knowing that in all likelihood we would never see one another again. In this sort of situation, goodbye is basically death.

62

TIME TO FIND THE EMBASSY. So we entered the fluted arches of the train terminal and asked our way through the crowd until we found an official who spoke English and knew where the embassy was. Turned out it was not an easy thing to find.

"Go north on Station Road," the official said. "Right on Love. Left on Shaheed Tajuddin Ahmed Avenue." He thought for a moment. "Shaheed turns into the Dhaka Highway. You'll want to follow that for a long, long time." He traced the path of an imaginary map with his finger. "And right on Kemal Ataturk Avenue," he said with a nod. "Kemal becomes Madani," he concluded. "It's on the left near the river. It's about ten kilometers."

"Thank you, sir," I said, hoping I'd been better at memorizing the instructions than I had been at memorizing, say, the periodic table in school. Rooble and I left the station and ventured out, stopping just long enough to eat our breakfast. Then we followed the directions until we were deep in the heart of the city. The streets were treelined and jammed with rickshaws—two-wheeled cabs pulled by men on foot or bicycle.

We came to a corner and waited for traffic to clear so we could cross. I looked left, and everything was clear. I stepped out into the street. Rooble grabbed me and pulled me back as a delivery truck whistled past my nose, inches away.

I swore. "Thank you, Rooble. You saved my life." He gave me the thumbs up. He didn't need to understand English to understand the gratitude in my voice.

The traffic here drives on the opposite side of the road, like in Britain. Motorcycles knitted their way through the small cracks in traffic, as did pedestrians. Accidents were almost guaranteed. Buses passed us as we walked. Like the trains, there were people hanging off the sides, and one or two on the roof, too. A policeman in a yellow vest riding a motorbike pestered a young man driving a small flatbed truck loaded with soft drinks.

The walk was taking a while since we weren't sure where we were going. By the word "we" I mean "me." Rooble had no idea what was happening, I don't think. He just trusted that we knew where we were going.

A few wrong turns. A little awkward bargaining for a snack on the way.

Eventually, we found ourselves in front of the embassy, which was a large, modern glass structure, with louvered screen over the outside. Very cool. The grounds were manicured with lush green grass and short exotic bushes and trees.

I approached the door, guarded by two armed sentries standing on either side.

"Hi," I said. One of the guards nodded. "I'm a citizen who's gotten stuck here accidentally, and I need to get home." The guards hands automatically dropped to the holsters of their weapons.

"You cannot come here without permission," the guard on the right said in squeaky English.

"I've lost my passport and I need help," I said. "May I speak to someone inside?"

"I'm sorry, sir, but you do not have permission to be here," the guard on the left said.

"I am a citizen, I am Canadian," I said. "I am Canadian and I need help."

"One moment," the guard said. "Wait here."

He entered the building and came out with some office-type person. I repeated my line: "I am a Canadian citizen and I need help."

"Hello, sir. My name is Mandy. How can I help you?" she said with a professional tone.

"I'm a Canadian citizen," I said.

"Do you have your passport with you?"

"No, I don't," I replied. "It was stolen." Good one, I thought. That should get her attention.

"I see," she said. Her nose wrinkled. My body odor may have started to attack her senses. "What about him?" She asked, pointing to Rooble.

"Ah, well, that's a long story," I said with a grin. "He's from Somalia, but he needs help, too."

"There is no Somalian Embassy in Bangladesh," she replied, without emotion.

"Oh. Well, that's a bit of a problem," I said. "But I am a Canadian citizen, and I need to get home." I pointed at Rooble. "I brought him with me because I thought you might know how to help him."

"Where are you from?" she asked, pursing her lips.

"St. John's, Newfoundland."

"What's your name?" She pulled out a pencil and paper. "What's your address there?" I dictated my address and phone number. "Let me make a few calls," she told me. "Wait here."

Through the front door, she disappeared into the glass bowels of the embassy. It must have been at least an hour before she returned with a woman, perhaps her boss, and pointed to us through the glass doors. The woman nodded and came out to talk with us where we waited.

"Hello. My name is Ms. Ratmundi. I work at this embassy. I'm told your name is Sean Bulger." I nodded. "We tried to reach someone using the phone number you provided. The number has been disconnected. However, we were able to talk to the St. John's Police Department and they told us that a Sean Bulger has been reported missing. His mom believes he ran away. How did you come to Bangladesh?" she asked.

"It's a very long story," I warned her.

"Please tell me," she said, almost like she meant it.

And so I began the story, a faster version than what I've laid it out here. She stopped to ask questions as we went. But she let me tell it the way it happened.

"That is an intriguing experience," she said. My heart sank. She didn't believe me. "And this boy, Rooble," she pointed at him. His face brightened at the sound of his name. "He came on board when your ship was attacked by pirates?"

"Yes," I said. "They left him behind. Forgot him, I guess. He was stone drunk at the time, though."

"Let me make a few more calls, and can I please take your picture?" She pulled out her smart phone and snapped a shot of me. "I'll see if I can get anything on Rooble, here." She pointed her phone at Rooble, who offered a shy grin.

"Wait," I said. "They won't recognize me." I ran my fingers through my hair like a runway model. "Now I'm ready." She snapped another shot. The morning sun started to gather heat and intensity.

"Wait here," she ordered. Rooble and I sat in the

shade on the grass as she disappeared into the building again. We waited another long while.

When she returned, she looked concerned. "You say your name is Sean Bulger. I've got visual ID. A school official IDed your photo. Unfortunately, we've been unable to locate your parents."

"My mom," I replied.

"Your mom?"

"I don't have a dad, or a stepdad right now. At least I didn't. I guess I might."

"I see," she said.

"My mom might have moved since I left home," I said. Or, passed out in her chair, or living under a bridge, for all I know, though I didn't say that to Ms. Ratmundi.

"There's one problem with your story," the woman said. "The Lyubov Orlova sank off the coast of Spain some time ago. It didn't make it to the Chittagong yards."

"It did," I corrected. "When the Bangledeshi crew found us, they took the the sensor and threw it into the ocean to make it look like the ship sank. If you check the Chittagong yards, the ship will still be there on the beach. I imagine that when we went through the Suez Canal, someone must have taken security footage of our passage there, too."

"What was the name of the ship-breaking yard?" she asked.

"I have no idea," I said. "I came in from the beach, and there were no signs. When we left, we left in a hurry. I wasn't looking at the sign."

"Because there are no young boys employed in the ship-breaking yards."

"There are," I insisted. "I traveled to Dhaka with a large group who'd been taken from their homes in the Swat Valley, in Pakistan. I'd probably still be there, except the pirate attack occurred. Rooble ended up setting us all free. Except he has no idea what he did, because we haven't been able to tell him. Nice kid. He smiles a lot." Hearing his name, Rooble smiled. "How would I end up with a Somali dude if my story wasn't true?" I asked.

"I don't know," she admitted.

Idea. Big gamble. "Rooble also brought an artifact along with him that I can show you. You can have it, actually. I don't know what to do with it now that we're here."

"OK," she said. "What is it?"

"Well, I told you Rooble came on board with the pirates. He had a weapon with him. This weapon was extremely important to our escape. It's in this bag."

The woman looked a little frightened. I passed her the gun, wrapped in bags. "Hold it here," I said. She took hold of the grip. "It's an AK-47," I announced. Her lips parted, as though she was going to say something. Her mouth closed again. "It's Rooble's, technically," I said. In my coat pocket I reached for the ammo clip. I stuck my hand in and felt Dennis, who instantly bit my finger with a vengeance. "Ow, you damn rodent," I cursed.

The woman looked at me, horrified and curious at the same time. "Sorry. Wrong pocket," I said. Out of the other pocket I pulled the empty banana clip.

She picked at the plastic bags as though they were too filthy to touch, which they were. She undid the knots and pulled the bags off the back of the weapon. It was enough to reveal I was telling the truth. The two guards' eyes widened. One of them muttered into the radio mouthpiece clipped to his chest. Suddenly, a swarm of security appeared. Rooble's smile vanished.

We were asked to get on the ground, face down, with our hands behind our heads. Of course, we complied. We were frisked. My coat was suddenly gone. They found Dennis. A man pulled him out of my pocket. Dennis let him have it. He picked Dennis up by the tail and was going to smash him on the concrete walkway leading into the embassy.

"Don't please," I yelled into the grass. "He's my pet. He's probably my second best friend, too." I rolled on to my side and held out my hand for Dennis. The man held the writhing ball of fur over my hand and lowered him slowly. Dennis sorted himself and sat on his haunches and snarled at the offending man. Then he ran over to me, laying on the ground, and jumped onto the side of my head and sat there. Old habits die hard.

The comical sight amused the group. They pointed and laughed.

When they were sure we were clean, and by that I mean free of weapons, we were allowed to resume sitting on the ground. Four armed guards surrounded us, not including the two we'd first met, who still stood either side of the front door, now with their holsters open, hands on their pistols..

The embassy staff again disappeared into the building for a long time. The sun rose higher in the sky and glowed with afternoon heat. We moved a few times to stay in the shadows as they shifted across the lawn. We were out of food and water. At some point, an embassy clerk brought out a couple of water bottles for us.

Eventually Ms. Ratmundi returned with another woman, introduced as Rebecca. who looked me over and asked, "Sean Bulger?"

"Yes," I replied.

"We've been able to confirm that you are who you say you are," she said. "You live in St. John's, Newfoundland."

"That's right," I exclaimed. I could feel a giddy hope start to rise in me.

"It turns out your cell phone just sent a text yesterday from Chittagong, too. Your mother and the Royal Canadian Mounted Police were monitoring your phone in order to track you. Plus, your coat was made in Canada." Rebecca pointed to Rooble. "As for your friend here, we are not able to confirm or deny anything about him, except what you've said about him. Somalia has no record of his being born, and, therefore, none of his disappearance. I can't get hold of any records for him. But that's anarchy for you."

"He needs to go somewhere," I said. "I didn't know what to do with him. I haven't even been able to talk to him. Can he come to Canada with me? He's worked hard to help us. I don't want to leave him here. He'll be so screwed if I do. I have to find help for him."

"It's OK," she said with some warmth. "You don't have to panic. We'll come up with a plan."

"I suppose he can't come home with me."

"I'm quite sure he can't, at least not yet. But it's also important that we talk with him and figure out what he wants to do."

I nodded. "That makes sense."

She pointed at the rat sitting politely on the toe of my sneaker, like he was trying to defend my right leg from harm. "That creature," she began.

"Dennis," I said.

"Ah, Dennis, then. Dennis will not be able to come with you. He won't be allowed into Canada. He hasn't had shots, and God knows what diseases he may be carrying. Has he bitten you or anything?"

I suppressed an urge to throw up. Instead tears started to flow. "Almost constantly," I said. I was trying hard not to blubber like a complete moron.

"We'll probably have to send you to a doctor, then, in case he's made you sick."

"What can I do with him?" I asked. "He's been my best friend during this nightmare."

"The proper thing to do is to put him down."

"You mean kill him?" I asked with outrage.

"But I suppose you could release him," she said quickly.

"Oh, that's awful," I said. I picked him off my shoe. I startled him and he dug into my finger like it was a chicken drumstick. "Ow, you... you...Dennis," I yelled through my tears. "You loveable jerk."

The embassy staff actually smiled.

"I don't have to let him go for a while, do I?"

Rebecca sighed. She conferred with another coworker. "We were going to put you up at a nice hotel. But if you like, we can get you a less fancy place, where rats won't be such a surprise."

"Yes," I agreed. "Send me to a rat-friendly hotel, please."

"This is a first in my entire career."

They invited us into the building while they changed arrangements to a local hotel. We were clearly so filthy that we stunk up the joint. Funny enough, once you live with body odor and filth long enough, you can't smell it any longer. For me, only a small portion of my smell was smellable.

After a few phone calls, the junior staff woman lifted her hand slowly and brought her index finger down to strike a final key on her computer keyboard. She walked to the printer and pulled out a piece of paper, which she folded like a letter. This piece of paper she passed to me, her nose wrinkling a little further with every step she took toward me. I took the paper, and she backed away to a safe distance.

"This letter will get you a rickshaw ride to the market, where you will be taken to a clothing store for two sets of clean, new clothes. You will then be taken to a hotel, where you will stay until we're able to sort everything out. You will not go out to eat, but you can order room service."

63

HINGS UNFOLDED LIKE SHE HAD explained. We were driven to the market. It took a few minutes to help Rooble understand that he could pick out some clothes. Once he caught on to the idea, it was hard to get him to stop. I picked out a couple of pairs of jeans and a couple of T-shirts. Clean underwear. Brand new socks. I'd dropped quite a bit of weight on the adventure so I wasn't sure what sizes to buy, but I wasn't allowed to try anything on, undoubtedly because of my stinking, filthy condition.

Then, we were off to the hotel. It seemed decent enough, though the curtains were stained. There were two beds, a couple of chairs, and a small desk. The window looked out onto a street jammed with telephone poles, with electrical lines running every which way.

The room had a TV, which hypnotized Rooble, so I got the shower first. I'd been wearing some of the clothes since my ordeal began. Though I'd hand-cleaned every-thing a few times, it was pretty ragged stuff. The shower offered only a hint of warm water, but it had soap and shampoo. I got in.

I can't tell you how warm water feels on your skin if you haven't had a shower in months. I soaped myself down from stem to stern. My tan was so deep in places it was hard to tell sometimes whether the color was from dirt or from sun. My feet were so grimy that water, soap, and scrub only took off the top layer of dirt. Some of the grime literally chipped off, like scabs.

How long I was in there, I'm not sure. When I came out, I felt like 12,300 tak. New clothes. You know what felt the best? Clean, new socks. From now on, that will be my favorite piece of clothing. Socks.

My old socks were bagged and sorry looking and

stunk like rotten cod. I offered one to Dennis. He accepted. However, he isn't the svelte figure he once was. I stretched it over his butt like spandex. He seemed pleased with his new look and began to explore the room.

By the time I got out of the shower, I could tell that the TV was turned off and Rooble was in deep conversation with another male voice. When I came out of the bathroom, I saw one guy sitting in a chair at the desk while the other guy chatted with Rooble, who was clearly delighted to talk to someone.

Dennis, who had been sleeping on the bed before I got into the shower, was still exploring somewhere. I felt fantastic, and browsed the room service menu.

"What would you like to eat?" I asked Rooble through the translator.

The translator took the menu and discussed it with Rooble.

"Cheeseburger and fries, with a Coke," he said.

"I'm getting the same thing," I agreed.

I called the order down to room service.

The cheeseburger and fries were disgusting looking, compared to what they'd look like at home, but to a guy who's eaten rats for months, it was excellent. I set aside part of my meal for Dennis, whenever he returned. The visitors left while Rooble and I savored our meals, then he went into the shower while I settled into bed.

In the middle of the night, I awoke to a fist of fur sitting on my chest. It was Dennis. Rooble had left the bathroom light on, so I could see that Dennis had lost his sock-spandex. Once he realized I was awake and had my attention, he leapt to the floor. A posse of rodents was hanging in a corner, their eyes glowing orange with the light from the bathroom.

"You found your squad," I said. "I guess these guys may be nicer to you, since they don't have to eat each other for food. They can eat stuff from the hotel, I'd bet. Is this going to be your new home?" I asked. "Is this where you want to live?"

Of course, rats don't understand humans talking. And I don't understand rat. But it felt like Dennis had come to say goodbye. That thought brought me fully awake.

"Little dude," I said to him, as I reached down to scratch between his ears. "We had a real runner, trout." He lay down and let me scratch his belly for a while. Then, as if it were time, he rolled back to his feet. And nosed my hand. "I won't forget you. Have a great life, will you? I'll try and do the same."

Rooble stirred as I talked. So I began to whisper. I didn't want him to witness this stretch of blubber. I scratched Dennis' haunches. And, my eyes had started to leak tears. Not manly, for sure.

Dennis stared at me, mockingly, perhaps, as if he was saying "Stop crying, you moron."

"I'll see you around, you stupid furry beast. Um." I paused. "I love you," I said. The words leapt out of my throat and into the air. Honestly, we were both a little embarrassed and awkward after they'd been said. Maybe that is why I had never said them to anyone before.

I passed him the chunk of hamburger and fries I'd saved him, which he instantly scarfed. "Goodbye, my friend."

After a couple of minutes, the mischief disappeared. That was the last I saw of Dennis.

64

THERE WAS PAPERWORK. THERE WERE phone calls. The embassy arranged for me to have a new cell phone to keep in touch, but I wasn't to go out into the city. Still. A new phone. For free. I ended up watching

TV in the hotel room for a long time. Rooble was the first to leave. The gentlemen who'd been helping him came on the second morning while I was in the shower and had taken him away without explaining anything to me. I heard their voices, but when I came out of the bathroom, Rooble and his stuff were gone. The Canadian embassy staff told me later that he'd been put on a list to come to Canada, and they gave me a case number so I could follow up on it when I got home.

I had two days alone. Apparently, the hold-up was finding my mom. They couldn't locate her anywhere. No surprises there. She'd gone missing a couple of weeks after I disappeared, apparently. I was a minor, which meant that, technically, she needed to give the embassy permission to do everything they needed to do to get me home. So, they officially made me a ward of the state, so that the embassy staff could do what they needed to do to return me to Canada.

One morning, a man showed up, asked me to grab my things, and took me to the embassy. There, Rebecca passed me a plane ticket. "You're going home today," she said.

"Thank you," I replied.

"We still haven't been able to get hold of your mom, so she won't be there to greet you," she said in a quiet tone.

"That's OK," I said. "It will be so good to be home." Tears came to my eyes. "I have so much homework to catch up on." Who would have ever thought I would look forward to doing homework?

Rebecca looked at me and grinned, and catching sight of my tears, offered this: "You'll be home before you know it, though it is a long flight. You've got a stopover in Cairo, one in Amsterdam, then home." She passed me a calling card. "You're going to call me at each stopover." Her number was scribbled on the calling card. "I just need to know every time you land, that you're going to make your next flight. Here's a little money for food," she added, passing me three Canadian twenty-dollar bills.

"Money I understand," I shrieked. I took out my wallet. "I'll trade you," I said. I passed her the 1000 tak. She held up her hand.

"It's the least I can do for all the help you've given me. I can pay some of this back," I said.

"It's easier for me if you don't," she said. "Keep it for a souvenir."

Before I knew it, I was on a small, crowded plane, heading towards Egypt. In Cairo, a few hours later, I called Rebecca as I was about to board the flight to Amsterdam. "Be careful," she said, as if she were my mother.

The plane to Amsterdam was pretty modern. It had the individual TV screens for each seat. I was flicking channels when I flipped passed an all-news channel. As I glanced at it, I thought I saw my yearbook photo. I had already hit the kids' channels before I could figure out how to flip my way back. As I did, I caught the tail end of the story that described my ordeal. I was on CNN.

I called Rebecca when I landed.

"The news networks have discovered your story," she said. "Most of North America has heard about you by now."

With the money she had given me, I chose a restaurant and ordered a huge turkey dinner with all the trimmings. Flavor. Holy man. Gravy. This is the food of the gods.

Then my flight home. I slept briefly. Then, shortly before we landed, I checked out the news channels again. I found Fox, and watched for a while. The story on me was hilarious. Clearly, they had trouble finding anyone who knew me. A couple of students I barely knew talked like they had known me all my life. And of course they were full of cod bits and tripe.

These people were saying I was a nice guy. That has

never been true, certainly not for the last few years.

I sucked. I lied, stole, did anything I could to stay drunk. But here these people were saying that I was nice. One even got sorta teary when she talked about me. Like I'd been a good person or something. I'd never done anything to help anyone, not even my mom.

They called me a hero, which just felt wrong. What was heroic in what I'd done? I survived. I made it. Surviving is not a brave decision. It's only one of two options, and the other option is much, much worse. Honestly, even if there had been crates of booze on that boat, I still might have survived. But in a stupor. Drunk as a skunk. Because we all know the kind of drinkers skunks can be.

If there was a hero in this story, it seems to me it was the boat. It had been orphaned at sea. But it did what it was supposed to do. It floated. It bred rats. It did the thing that ships were supposed to do. And it grounded me. Literally. It grounded me off alchohol. A floating detox. It kept me away from things long enough to help me understand that I loved those things. And in the end, it gave its life. Eventually, it'll be reborn as a bridge, or another boat, or a building or something.

The boat told me how to survive, though it didn't talk. It told me to eat rats, just because that's all there was to eat. It even gave me a book to figure it all out. It told me to stop drinking and clear my head. Out on the drink, I discovered sobriety. The boat showed me that I had to work to solve my problems. These are things I could have learned at home, but I needed the ship to help me pay attention. Yeah. The ship was the hero. The best stepparent I ever had. Brought out the best in me. Made me more than I was.

My reflections were abruptly interrupted when the plane thudded onto the tarmac like a dictionary dropped on a floor. Not exactly smooth. Then waffled to a stop at the terminal. Like all birds, this one was elegant in the air, but awkward on land. The passengers leapt to their feet immediately, jostling for pole position on the exit. I couldn't be bothered. I was clean. I was full. No family to meet me. No rush, right? The glut of passengers streamed down the aisles. Once the plane was empty, I stepped into the aisle and walked forward. The flight attendant was just about to leave his post at the airplane door. He looked me over.

"You forget your luggage, sir?" the flight attendant asked.

I shook my head. It all fit into a bag in my hand. Long vacation. I did it with only one pair of underwear.

As I walked across the jet bridge from the plane door to the terminal gate, I saw a man standing patiently at the end of the hallway. He nodded when he saw me.

"Sean Bulger?"

I nodded.

"My name's Mitch, and I'm from Social Services. We're acting in place of your mom, so for now, you need to come with me."

"Sure," I said. I pulled the cell phone from my pocket and dialed Rebecca. A sleepy voice answered. "Hello?"

"Rebecca?"

"Yes?" she croaked.

"I made it," I said. "A guy named Mitch from Social Services met me after we landed."

"That's great, Sean," she said. "You're home."

"I'm home, thanks to you. Thank you for all you did to get me here."

"You're welcome," she said. "Have a good life."

"I plan to," I said. "You, too."

"I will," she promised. "Goodbye."

"Bye."

Mitch stopped before we entered the public side of the the terminal. "Ah, we're not going to go in there," he said. "It's a zoo."

"A zoo?" I asked.

"The media interest in your story is insane. We're going to go out the back way." We met a man who led us down some stairs and through a labrynth of passageways and doors, until we were let out through a secure exit for employees. We scooted through the a corner of the lobby, past a huge throng of people and exited another set of doors to a secure parking area where Mitch had left his car—a sad looking Ford Tempo.

We got into the car, and Mitch set the car key in the ignition. He turned to look at me. "You a bit peckish, Sean?"

"A might, I'd say. I dreamt of a good scoff."

He chuckled. "I'd bet you did. Heard you ate rats."

"It's true."

"Got to hear this story of yours for myself. I'll buy you a burger if you tell me your tale."

"That, sir, is a deal."

65

AFTER A GOOD WELCOME-HOME BROUHAHA, I found myself with a day off. It was a rare sort of June day for St. John's—sunny, and somewhat warm. I'd bought myself a little kibble and headed up to my old apartment. The grass around the building had turned green.

I brought a lawn chair and a good book called Holes, and I set up beside the dumpster in back of the old building. Poured a little kibble beside my chair.

"Sailor, buddy. I came back for you." I made a few kissing sounds. If I were Sailor I'd be hanging out behind the row of apartments here. Scrubbing food from the dumpsters. Living in the brushwood behind. "Sailor, you old boot. I'm waiting."

I can only guess at what my mom had done with the beast before she cleared out. Apparently, she's in rehab. I'm tucked into a group home now, and the counsellors think I should wait until she finishes her program to visit her.

I'm stuck redoing grade eleven —at least, they say, until they're sure I know enough to move on. But I couldn't give a rat's ass. 'Cause I'm alive. I'm clean. I'm even starting to make friends with some of those kids who called me nice on the news. Somehow all the hard parts of that voyage have turned pretty. I like to think of them now. And if I had to do it all over again, I wouldn't change a thing.

The day grew long, and evening came on. I read my book. Every chapter I'd make a meowing sound and throw in a few kisses. Finally daylight was too weak to read and I clicked on my new LED flashlight. The day wore into night, dark as my mother's anger. Kiss, meow. Kiss, meow. A few tenants gave me odd looks as they tossed their garbage into the bin. I didn't recognize any of them, but this wasn't the kind of building that retained residents for long. I realized it was 9.30. Curfew at my new digs was 10. I guessed I'd have to go and try again another day. "Come on, Sailor," I called out, as I tucked my book under my arm and folded the chair. "I'm comin' back, ya hear?"

As I turned to walk around the building to the street out front, I tripped on something. I went ass over tea kettle. And ended up on my face in the grass. A moment passed. A tiny skull knocked against mine. And then in my ear, a wet dab and a quiet rumble. Purring. Flea-bitten fur rubbed over my ear.

I rolled over onto my back. Sailor climbed onto my chest. His eyes glowed like green dimes in the streetlight.

"Well hello, old sock," I purred. "You still here, eh?" I ran my hand over his back a few times, and he leaned into my stroke. And then he attacked my hand with the vengeance of a starving rat. His teeth settled firmly into the flap of skin between my thumb and forefinger.

"Ow!" I complained. The attack felt like a question: "Where the hell have you been?"

I balled his body as he clung by his teeth to my skin and held him to my chest. He slowly released his bite and began to lick my hand.

"Sorry, old sock," I said. He buried his head in the palm of my hand. "Took me a while, buddy." I sighed. "Too long. But, sometimes you sail away to find home. Sometimes home sails away to find you."

ABOUT THE AUTHOR

A professor of English at Mount Royal University, Bunn is the author of four previous books: a YA historical adventure, *Kill Shot* (Bitingduck Press, 2015); the teen magical adventure *Duck Boy* (Bitingduck Press, 2012); *Hymns of Home*, a collection of essays on family, technology, and the environment that reached Calgary's bestseller list twice in Summer 2013 (Bitingduck Press, 2013); and an illustrated children's book, *Canoë Lune* (Le Canotier, 2001). He is active in the Young Alberta Book Society and raises bees.

Visit Bill on the web:

Blog: http://billbunn.net/

Facebook: https://www.facebook.com/billbunnauthor

LinkedIn:
http://www.linkedin.com/pub/bill-bunn/22/20b/863

Twitter: @Moon_canoe

CPSIA information can be obtained
at www.ICGtesting.com
Printed in the USA
LVHW01s2141010218
564851LV00002B/3/P